TIVERTON
TALES

TIVERTON
TALES

BY

ALICE BROWN

THE GREGG PRESS / RIDGEWOOD, N. J.

First published in 1899 by Houghton, Mifflin & Co.
Republished in 1967 by
The Gregg Press Incorporated
171 East Ridgewood Avenue
Ridgewood, New Jersey, U.S.A.
Copyright© 1967 by
The Gregg Press, Inc.

Library of Congress Catalog Card Number: 67-29259

Printed in United States of America

AMERICANS
IN
FICTION

INTRODUCTION BY PROFESSOR CLARENCE GOHDES
Editor of *American Literature* Magazine

In the domain of literature the play may once have been the chief abstract and chronicle of the times, but during the nineteenth and twentieth centuries the novel has usurped the chief place in holding the mirror up to the homely face of society. On this account, if for no other, the Gregg Press series of reprints of American fiction merits the attention of all students of Americana and of librarians interested in building up adequate collections dealing with the social and literary history of the United States. Most of the three score and ten novels or volumes of short stories included in the series enjoyed considerable fame in their day but have been so long out of print as to be virtually unobtainable in the original editions.

Included in the list are works by writers not presently fashionable in critical circles — but nevertheless well known to literary historians — among them Joel Chandler Harris, Harriet Beecher Stowe, Thomas Bailey Aldrich, and William Gilmore Simms. A substantial element in the list consists of authors who are known especially for their graphic portrayal of a particular American setting, such as Gertrude Atherton (California), Arlo Bates (Boston), Alice Brown (New England), Edward Eggleston (Indiana), Mary Wilkins Freeman (New England), Henry B. Fuller (Chicago), Richard M. Johnston (Georgia), James Lane Allen (Kentucky), Mary N. Murfree (Tennessee), and Thomas Nelson Page (Virginia). There is even a novel by Frederic Remington, one of the most popular painters of the Western cowboy and Indian — and another, an impressive minor classic on the early mining region of Colorado, from the pen of Mary Hallock Foote. The professional student of American literature will rejoice in the opportunity afforded by the collection to extend his reading of fiction belonging to what is called the "local-color movement" — a major current in the development of the national belles-lettres.

Among the titles in the series are also a number of famous historical novels. Silas Weir Mitchell's *Hugh Wynne* is one of the best fictional treatments of the American Revolution. John Esten Cooke is the foremost Southern writer of his day who dealt with the Civil War. The two books by Thomas Dixon are among the most famous novels on the Reconstruction Era, with sensational disclosures of the original Ku Klux Klan in action. They supplied the grist for the first great movie "spectacular" — *"The Birth of a Nation* (1915).

Paul Leicester Ford's *The Honorable Peter Stirling* is justly ranked among the top American novels which portray American politics in action — a subject illuminated by other novelists in the Gregg list — A. H. Lewis, Frances H. Burnett, and Alice Brown, for example. Economic problems are forcefully put before the reader in works by Aldrich, Mrs. Freeman, and John Hay, whose novels illustrate the ominous concern over the early battles between labor and capital. From the sweatshops of Eastern cities in which newly arrived immigrants toiled for pittances, to the Western mining camps where the laborers packed revolvers, the working class of the times enters into various other stories in the Gregg list. The capitalist class, also, comes in for attention, with an account of a struggle for the ownership of a railroad in Samuel Merwin's *The Short-Line War* and with the devastating documentation of the foibles of the newly rich and their wives in the narratives of David Graham Phillips. It was Phillips whose annoying talent for the exposure of abuses led Theodore Roosevelt to put the term "muck-raker" into currency.

While it is apparent that local-color stories, the historical novel, and the economic novel have all been borne in mind in choosing the titles for this important series of reprints, it is evident that careful consideration has also been given to treatments of various minority elements in the American population. The Negro, especially, but also the Indian, the half-breed, Creoles, Cajuns — and even the West Coast Japanese — appear as characters in various of these novels or volumes of short stories and sketches. Joel Chandler Harris's *Free Joe* will open the eyes of readers who know that author solely as the creator of humorous old Uncle Remus. And there is a revelatory volume of dialect tales, written by a Negro author, *The Conjure Woman* by Charles W. Chesnutt.

In literary conventions and the dominating attitudes toward life, the works in the Gregg series range from the adventurous romance illustrated so well by Mayne Reid or the polite urbanity of Owen Wister to the mordant irony of Kate Chopin and the grimmer realism of Joseph Kirkland's own experiences on bloody Civil War battlefields or the depressing display of New York farm life by Harold Frederic. In short, the series admirably illustrates the general qualities of the fiction produced in the United States during the era covered, just as it generously mirrors the geographical regions, the people, and the problems of the times.

TO M. H. R.

A MASTER MAGICIAN

CONTENTS

TIVERTON TALES

DOORYARDS

TIVERTON has breezy, upland roads, and
damp, sweet valleys; but should you tarry
there a summer long, you might find it wasteful
to take many excursions abroad. For, having
once received the freedom of family living, you
will own yourself disinclined to get beyond
dooryards, those outer courts of domesticity.
Homely joys spill over into them, and, when
children are afoot, surge and riot there. In
them do the common occupations of life find
niche and channel. While bright weather holds,
we wash out of doors on a Monday morning,
the wash-bench in the solid block of shadow
thrown by the house. We churn there, also,
at the hour when Sweet-Breath, the cow, goes
afield, modestly unconscious of her own sover-
eignty over the time. There are all the varying fortunes of butter-making recorded. Sometimes it comes merrily to the tune of

> " Come, butter, come !
> Peter stands a-waiting at the gate,
> Waiting for his butter-cake.
> Come, butter, come !"

chanted in time with the dasher; again it doth
willfully refuse, and then, lest it be too cool,
we contribute a dash of hot water, or too hot,
and we lend it a dash of cold. Or we toss in a
magical handful of salt, to encourage it. Possibly, if we be not the thriftiest of household-
ers, we feed the hens here in the yard, and then
"shoo" them away, when they would fain take
profligate dust-baths under the syringa, leaving
unsightly hollows. But however, and with what
complexion, our dooryards may face the later
year, they begin it with purification. Here are
they an unfailing index of the severer virtues;
for, in Tiverton, there is no housewife who, in
her spring cleaning, omits to set in order this
outer pale of the temple. Long before the
merry months are well under way, or the cows
go kicking up their heels to pasture, or plants
are taken from the south window and clapped
into chilly ground, orderly passions begin to
riot within us, and we "clear up" our yards.
We gather stray chips, and pieces of bone
brought in by the scavenger dog, who sits now
with his tail tucked under him, oblivious of
such vagrom ways. We rake the grass, and
then, gilding refined gold, we sweep it. There
is a tradition that Miss Lois May once went to
the length of trimming her grass about the
doorstone and clothes-pole with embroidery
scissors; but that was a too-hasty encomium
bestowed by a widower whom she rejected

next week, and who qualified his statement by saying they were pruning-shears.

After this preliminary skirmishing arises much anxious inspection of ancient shrubs and the faithful among old-fashioned plants, to see whether they have "stood the winter." The fresh, brown "piny" heads are brooded over with a motherly care; wormwood roots are loosened, and the horse-radish plant is given a thrifty touch. There is more than the delight of occupation in thus stirring the wheels of the year. We are Nature's poor handmaidens, and our labor gives us joy.

But sweet as these homespun spots can make themselves, in their mixture of thrift and prodigality, they are dearer than ever at the points where they register family traits, and so touch the humanity of us all. Here is imprinted the story of the man who owns the farm, that of the father who inherited it, and the grandfather who reclaimed it from waste; here have they and their womenkind set the foot of daily living and traced indelible paths. They have left here the marks of tragedy, of pathos, or of joy. One yard has a level bit of grassless ground between barn and pump, and you may call it a battlefield, if you will, since famine and desire have striven there together. Or, if you choose to read fine meanings into threadbare things, you may see in it a field of the cloth of gold, where simple love of life and

childlike pleasure met and sparkled for no eye
to see. It was a croquet ground, laid out in
the days when croquet first inundated the land,
and laid out by a woman. This was Della
Smith, the mother of two grave children, and
the wife of a farmer who never learned to
smile. Eben was duller than the ox which
ploughs all day long for his handful of hay
at night and his heavy slumber; but Della,
though she carried her end of the yoke with a
gallant spirit, had dreams and desires forever
bursting from brown shells, only to live a moment in the air, and then, like bubbles, die.
She had a perpetual appetite for joy. When
the circus came to town, she walked miles to
see the procession; and, in a dream of satisfied
delight, dropped potatoes all the afternoon, to
make up. Once, a hand-organ and monkey
strayed that way, and it was she alone who
followed them; for the children were little,
and all the saner house-mothers contented
themselves with leaning over the gates till the
wandering train had passed. But Della drained
her draught of joy to the dregs, and then tilted
her cup anew. With croquet came her su-
premest joy, — one that leavened her days till
God took her, somewhere, we hope, where
there is playtime. Della had no money to
buy a croquet set, but she had something far
better, an alert and undiscouraged mind. On
one dizzy afternoon, at a Fourth of July picnic,

when wickets had been set up near the wood, she had played with the minister, and beaten him. The game opened before her an endless vista of delight. She saw herself perpetually knocking red-striped balls through an eternity of wickets; and she knew that here was the one pastime of which no soul could tire. Afterwards, driving home with her husband and two children, still in a daze of satisfied delight, she murmured absently: —

"Wonder how much they cost?"

"What?" asked Eben, and Della turned, flushed scarlet, and replied: —

"Oh, nothin'!"

That night, she lay awake for one rapt hour, and then she slept the sleep of conquerors. In the morning, after Eben had gone safely off to work, and the children were still asleep, she began singing, in a monotonous, high voice, and took her way out of doors. She always sang at moments when she purposed leaping the bounds of domestic custom. Even Eben had learned that, dull as he was. If he heard that guilty crooning from the buttery, he knew she might be breaking extra eggs, or using more sugar than was conformable.

"What you doin' of?" he was accustomed to call. But Della never answered, and he did not interfere. The question was a necessary concession to marital authority; he had no wish to curb her ways.

Della scudded about the yard like a willful wind. She gathered withes from a waiting pile, and set them in that one level space for wickets. Then she took a handsaw, and, pale about the lips, returned to the house and to her bedroom. She had made her choice. She was sacrificing old associations to her present need ; and, one after another, she sawed the ornamenting balls from her mother's high-post bedstead. Perhaps the one element of tragedy lay in the fact that Della was no mechanician, and she had not foreseen that, having one flat side, her balls might decline to roll. But that dismay was brief. A weaker soul would have flinched ; to Della it was a futile check, a pebble under the wave. She laid her balls calmly aside. Some day she would whittle them into shape ; for there were always coming to Della days full of roomy leisure and large content. Meanwhile apples would serve her turn, — good alike to draw a weary mind out of its channel or teach the shape of spheres. And so, with two russets for balls and the clothes-slice for a mallet (the heavy sledge-hammer having failed), Della serenely, yet in triumph, played her first game against herself.

"Don't you drive over them wickets !" she called imperiously, when Eben came up from the lot in his dingle cart.

"Them what ? " returned he, and Della had to go out to explain. He looked at them gravely; hers had been a ragged piece of work.

"What under the sun'd you do that for?" he inquired. "The young ones would n't turn their hand over for 't. They ain't big enough." "Well, I be," said Della briefly. "Don't you drive over 'em."

Eben looked at her and then at his path to the barn, and he turned his horse aside.

Thereafter, until we got used to it, we found a vivid source of interest in seeing Della playing croquet, and always playing alone. That was a very busy summer, because the famous drought came then, and water had to be carried for weary rods from spring and river. Sometimes Della did not get her playtime till three in the afternoon, sometimes not till after dark; but she was faithful to her joy. The croquet ground suffered varying fortunes. It might happen that the balls were potatoes, when apples failed to be in season; often her wickets broke, and stood up in two ragged horns. Sometimes one fell away altogether, and Della, like the planets, kept an unseen track. Once or twice, the mistaken benevolence of others gave her real distress. The minister's daughter, noting her solitary game, mistook it for forlornness, and, in the warmth of her maiden heart, came to ask if she might share. It was a timid though official benevolence; but Della's bright eyes grew dark. She clung to her kitchen chair.

"I guess I won't," she said, and, in some dim way, everybody began to understand that this was but an intimate and solitary joy. She had grown so used to spreading her banquets for one alone that she was frightened at the sight of other cups upon the board; for although loneliness begins in pain, by and by, perhaps, it creates its own species of sad and shy content.

Della did not have a long life; and that was some relief to us who were not altogether satisfied with her outlook here. The place she left need not be always desolate. There was a good maiden sister to keep the house, and Eben and the children would be but briefly sorry. They could recover their poise; he with the health of a simple mind, and they as children will. Yet he was truly stunned by the blow; and I hoped, on the day of the funeral, that he did not see what I did. When we went out to get our horse and wagon, I caught my foot in something which at once gave way. I looked down — at a broken wicket and a withered apple by the stake.

Quite at the other end of the town is a dooryard which, in my own mind, at least, I call the traveling garden. Miss Nancy, its presiding mistress, is the victim of a love of change; and since she may not wander herself, she transplants shrubs and herbs from nook to nook. No sooner does a green thing get safely rooted than Miss Nancy snatches it up and sets it elsewhere. Her yard is a varying pageant of plants in all stages of misfortune. Here is a shrub, with faded leaves, torn from the lap of prosperity in a well-sunned corner to languish under different conditions. There stands a hardy bush, shrinking, one might guess, under all its bravery of new spring green, from the premonition that Miss Nancy may move it to-morrow. Even the ladies'-delights have their months of garish prosperity, wherein they sicken like country maids; for no sooner do they get their little feet settled in a dark, still corner than they are summoned out of it, to sunlight bright and strong. Miss Nancy lives with a bedridden father, who has grown peevish through long patience; can it be that slow, senile decay which has roused in her a fierce impatience against the sluggishness of life, and that she hurries her plants into motion because she herself must halt? Her father does not theorize about it. He says, "Nancy never has no luck with plants." And that, indeed, is true.

There is another dooryard with its infallible index finger pointing to tell a tale. You can scarcely thread your way through it for vehicles of all sorts congregated there to undergo slow decomposition at the hands of wind and wea-ther. This farmer is a tradesman by nature, and though, for thrift's sake, his fields must be

tilled, he is yet inwardly constrained to keep
on buying and selling, albeit to no purpose.
He is everlastingly swapping and bargaining,
giving play to a faculty which might, in its
legitimate place, have worked out the definite
and tangible, but which now goes automatically
clicking on under vain conditions.   The house,
too, is overrun with useless articles, presently
to be exchanged for others as unavailing, and
in the farmer's pocket ticks a watch which
to-morrow will replace with another more prob-
lematic still.   But in the yard are the undis-
putable evidences of his wild unthrift.   Old
rusty mowing-machines, buggies with torn and
flapping canvas, sleighs ready to yawn at every
crack, all are here : poor relations in a broken-
down family.   But children love this yard.
They come, hand in hand, with a timid confidence in their right, and ask at the back door
for the privilege of playing in it.   They take
long, entrancing journeys in the mouldy old
chaise ; they endure Siberian nights of sleigh-
ing, and throw out their helpless dolls to the
pursuing wolves ; or the more mercantile-
minded among the boys mount a three-wheeled
express wagon, and drive noisily away to traffic
upon the road.   This, in its dramatic possibilities, is not a yard to be despised.

Not far away are two neighboring houses
once held in affectionate communion by a
straight path through the clover and a gap in

the wall. This was the road to much friendly gossip, and there were few bright days which did not find two matrons met at the wall, their heads together over some amiable yarn. But now one house is closed, its windows boarded up, like eyes shut down forever, and the grass has grown over the little path : a line erased, perhaps never to be renewed. It is easier to wipe out a story from nature than to wipe it from the heart ; and these mutilated pages of the outer life perpetually renew in us the pangs of loss and grief.

But not all our dooryard reminiscences are instinct with pain. Do I not remember one swept and garnished plot, never defiled by weed or disordered with ornamental plants, where stood old Deacon Pitts, upon an historic day, and woke the echoes with a herald's joy? Deacon Pitts had the ghoulish delight of the ennuied country mind in funerals and the mortality of man ; and this morning the butcher had brought him news of death in a neighboring town. The butcher had gone by, and I was going ; but Deacon Pitts stood there, dramatically intent upon his mournful morsel. I judged that he was pondering on the possibility of attending the funeral without the waste of too much precious time now due the crops. Suddenly, as he turned back toward the house, bearing a pan of liver, his pondering eye caught sight of his aged wife toiling across

the fields, laden with pennyroyal. He set the
pan down hastily — yea, even before the ad-
vancing cat! — and made a trumpet of his
hands.

"Sarah!" he called piercingly. "Sarah!
Mr. Amasa Blake's passed away! Died yesterday!"

I do not know whether he was present at
that funeral, but it would be strange if he
were not; for time and tide both served him,
and he was always on the spot. Indeed, one
day he reached a house of mourning in such
season that he found the rooms quite empty,
and was forced to wait until the bereaved
family should assemble. There they sat, he
and his wife, a portentous couple in their dead
black and anticipatory gloom, until even their
patience had well-nigh fled. And then an
arriving mourner overheard the deacon, as he
bent forward and challenged his wife in a sus-
picious and discouraged whisper: —

"Say, Sarah, ye don't s'pose it's all goin' to
fush out, do ye?"

They had their funeral.

To the childish memory, so many of the yards
are redolent now of wonder and a strange,
sweet fragrance of the fancy not to be described! One, where lived a notable cook,
had, in a quiet corner, a little grove of caraway.
It seemed mysteriously connected with the
oak-leaf cookies, which only she could make;

and the child, brushing through the delicate bushes grown above his head, used to feel vaguely that, on some fortunate day, cookies would be found there, "a-blowin' and a-growin'." That he had seen them stirred and mixed and taken from the oven was an empty matter; the cookies belonged to the caraway grove, and there they hang ungathered still. In the very same yard was a hogshead filled with rain-water, where insects came daily to their death and floated pathetically in a film of gauzy wings. The child feared this innocent black pool, feared it too much to let it alone; and day by day he would hang upon the rim with trembling fingers, and search the black, smooth depths, with all Ophelia's pangs. And to this moment, no rushing river is half so ministrant to dread as is a still, dull hogshead, where insects float and fly.

These are our dooryards. I wish we lived in them more; that there were vines to sing under, and shade enough for the table, with its wheaten loaf and good farm butter, and its smoking tea. But all that may come when we give up our frantic haste, and sit down to look, and breathe, and listen.

A MARCH WIND

WHEN the clouds hung low, or chimneys refused to draw, or the bread soured over night, a pessimistic public, turning for relief to the local drama, said that Amelia Titcomb had married a tramp. But as soon as the heavens smiled again, it was conceded that she must have been getting lonely in her middle age, and that she had taken the way of wisdom so to furbish up mansions for the coming years. Whatever was set down on either side of the page, Amelia did not care. She was wholeheartedly content with her husband and their farm.

It had happened, one autumn day, that she was trying, all alone, to clean out the cistern. This was while she was still Amelia Titcomb, innocent that there lived a man in the world who could set his foot upon her maiden state, and flourish there. She was an impatient creature. She never could delay for a fostering time to put her plants into the ground, and her fall cleaning was done long before the flies were gone. So, to-day, while other house mistresses sat cosily by the fire, awaiting a milder season, she was toiling up and down the ladder

set in the cistern, dipping pails of sediment
from the bottom, and, hardy as she was, almost
repenting her of a too-fierce desire. Her
thick brown hair was roughened and blown
about her face, her cheeks bloomed out in a
frosty pink, and the plaid kerchief, tied in a
hard knot under her chin, seemed foolishly
ineffectual against the cold. Her hands ached,
holding the pail, and she rebelled inwardly
against the inclemency of the time. It never
occurred to her that she could have put off this
exacting job. She would sooner have expected
Heaven to put off the weather. Just as she
reached the top of the cistern, and lifted her
pail of refuse over the edge, a man appeared
from the other side of the house, and stood
confronting her. He was tall and gaunt, and
his deeply graven face was framed by grizzled
hair. Amelia had a rapid thought that he was
not so old as he looked; experience, rather
than years, must have wrought its trace upon
him. He was leading a little girl, dressed with
a very patent regard for warmth, and none
for beauty. Amelia, with a quick, feminine
glance, noted that the child's bungled skirt and
hideous waist had been made from an old army
overcoat. The little maid's brown eyes were
sweet and seeking; they seemed to petition
for something. Amelia's heart did not re-
spond; at that time, she had no reason for
thinking she was fond of children. Yet she

felt a curious disturbance at sight of the pair.
She afterwards explained it adequately to the
man, by asserting that they looked as odd as
Dick's hatband.

"Want any farmwork done?" asked he.
"Enough to pay for a night's lodgin'?" His
voice sounded strangely soft from one so large
and rugged. It hinted at unused possibilities.
But though Amelia felt impressed, she was
conscious of little more than her own cold and
stiffness, and she answered sharply, —

"No, I don't. I don't calculate to hire,
except in hayin' time, an' then I don't take
tramps."

The man dropped the child's hand, and
pushed her gently to one side.

"Stan' there, Rosie," said he. Then he
went forward, and drew the pail from Amelia's
unwilling grasp. "Where do you empt' it?"
he asked. "There? It ought to be carried
further. You don't want to let it gully down
into that beet bed. Here, I'll see to it."

Perhaps this was the very first time in
Amelia's life that a man had offered her an
unpaid service for chivalry alone. And somehow, though she might have scoffed, knowing
what the tramp had to gain, she believed in
him and in his kindliness. The little girl
stood by, as if she were long used to doing as
she had been told, with no expectation of difficult reasons; and the man, as soberly, went

about his task. He emptied the cistern, and cleansed it, with plentiful washings. Then, as if guessing by instinct what he should find, he went into the kitchen, where were two tubs full of the water which Amelia had pumped up at the start. It had to be carried back again to the cistern; and when the job was quite finished, he opened the bulkhead, set the tubs in the cellar, and then, covering the cistern and cellar-case, rubbed his cold hands on his trousers, and turned to the child.

"Come, Rosie," said he, "we'll be goin'."

It was a very effective finale, but still Amelia suspected no trickery. The situation seemed to her, just as the two new actors did, entirely simple, like the course of nature. Only, the day was a little warmer because they had appeared. She had a new sensation of welcome company. So it was that, quite to her own surprise, she answered as quickly as he spoke, and her reply also seemed an inevitable part of the drama: —

"Walk right in. It's 'most dinner-time, an' I'll put on the pot." The two stepped in before her, and they did not go away.

Amelia herself never quite knew how it happened; but, like all the other natural things of life, this had no need to be explained. At first, there were excellent reasons for delay. The man, whose name proved to be Enoch Willis, was a marvelous hand at a blow, and

she kept him a week, splitting some pine knots
that defied her and the boy who ordinarily
chopped her wood.   At the end of the week,
Amelia confessed that she was "terrible tired
seein' Rosie round in that gormin' kind of a
dress;" so she cut and fitted her a neat little gown from her own red cashmere.   That
was the second reason.   Then the neighbors
heard of the mysterious guest, and dropped in,
to place and label him.   At first, following the
lead of undiscouraged fancy, they declared that
he must be some of cousin Silas's connections
from Omaha; but even before Amelia had
time to deny that, his ignorance of local tradition denied it for him.   He must have heard
of this or that, by way of cousin Silas; but
he owned to nothing defining place or time,
save that he had been in the war — "all through
it."   He seemed to be a man quite weary of
the past and indifferent to the future.   After
a half hour's talk with him, unseasonable callers were likely to withdraw, perhaps into the
pantry, whither Amelia had retreated to escape
catechism, and remark jovially, "Well, 'Melia,
you ain't told us who your company is!"

"Mr. Willis," said Amelia.   She was emulating his habit of reserve.   It made a part of
her new loyalty.

Even to her, Enoch had told no tales; and
strangely enough, she was quite satisfied.   She
trusted him.   He did say that Rosie's mother

was dead; for the last five years, he said, she
had been out of her mind. At that, Amelia's
heart gave a fierce, amazing leap. It struck a
note she never knew, and wakened her to life
and longing. She was glad Rosie's mother
had not made him too content. He went on
a step or two into the story of his life. His
wife's last illness had eaten up the little place,
and after she went, he got no work. So, he
tramped. He must go again. Amelia's voice
sounded sharp and thin, even to her, as she
answered, —

"Go! I dunno what you want to do that
for. Rosie's terrible contented here."

His brown eyes turned upon her in a kindly
glance.

"I've got to make a start somewhere,"
said he. "I've been thinkin' a machine
shop's the best thing. I shall have to depend
on somethin' better 'n days' works."

Amelia flushed the painful red of emotion
without beauty.

"I dunno what we're all comin' to," said
she brokenly.

Then the tramp knew. He put his gnarled
hand over one of hers. Rosie looked up curiously from the speckled beans she was count-
ing into a bag, and then went on singing to
herself an unformed, baby song. "Folks 'll
talk," said Enoch gently. "They do now.
A man an' woman ain't never too old to be

hauled up, an' made to answer for livin'. If I
was younger, an' had suthin' to depend on,
you 'd see ; but I 'm no good now. The better part o' my life 's gone."

Amelia flashed at him a pathetic look, half
agony over her own lost pride, and all a longing of maternal love.

"I don't want you should be younger," said
she. And next week they were married.

Comment ran races with itself, and brought
up nowhere. The treasuries of local speech
were all too poor to clothe so wild a venture.
It was agreed that there 's no fool like an old
fool, and that folks who ride to market may
come home afoot. Everybody forgot that
Amelia had had no previous romance, and dis-
mally pictured her as going through the woods,
and getting a crooked stick at last. Even the
milder among her judges were not content
with prophesying the betrayal of her trust
alone. They argued from the tramp nature to
inevitable results, and declared it would be a
mercy if she were not murdered in her bed.
According to the popular mind, a tramp is a
distinct species, with latent tendencies toward
crime. It was recalled that a white woman
had, in the old days, married a comely Indian,
whose first drink of fire-water, after six months
of blameless happiness, had sent him raging
home, to kill her " in her tracks." Could a
tramp, pledged to the traditions of an awful

brotherhood, do less ? No, even in honor, no ! Amelia never knew how the tide of public apprehension surged about her, nor how her next-door neighbor looked anxiously out, the first thing on rising, to exclaim, with a sigh of relief, and possibly a dramatic pang, " There ! her smoke 's a-goin'."

Meantime, the tramp fell into all the usages of life indoors ; and without, he worked revolution. He took his natural place at the head of affairs, and Amelia stood by, rejoicing. Her besetting error of doing things at the wrong moment had disarranged great combinations as well as small. Her impetuosity was constantly misleading her, bidding her try, this one time, whether harvest might not follow faster on the steps of spring. Enoch's mind was of another cast. For him, tradition reigned, and law was ever laying out the way. Some months after their marriage, Amelia had urged him to take away the winter banking about the house, for no reason save that the Mardens clung to theirs ; but he only replied that he 'd known of cold snaps way on into May, and he guessed there was no particular hurry. The very next day brought a bitter air, laden with sleet, and Amelia, shivering at the open door, exulted in her feminine soul at finding him triumphant on his own ground. Enoch seemed, as usual, unconscious of victory. His immobility had no personal flavor. He merely

acted from an inevitable devotion to the laws
of life; and however often they might prove
him right, he never seemed to reason that
Amelia was consequently wrong.   Perhaps
that was what made it so pleasant to live with
him.

It was "easy sleddin'" now.   Amelia grew
very young.   Her cheeks gained a bloom, her
eyes brightened.   She even, as the matrons
noticed, took to crimping her hair.   They
looked on with a pitying awe.   It seemed a
fearsome thing, to do so much for a tramp
who would only kill you in the end.   Amelia
stepped deftly about the house.   She was a large
woman, whose ways had been devoid of grace;
but now the richness of her spiritual condition
informed her with a charm.   She crooned a
little about her work.   Singing voice she had
none, but she grew into a way of putting words
together, sometimes a line from the psalms,
sometimes a name she loved, and chanting the
sounds, in unrecorded melody.   Meanwhile,
little Rosie, always irreproachably dressed,
with a jealous care lest she fall below the popular standard, roamed in and out of the house,
and lightened its dull intervals.   She, like the
others, grew at once very happy, because, like
them, she accepted her place without a qualm,
as if it had been hers from the beginning.
They were simple natures, and when their joy
came, they knew how to meet it.

But if Enoch was content to follow the beaten ways of life, there was one window through which he looked into the upper heaven of all : thereby he saw what it is to create. He was a born mechanician. A revolving wheel would set him to dreaming, and still him to that lethargy of mind which is an involuntary sharing in the things that are. He could lose himself in the life of rhythmic motion ; and when he discovered rusted springs, or cogs unprepared to fulfill their purpose, he fell upon them with the ardor of a worshiper, and tried to set them right. Amelia thought he should have invented something, and he confessed that he had invented many things, but somehow failed in getting them on the market. That process he mentioned with the indifference of a man to whom a practical outcome is vague, and who finds in the ideal a bright reality. Even Amelia could see that to be a maker was his joy ; to reap rewards of making was another and a lower task.

One cold day in the early spring, he went " up garret " to hunt out an old saddle, gathering mildew there, and came upon a greater treasure, a disabled clock. He stepped heavily down, bearing it aloft in both hands.

" See here, 'Melia," asked he, " why don't this go ? "

Amelia was scouring tins on the kitchen table. There was a teasing wind outside, with a flurry of snow, and she had acknowledged that the irritating weather made her as nervous as a witch. So she had taken to a job to quiet herself.

"That clock?" she replied. "That was gran'-ther Eli's. It give up strikin', an' then the hands stuck, an' I lost all patience with it. So I bought this nickel one, an' carted t' other off into the attic. 'T ain't worth fixin'."

"Worth it!" repeated Enoch. "Well, I guess I'll give it a chance."

He drew a chair to the stove, and there hesitated. "Say, 'Melia," said he, "should you jest as soon I'd bring in that old shoemaker's bench out o' the shed? It's low, an' I could reach my tools off'n the floor."

Amelia lacked the discipline of contact with her kind, but she was nevertheless smooth as silk in her new wifehood.

"Law, yes, bring it along," said she. "It's a good day to clutter up. The' won't be nobody in."

So, while Enoch laid apart the clock with a delicacy of touch known only to square, mechanical fingers, and Rosie played with the button-box on the floor, assorting colors and matching white with white, Amelia scoured the tins. Her energy kept pace with the wind; it whirled in gusts and snatches, yet her precision never failed.

"Made up your mind which cow to sell?"

she asked, opening a discussion still unsettled, after days of animated talk.

"Ain't much to choose," said Enoch. He had frankly set Amelia right on the subject of livestock; and she smilingly acquiesced in his larger knowledge. "Elbridge True's got a mighty nice Alderney, an' if he's goin' to sell milk another year, he'll be glad to get two good milkers like these. What he wants is ten quarts apiece, no matter if it's bluer 'n a whetstone. I guess I can swap off with him; but I don't want to run arter him. I put the case last Thursday. Mebbe he'll drop round."

"Well," concluded Amelia, "I guess you 're pretty sure to do what's right."

The forenoon galloped fast, and it was half past eleven before she thought of dinner.

"Why," said she, "ain't it butcher day? I 've been lottin' on a piece o' liver."

"Butcher day is Thursday," said Enoch. "You 've lost count."

"My land!" responded Amelia. "Well, I guess we can put up with some fried pork an' apples." There came a long, insistent knock at the outer door. "Good heavens! Who's there! Rosie, you run to the side-light, an' peek. It can't be a neighbor. They 'd come right in. I hope my soul it ain't company, a day like this."

Rosie got on her fat legs with difficulty. She held her pinafore full of buttons, but disaster lies in doing too many things at once; there came a slip, a despairing clutch, and the buttons fell over the floor. There were a great many round ones, and they rolled very fast. Amelia washed the sand from her parboiled fingers, and drew a nervous breath. She had a presentiment of coming ill, painfully heightened by her consciousness that the kitchen was "riding out," and that she and her family rode with it. Rosie came running back from her peephole, husky with importance. The errant buttons did not trouble her. She had an eternity of time wherein to pick them up; and, indeed, the chances were that some tall, benevolent being would do it for her.

"It's a man," she said. "He's got on a light coat with bright buttons, and a fuzzy hat. He's got a big nose."

Now, indeed, despair entered into Amelia, and sat enthroned. She sank down on a straight-backed chair, and put her hands on her knees, while the knock came again, a little querulously.

"Enoch," said she, "do you know what's happened? That's cousin Josiah Pease out there." Her voice bore the tragedy of a thousand past encounters; but that Enoch could not know.

"Is it?" asked he, with but a mild appearance of interest. "Want me to go to the door?"

"Go to the door!" echoed Amelia, so stri-
dently that he looked up at her again. "No; I
don't want anybody should go to the door till
this room's cleared up. If 't w'an't so ever-
lastin' cold, I'd take him right into the clock-
room, an' blaze a fire; but he'd see right
through that. You gether up them tools an'
things, an' I'll help carry out the bench."

If Enoch had not just then been absorbed
in a delicate combination of brass, he might
have spoken more sympathetically. As it was,
he seemed kindly, but remote.

"Look out!" said he, "you'll joggle. No,
I guess I won't move. If he's any kind of a
man, he'll know what 't is to clean a clock."

Amelia was not a crying woman, but the
hot tears stood in her eyes. She was experi-
encing, for the first time, that helpless pang
born from the wounding of pride in what we
love.

"Don't you see, Enoch?" she insisted.
"This room looks like the Old Boy — an' so do
you — an' he'll go home an' tell all the folks
at the Ridge. Why, he's heard we're married,
an' come over here to spy out the land. He
hates the cold. He never stirs till 'way on
into June; an' now he's come to find out."

"Find out what?" inquired Enoch absorb-
edly. "Well, if you're anyways put to 't, you
send him to me." That manly utterance enun-
ciated from a "best-room" sofa, by an Enoch

clad in his Sunday suit, would have filled
Amelia with rapture; she could have leaned
on it as on the Tables of the Law.   But, alas!
the scene-setting was meagre, and though
Enoch was very clean, he had no good clothes.
He had pointedly refused to buy them with
his wife's money until he should have worked
on the farm to a corresponding amount.   She
had loved him for it; but every day his outer
poverty hurt her pride.   "I guess you better
ask him in," concluded Enoch.   "Don't you
let him bother you."

Amelia turned about with the grand air of a
woman repulsed.

"He *don't* bother me," said she, "an' I *will*
let him in."   She walked to the door, stepping
on buttons as she went, and conscious, when
she broke them, of a bitter pleasure.   It added
to her martyrdom.

She flung open the door, and called herself
a fool in the doing; for the little old man
outside was in the act of turning away.   In
another instant, she might have escaped.   But
he was only too eager to come back again, and
it seemed to Amelia as if he would run over
her, in his desire to get in.

"There! there! 'Melia," said he, pushing
past her, "can't stop to talk till I git near the
fire.   Guess you were settin' in the kitchen,
wa'n't ye?   Don't make no stranger o' me.
That your man?"

She had shut the door, and entered, exasperated anew by the rising wind. "That's my husband," said she coldly. "Enoch, here's cousin Josiah Pease."

Enoch looked up benevolently over his spectacles, and put out a horny left hand, the while the other guarded his heap of treasures. "Pleased to meet you, sir," said he. "You see I'm tinkerin' a clock."

To Enoch, the explanation was enough. All the simple conventions of his life might well wait upon a reason potent as this. Josiah Pease went to the stove, and stood holding his tremulous hands over a cover. He was a little man, eclipsed in a butternut coat of many capes, and his parchment face shaded gradually up from it, as if into a harder medium. His eyes were light, and they had an exceedingly uncomfortable way of darting from one thing to another, like some insect born to spear and sting. His head was entirely bald, all save a thin fringe of hair not worth mentioning, since it disappeared so effectually beneath his collar; and his general antiquity was grotesquely emphasized by two sets of aggressive teeth, displaying their falsity from every crown.

Amelia took out the broom, and began sweeping up buttons. She had an acrid consciousness that by sacrificing them she was somehow completing the tragedy of her day. Rosie gave a little cry; but Amelia pointed to

the corner where stood the child's chair, ex-
humed from the attic, after forty years of rest.
"You set there," she said, in an undertone,
"an' keep still."

Rosie obeyed without a word. Such an
atmosphere had not enveloped her since she
entered this wonderful house. Remembering
vaguely the days when her own mother had
"spells," and she and her father effaced themselves until times should change, she folded
her little hands, and lapsed back into a condition of mental servitude.

Meanwhile, Amelia followed nervously in
the track of Enoch's talk with cousin Josiah,
though her mind kept its undercurrent of foolish musing. Like all of us, snatched up by
the wheels of great emergencies, she caught
at trifles while they whirled her round. Here
were "soldier-buttons." All the other girls
had collected them, though she, having no lover
in the war, had traded for her few. Here were
the gold-stones that held her changeable silk,
there the little clouded pearls from her sister's
raglan. Annie had died in youth; its gla-
mour still enwrapped her. Poor Annie! But
Rosie had seemed to bring her back. Amelia
swept litter, buttons and all, into the dustpan,
and marched to the stove to throw her booty
in. Nobody marked her save Rosie, whose
playthings were endangered; but Enoch's very
obtuseness to the situation was what stayed her

hand. She carried the dustpan away into a closet, and came back, to gather up her tins. A cold rage of nervousness beset her, so overpowering that she herself was amazed at it.

Meantime, Josiah Pease had divested himself of his coat, and drawn the grandfather chair into a space behind the stove.

"You a clock-mender by trade?" he asked of Enoch.

"No," said Enoch absently, "I ain't got any reg'lar trade."

"Jest goin' round the country?" amended cousin Josiah, with the preliminary insinuation Amelia knew so well. He was, it had been said, in the habit of inventing lies, and challenging other folks to stick to 'em. But Enoch made no reply. He went soberly on with his work.

"Law, 'Melia, to think o' your bein' married," continued Josiah, turning to her. "I never should ha' thought that o' you."

"I never thought it of myself," said Amelia tartly. "You don't know what you'll do till you're tried."

"No! no!" said Josiah Pease. "Never in the world. You remember Sally Flint, how plain-spoken she is? Well, Betsy Marden's darter Ann rode down to the poor-house t' other day with some sweet trade, an' took a young sprig with her. He turned his back a minute, to look out o' winder, an' Sally spoke right up,

as ye might say, afore him. 'That your beau?'
says she. Well, o' course Ann couldn't own
it, an' him right there, so to speak. So she
shook her head. 'Well, I'm glad on 't,' says
Sally. 'If I couldn't have anything to eat,
I'd have suthin' to look at!' He was the
most unsignifyin'est creatur' you ever put your
eyes on. But they say Ann's started in on her
clo'es."

Amelia's face had grown scarlet. "I dunno's
any such speech is called for here," said she,
in a furious self-betrayal. Josiah Pease had
always been able to storm her reserves.

"Law, no," answered he comfortably. "It
come into my mind, — that's all."

She looked at Enoch with a passionate sympathy, knowing too well how the hidden sting
was intended to work. But Enoch had not
heard. He was absorbed in a finer problem of
brass and iron ; and though Amelia had wished
to save him from hurt, in that instant she
scorned him for his blindness. "I guess I
shall have to ask you to move," she said to her
husband coldly. "I've got to git to that stove,
if we're goin' to have any dinner to-day."

It seemed to her that even Enoch might
take the hint, and clear away his rubbish.
Her feelings might have been assuaged by a
clean hearth and some acquiescence in her own
mood. But he only moved back a little, and
went on fitting and musing. He was not think-

ing of her in the least, nor even of Josiah Pease. His mind had entered its brighter, more alluring world. She began to fry her pork and apples, with a perfunctory attempt at conversation. "You don't often git round so early in the spring," said she.

"No," returned cousin Josiah. "I kind o' got started out, this time, I don't rightly know why. I guess I've had you in mind more of late, for some Tiverton folks come over our way, tradin', an' they brought all the news. It sort o' stirred me up to come."

Amelia turned her apples vigorously, well aware that the slices were breaking. That made a part of her bitter day.

"Folks need n't take the trouble to carry news about me," she said. There was an angry gleam in her eyes. "If anybody wants to know anything, let 'em come right here, an' I'll settle 'em." The ring of her voice penetrated even to Enoch's perception, and he looked up in mild surprise. She seemed to have thrown open, for an instant, a little window into a part of her nature he had never seen.

"How good them apples smell!" said Josiah innocently. "Last time I had 'em was down to cousin Amasa True's, he that married his third wife, an' she run through all he had. I went down to see 'em arter the vandoo, — you know they got red o' most everything, — an'

they had fried pork an' apples for dinner. Old
Bashaby dropped in. 'Law!' says she. 'Fried
pork an' apples! Well, I call that livin' pretty
nigh the wind!'" Josiah chuckled. He was
very warm now, and the savory smell of the
dish he decried was mounting to what served
him for fancy. "'Melia, you ain't never had
your teeth out, have ye?" he asked, as one
who spoke from richer memories.

"I guess my teeth 'll last me as long as I
want 'em," said Amelia curtly.

"Well, I did n't know. They looked real
white an' firm last time I see 'em, but you
never can tell how they be underneath. I
knew the folks would ask me when I got
home. I thought I 'd speak."

"Dinner 's ready," said Amelia. She turned
an alien look upon her husband. "You want
to wash your hands?"

Enoch rose cheerfully. He had got to a
hopeful place with the clock.

"Set ri' down," said he. "Don't wait a
minute. I 'll be along."

So Amelia and the guest began their meal,
while little Rosie climbed, rather soberly, into
her higher chair, and held out her plate.

"You wait," said Amelia harshly. "Can't
you let other folks eat a mouthful before you
have to have yours?" Yet as she said it, she
remembered, with a remorseful pang, that she
had always helped the child first; it had been
so sweet to see her pleased and satisfied.

Josiah was never talkative during meals.
Not being absolute master of his teeth, his
mind dwelt with them. Amelia remembered
that, with a malicious satisfaction. But he
could not be altogether dumb. That, people
said, would never happen to Josiah Pease
while he was above ground.

"That his girl?" he asked, indicating Rosie
with his knife, in a gustatory pause.

"Whose?" inquired Amelia willfully.

"His." He pointed again, this time to the
back room, where Enoch was still washing his
hands.

"Yes."

"Mother dead?"

Amelia sprang from her chair, while Rosie
looked at her with the frightened glance of a
child to whom some half-forgotten grief has
suddenly returned.

"Josiah Pease!" said Amelia. "I never
thought a poor, insignificant creatur' like you
could rile me so, — when I know what you 're
doin' it for, too. But you 've brought it about.
Her mother dead? Ain't I been an' married
her father?"

"Law, Amelia, do se' down!" said Josiah
indulgently. There was a mince-pie warming
on the back of the stove. He saw it there.
"I did n't mean nuthin'. I'll be bound you
thought she 's dead, or you would n't ha' took
such a step. I only meant, did ye see her

death in the paper, for example, or anything
like that?"

"'Melia," called Enoch, from the doorway,
"I won't come in to dinner jest now. Elbridge True's drove into the yard. I guess he's
got it in mind to talk it over about them cows.
I don't want to lose the chance."

"All right," answered Amelia. She took
her seat again, while Enoch's footsteps went
briskly out through the shed. With the clanging of the door, she felt secure. If she had to
deal with Josiah Pease, she could do it better
alone, clutching at the certainty that was with
her from of old, that, if you could only keep
your temper with cousin Josiah, you had one
chance of victory. Flame out at him, and you
were lost. "Some more potatoes?" asked she,
with a deceptive calm.

"Don't care if I do," returned Josiah, selecting greedily, his fork hovering in air. "Little
mite watery, ain't they? Dig 'em yourself?"

"We dug 'em," said Amelia coldly.

Rosie stepped down from her chair, unno-
ticed. To Amelia, she was then no bigger
than some little winged thing flitting about
the room in time of tragedy. Our greatest
emotions sometimes stay unnamed. At that
moment, Amelia was swayed by as tumultuous
a love as ever animated damsel of verse or
story; but it merely seemed to her that she
was an ill-used woman, married to a man for

whom she was called on to be ashamed. Rosie tiptoed into the entry, put on her little shawl and hood, and stole out to play in the corn-house. When domestic squalls were gathering, she knew where to go. The great outdoors was safer. Her past had taught her that.

"Don't like to eat with folks, does he? Well, it's all in what you're brought up to."

Amelia was ready with her counter-charge. "Have some tea?"

She poured it as if it were poison, and Josiah became conscious of her tragic self-control.

"You ain't eat a thing," said he, with an ostentatious kindliness. He bent forward a little, with the air of inviting a confidence. "Got suthin' on your mind, ain't you, 'Melia?" he whispered. "Kind o' worried? Find he's a drinkin' man?"

Amelia was not to be beguiled, even by that anger which veils itself as justice. She looked at him steadily, with scorching eyes.

"You ain't took any sugar," said she. "There 't is, settin' by you. Help yourself."

Josiah addressed himself to his tea, and then Amelia poured him another cup. She had some fierce satisfaction in making it good and strong. It seemed to her that she was heartening her adversary for the fray, and she took pleasure in doing it effectually. So great

was the spirit within her that she knew he
could not be too valiant, for her keener joy in
laying him low. Then they rose from the
table, and Josiah took his old place by the
stove, while Amelia began carrying the dishes
to the sink. Her mind was a little hazy now ;
her next move must depend on his, and cousin
Josiah, somewhat drowsy from his good dinner,
was not at once inclined to talk. Suddenly
he raised his head snakily from those sunken
shoulders, and pointed a lean finger to the
window.

"'Melia!" cried he sharply. "I 'll be buttered if he ain't been and traded off both your
cows. My Lord! be you goin' to stan' there
an' let them two cows go?"

Amelia gave one swift glance from the
window, following the path marked out by
that insinuating index. It was true. Elbridge
was driving her two cows out of the yard, and
her husband stood by, watching him. She
walked quietly into the entry, and Josiah laid
his old hands together in the rapturous certainty that she was going to open the door,
and send her anger forth. But Amelia only
took down his butternut coat from the nail,
and returned with it, holding it ready for him
to insert his arms.

"Here's your coat," said she, with that
strange, deceptive calmness. "Stan' up, an'
I 'll help you put it on."

Josiah looked at her with helplessly open mouth, and eyes so vacuous that Amelia felt, even at that moment, the grim humor of his plight.

"I was in hopes he'd harness up" — he began, but she ruthlessly cut him short.

"Stan' up! Here, put t' other arm in fust. This han'kercher yours? Goes round your neck? There 't is. Here's your hat. Got any mittens? There they be, in your pocket. This way. This is the door you come in, an' this is the door you'll go out of." She preceded him, her head thrown up, her shoulders back. Amelia had no idea of dramatic values, but she was playing an effective part. She reached the door and flung it open, but Josiah, a poor figure in its huddled capes, still stood abjectly in the middle of the kitchen. "Come!" she called peremptorily. "Come, Josiah Pease! Out you go." And Josiah went, though, contrary to his usual habit, he did not talk. He quavered uncertainly down the steps, and Amelia called a halt. "Josiah Pease!"

He turned, and looked up at her. His mouth had dropped, and he was nothing but a very helpless old child. Vicious as he was, Amelia realized the mental poverty of her adversary, and despised herself for despising him. "Josiah Pease!" she repeated. "This is the end. Don't you darken my doors ag'in. I've done with you, — egg an' bird!" She

closed the door, shutting out Josiah and the
keen spring wind, and went back to the window, to watch him down the drive.   His back
looked poor and mean.   It emphasized the pet-
tiness of her victory.   Even at that moment,
she realized that it was the poorer part of her
which had resented attack on a citadel which
should be impregnable as time itself.   Just
then Enoch stepped into the kitchen behind
her, and his voice jarred upon her tingling
nerves.

"Well," said he, more jovially than he was
wont to speak, "I guess I've made a good
trade for ye.   Company gone?   Come here
an' se' down while I eat, an' I'll tell ye all
about it."

Amelia turned about and walked slowly up
to him, by no volition of her conscious self.
Again love, that august creature, veiled itself
in an unjust anger, because it was love and
nothing else.

"You've made a good bargain, have you?"
she repeated.   "You've sold my cows, an'
had 'em drove off the place without if or but.
That's what you call a good bargain!"   Her
voice frightened her.   It amazed the man who
heard.   These two middle-aged people were
waking up to passions neither had felt in
youth.   Life was strong in them because love
was there.

"Why, 'Melia!" said the man.   "Why,
'Melia!"

Amelia was hurried on before the wind of
her destiny. Her voice grew sharper. Little
white stripes, like the lashes from a whip,
showed themselves on her cheeks. She seemed
to be speaking from a dream, which left her
no will save that of speaking.

"It's been so ever sence you set foot in
this house. Have I had my say once? Have I
been mistress on my own farm? No! You
took the head o' things, an' you've kep' it.
What's mine is yours."

Her triumph over Josiah seemed to be
strangely repeated; the scene was almost identical. The man before her stood with his
hands hanging by his sides, the fingers limp,
in an attitude of the profoundest patience. He
was thinking things out. She knew that.
Her hurrying mind anticipated all he might
have said, and would not. And because he
had too abiding a gentleness to say it, the
insanity of her anger rose anew. "I'm the
laughin'-stock o' the town," she went on bitterly. "There ain't a man or woman in it
that don't say I've married a tramp."

Enoch winced, with a sharp, brief quiver of
the lips; but before she could dwell upon the
sight, to the resurrection of her tenderness, he
turned away from her, and went over to the
bench.

"I guess I'll move this back where't was,"
he said, in a very still voice, and Amelia stood

watching him, conscious of a new and bitterer
pang : a fierce contempt that he could go on
with his poor, methodical way of living, when
greater issues waited at the door.   He moved
the bench into its old place, gathered up the
clock, with its dismantled machinery, and carried it into the attic.   She heard his step on
the stairs, regular and unhalting, and despised
him again ; but in all those moments, the
meaning of his movements had not struck her.
When he came back, he brought in the broom ;
and while he swept up the fragments of his
work, Amelia stood and watched him.   He
carried the dustpan and broom away to their
places, but he did not reënter the room.   He
spoke to her from the doorway, and she could
not see his face.

"I guess you won't mind if I leave the clock
as 't is.   It needs some new cogs, an' if anybody should come along, he would n't find it
any the worse for what I 've done.   I 've jest
thought it over about the cows, an' I guess I 'll
leave that, too, jest as it is.   I made you a
good bargain, an' when you come to think it
over, I guess you 'd ruther it 'd stan' so than
run the resk of havin' folks make a handle of
it.   Good-by, 'Melia.   You 've been good to
me, — better 'n anybody ever was in the world."

She heard his step, swift and steady, through
the shed and out at the door.   He was gone.
Amelia turned to the window, to look after

him, and then, finding he had not taken the
driveway, she ran into the bedroom, to gaze
across the fields.   There he was, a lonely
figure, striking vigorously out.   He seemed
glad to go ; and seeing his haste, her heart
hardened against him.   She gave a little dis-
dainful laugh.

"Well," said Amelia, "*that*'s over.   I'll
wash my dishes now."

Coming back into the kitchen, with an assured step, she moved calmly about her work,
as if the world were there to see.   Her pride
enveloped her like a garment.   She handled
the dishes as if she scorned them, yet her
method and care were exquisite.   Presently
there came a little imperative pounding at the
side door.   It was Rosie.   She had forgotten
the cloudy atmosphere of the house, and being
cold, had come, in all her old, imperious certainty of love and warmth, to be let in.   Amelia
stopped short in her work, and an ugly frown
roughened her brow.   Josiah Pease, with all
his evil imaginings, seemed to be at her side,
his lean forefinger pointing out the baseness
of mankind.   In that instant, she realized
where Enoch had gone.   He meant to take
the three o'clock train where it halted, down
at the Crossing, and he had left the child
behind.   Tearing off her apron, she threw it
over her head.   She ran to the door, and, opening it, almost knocked the child down, in her

haste to be out and away. Rosie had lifted her frosty face in a smile of welcome, but Amelia did not see it. She gathered the child in her arms, and hurried down the steps, through the bars, and along the narrow path toward the pine woods. The sharp brown stubble of the field merged into the thin grasses of the greener lowland, and she heard the trickling of the little dark brook, where gentians lived in the fall, and where, still earlier, the cardinal flower and forget-me-not crowded in lavish color. She knew every inch of the way; her feet had an intelligence of their own. The farm was a part of her inherited life; but at that moment, she prized it as nothing beside that newly discovered wealth which she was rushing to cast away. Rosie had not striven in the least against her capture. She knew too much of life, in some patient fashion, to resist it, in any of its phases. She put her arms about Amelia's neck, to cling the closer, and Amelia, turning her face while she staggered on, set her lips passionately to the little sleeve.

"You cold?" asked she — "*dear?*" But she told herself it was a kiss of farewell.

She stepped deftly over the low stone wall into the Marden woods, and took the slippery downward path, over pine needles. Sometimes a rounded root lay above the surface, and she stumbled on it ; but the child only tightened

her grasp. Amelia walked and ran with the
prescience of those without fear ; for her eyes
were unseeing, and her thoughts hurrying
forward, she depicted to herself the little drama
at its close. She would be at the Crossing and
away again, before the train came in ; nobody
need guess her trouble. Enoch must be there,
waiting. She would drop the child at his side,
— the child he had deserted, — and before he
could say a word, turn back to her desolate
home. And at the thought, she kissed the
little sleeve again, and thought how good it
would be if she could only be there again,
though alone, in the shielding walls of her
house, and the parting were over and done.
She felt her breath come chokingly.

"You'll have to walk a minute," she whispered, setting the child down at her side.
"There's time enough. I can't hurry."

At that instant, she felt the slight warning
of the ground beneath her feet, shaken by
another step, and saw, through the pines, her
husband running toward her. Rosie started
to meet him, with a little cry, but Amelia thrust
her aside, and hurried swiftly on in advance,
her eyes feeding upon his face. It had miraculously changed. Sorrow, the great despair
of life, had eaten into it, and aged it more than
years of patient want. His eyes were like
lamps burned low, and the wrinkles under
them had guttered into misery. But to Amelia,

his look had all the sweet familiarity of faces
we shall see in Paradise. She did not stop
to interpret his meeting glance, nor ask him
to read hers. Coming upon him like a whirl-
wind, she put both her shaking hands on his
shoulders, and laid her wet face to his.

"Enoch! Enoch!" she cried sharply, "in
the name of God, come home with me!"

She felt him trembling under her hands, but
he only put up his own, and very gently loosed
the passionate grasp. "There! there!" he
said, in a whisper. "Don't feel so bad. It's
all right. I jest turned back for Rosie. Mebbe
you won't believe it, but I forgot all about
her."

He lowered his voice, for Rosie had gone
close to him, and laid her hands clingingly
upon his coat. She did not understand, but
she could wait. A branch had almost barred
the path, and Amelia, her dull gaze fallen,
noted idly how bright the moss had kept, and
how the scarlet cups enriched it. Her strength
would not sustain her, void of his, and she
sank down on the wood, her hands laid limply
in her lap. "Enoch," she said, from her new
sense of the awe of life, "don't lay up anything ag'inst me. You couldn't if you knew."

"Knew what?" asked Enoch gently. He
did not forget that circumstance had laid a
blow at the roots of his being; but he could
not turn away while she still suffered.

Amelia began, stumblingly, —

"He talked about you. I could n't stan' it."

"Did you believe it?" he queried sternly.

"There wa'n't anything to believe. That's neither here nor there. But — Enoch, if anybody should cut my right hand off — Enoch" — Her voice fell brokenly. She was a New England woman, accustomed neither to analyze nor talk. She could only suffer in the elemental way of dumb things who sometimes need a language of the heart. One thing she knew. The man was hers; and if she reft herself away from him, then she must die.

He had taken Rosie's hand, and Amelia was aware that he turned away.

"I don't want to bring up anything," he said hesitatingly, "but I could n't stan' bein' any less 'n other men would, jest because the woman had the money, an' I had n't. I dunno 's 't was exactly fair about the cows, but somehow you kind o' set me at the head o' things, in the beginnin', an' it never come into my mind" —

Amelia sat looking wanly past him. She began to see how slightly argument would serve. Suddenly the conventions of life fell away from her and left her young.

"Enoch," she said vigorously, "you 've got to take me. Somehow, you 've got to. Talkin' won't make you see that what I said never

meant no more than the wind that blows. But
you've got to keep me, or remember, all your
life, how you murdered me by goin' away.
The farm's come between us. Le's leave it!
It's 'most time for the cars. You take me
with you now. If you tramp, I'll tramp. If
you work out, so 'll I. But where you go, I've
got to go, too."

Some understanding of her began to creep
upon him; he dropped the child's hand, and
came a step nearer. Enoch, in these latter
days of his life, had forgotten how to smile;
but now a sudden, mirthful gleam struck upon
his face, and lighted it with the candles of
hope. He stood beside her, and Amelia did
not look at him.

"Would you go with me, 'Melia?" he
asked.

"I'm goin'," said she doggedly. Her case
had been lost, but she could not abandon it.
She seemed to be holding to it in the face of
righteous judgment.

"S'pose I don't ask you?"

"I'll foller on behind."

"Don't ye want to go home, an' lock up,
an' git a bunnit?"

She put one trembling hand to the calico
apron about her head.

"No."

"Don't ye want to leave the key with some
o' the neighbors?"

"I don't want anything in the world but you," owned Amelia shamelessly.

Enoch bent suddenly, and drew her to her feet. "'Melia," said he, "you look up here."

She raised her drawn face and looked at him, not because she wished, but because she must. In her abasement, there was no obedience which she would deny him. But she could only see that he was strangely happy, and so the more removed from her own despair. Enoch swiftly passed his arm about her, and turned her homeward. He laughed a little. Being a man, he must laugh when that bitter ache in the throat presaged more bitter tears.

"Come, 'Melia," said he, "come along home, an' I'll tell you all about the cows. I made a real good bargain. Come, Rosie."

Amelia could not answer. It seemed to her as if love had dealt with her as she had not deserved; and she went on, exalted, afraid of breaking the moment, and knowing only that he was hers again. But just before they left the shadow of the woods, he stopped, holding her still, and their hearts beat together.

"'Melia," said he brokenly, "I guess I never told you in so many words, but it's the truth: if God Almighty was to make me a woman, I'd have her you, not a hair altered. I never cared a straw for any other. I know that now. You're all there is in the world."

When they walked up over the brown field,

the sun lay very warmly there with a promise
of spring fulfilled. The wind had miraculously died, and soft clouds ran over the sky in
flocks. Rosie danced on ahead, singing her
queer little song, and Enoch struggled with
himself to speak the word his wife might
wish.

"'Melia," said he at last, "there ain't anything in my life I could n't tell you. I jest
ain't dwelt on it, that's all. If you want to
have me go over it " —

"I don't want anything," said Amelia firmly.
Her eyes were suffused, and yet lambent. The
light in them seemed to be drinking up their
tears. Her steps, she knew, were set within
a shining way. At the door only she paused
and fixed him with a glance. "Enoch," said
she threateningly, "whose cows were them
you sold to-day?"

He opened his lips, but she looked him
down. One word he rejected, and then another. His cheeks wrinkled up into obstinate
smiling, and he made the grimace of a child
over its bitter draught.

"'Melia, it ain't fair," he complained. "No,
it ain't. I'll take one of 'em, if you say so,
or I'll own it don't make a mite o' difference
whose they be. But as to lyin'" —

"Say it!" commanded Amelia. "Whose
were they?"

"Mine!" said Enoch. .They broke into

laughter, like children, and held each other's hands.

"I ain't had a mite o' dinner," said Amelia happily, as they stepped together into the kitchen. "Nor you! An' Rosie didn't eat her pie. You blaze up the fire, an' I'll fry some eggs."

THE MORTUARY CHEST

"Now we 've got red o' the men-folks," said
Mrs. Robbins, "le's se' down an' talk it over."
The last man of all the crowd accustomed to
seek the country store at noontime was closing
the church door behind him as she spoke.
"Here, Ezry," she called after him, "you
hurry up, or you won't git there afore cockcrow
to-morrer, an' I would n't have that letter miss
for a good deal."

Mrs. Robbins was slight, and hung on wires,
— so said her neighbors.   They also remarked
that her nose was as pickèd as a pin, and that
anybody with them freckles and that red hair
was sure to be smart.   You could always tell.
Mrs. Robbins knew her reputation for extreme
acuteness, and tried to live up to it.

"Law! don't you go to stirrin' on him up,"
said Mrs. Solomon Page comfortably, putting
on the cover of her butter-box, which had con-
tained the family lunch.   "If the store's
closed, he can slip the letter into the box, an'
three cents with it, an' they 'll put a stamp on
in the mornin'."

By this time, there was a general dusting of
crumbs from Sunday gowns, a settling of boxes

and baskets, and the feminine portion of the
East Tiverton congregation, according to ancient custom, passed into the pews nearest the
stove, and arranged itself more compactly for
the midday gossip. This was a pleasant inter-
lude in the religious decorum of the day; no
Sunday came when the men did not trail off
to the store for their special council, and the
women, with a restful sense of sympathy
alloyed by no disturbing element, settled down
for an exclusively feminine view of the universe.
Mrs. Page took the head of the pew, and disposed her portly frame so as to survey the
scene with ease. She was a large woman,
with red cheeks and black, shining hair. One
powerful arm lay along the back of the pew,
and, as she talked, she meditatively beat the
rail in time. Her sister, Mrs. Ellison, according to an intermittent custom, had come over
from Saltash to attend church, and incidentally
to indulge in a family chat. It was said that
Tilly rode over about jes' so often to get the
Tiverton news for her son Leonard, who fur-
nished local items to the Sudleigh "Star;" and,
indeed, she made no secret of sitting down
in social conclave with a bit of paper and a
worn pencil in hand, to jog her memory. She,
too, had smooth black hair, but her dark eyes
were illumined by no steadfast glow; they
snapped and shone with alert intelligence, and
her great forehead dominated the rest of her

face, scarred with a thousand wrinkles by intensity of nature rather than by time. A pleasant warmth had diffused itself over the room, so cold during the morning service that foot-stoves had been in requisition. Bonnet strings were thrown back and shawls unpinned. The little world relaxed and lay at ease.

"What's the news over your way, sister?" asked Mrs. Ellison, as an informal preliminary.

"Tilly don't want to give; she'd rather take," said Mrs. Baxter, before the other could answer. "She's like old Mis' Pepper. Seliny Hazlitt went over there, when she was fust married an' come to the neighborhood, an' asked her if she'd got a sieve to put squash through. Poor Seliny! she did n't know a sieve from a colander, in them days."

"I guess she found out soon enough," volunteered Mrs. Page. "*He* was one o' them kind o' men that can keep house as well as a woman. I'd ruther live with a born fool."

"Well, old Mis' Pepper she ris up an' smoothed down her apron (recollect them little dots she used to wear? — made her look as broad as a barn door!), an' she says, 'Yes, we've got a sieve for flour, an' a sieve for meal, an' a sieve for rye, an' a sieve for blue-monge, an' we could have a sieve for squash if we was a mind to, *but I don't wish to lend.*' That's the way with Tilly. She's terrible cropein' about news, but she won't lend."

"How's your cistern?" asked Mrs. John Cole, who, with an exclusively practical turn of mind, saw no reason why talk should be consecutive. "Got all the water you want?"

"Yes," said Mrs. Page; "that last rain filled it up higher 'n it 's been sence November."

But Mrs. Ellison was not to be thrown off the track.

"Ain't there been consid'able talk over here about Parson Bond?" she asked.

Miss Sally Ware, a plump and pleasing maiden lady, whose gold beads lay in a crease especially designed for them, stirred uneasily in her seat and gave her sisters an appealing glance. But she did not speak, beyond uttering a little dissentient noise in her throat. She was loyal to her minister. An embarrassed silence fell like a vapor over the assemblage. Everybody longed to talk; nobody wanted the responsibility of beginning. Mrs. Page was the first to gather her forces.

"Now, Tilly," said she, with decision, "you ain't comin' over here to tole us into haulin' our own pastor over the coals, unless you'll say right out you won't pass it on to Saltash folks. As for puttin' it in the paper, it ain't the kind you can."

Tilly's eyes burned.

"I guess I know when to speak an' when not to," she remarked. "Now don't beat about the bush; the men-folks 'll be back to-

rights. I never in my life give Len a mite o'
news he could n't ha' picked up for himself."

"Well, some master silly pieces have got
into the paper, fust an' last," said Mrs. Robbins. "Recollect how your Len come 'way
over here to git his shoes cobbled, the week
arter Tom Brewer moved int' the Holler, an'
folks had n't got over swappin' the queer things
he said? an' when Tom got the shoes done
afore he promised, Len says to him, 'You 're
better 'n your word.' 'Well,' says Tom, 'I flew
at 'em with all the venom o' my specie.' An'
it wa'n't a fortnight afore that speech come
out in a New York paper, an' then the Sudleigh 'Star' got hold on 't, an' so 't went. If
folks want that kind o' thing, they can git a
plenty, *I* say." She set her lips defiantly, and
looked round on the assembled group. This
was something she had meant to mention;
now she had done it.

The informal meeting was aghast. A flavor
of robust humor was accustomed to enliven it,
but not of a sort to induce dissension.

"There! there!" murmured Sally Ware.
"It 's the Sabbath day!"

"Well, nobody 's breakin' of it, as I know
of," said Mrs. Ellison. Her eyes were brighter
than usual, but she composed herself into a
careful disregard of annoyance. When desire
of news assailed her, she could easily conceal
her personal resentments, cannily sacrificing

small issues to great. "I guess there's no danger o' Parson Bond's gittin' into the paper, so long's he behaves himself; but if anybody's got eyes, they can't help seein'. I hadn't been in the Bible class five minutes afore I guessed how he was carryin' on. Has he begun to go with Isabel North, an' his wife not cold in her grave?"

"Well, I think, for my part, he does want Isabel," said Mrs. Robbins sharply, "an' I say it's a sin an' a shame. Why, she ain't twenty, an' he's sixty if he's a day. My soul! Sally Ware, you better be settin' your cap for my William Henry. He's 'most nineteen."

Miss Ware flushed, and her plump hands tightened upon each other under her shawl. She was never entirely at ease in the atmosphere of these assured married women; it was always a little bracing.

"Well, how's she take it?" asked Tilly, turning from one to the other. "Tickled to death, I s'pose?"

"Well, I guess she ain't!" broke in a younger woman, whose wedding finery was not yet outworn. "She's most sick over it, and so she has been ever since her sister married and went away. I believe she'd hate the sight of him, if 't wasn't the minister; but *'t is* the minister, and when she's put face to face with him, she can't help saying yes and no."

"I dunno'," said Mrs. Page, with her unc-

tuous laugh. "Remember the party over to
Tiverton t' other night, an' them tarts? You
see, Rosanna Maria Pike asked us all over; an'
you know how flaky her pie-crust is. Well,
the minister was stan'in' side of Isabel when
the tarts was passed. He was sort o' shinin'
up to her that night, an' I guess he felt a mite
twittery; so when the tarts come to him, he
reached out kind o' delicate, with his little
finger straight out, an' tried to take one. An'
a ring o' crust come off on his finger. Then
he tried it ag'in, an' got another ring. Everybody 'd ha' laughed, if it had n't been the minister; but Isabel she tickled right out, an'
says, 'You don't take jelly, do you, Mr. Bond?'
An' he turned as red as fire, an' says, 'No, I
thank you.'"

"She would n't ha' said it, if she had n't ha'
been so nervous," remarked Miss Sally, taking
a little parcel of peppermints from her pocket,
and proceeding to divide them.

"No, I don't s'pose she would," owned Mrs.
Page reflectively. "But if what they say is
true, she 's been pretty sassy to him, fust an'
last. Why, you know, no matter how the parson begins his prayer, he 's sure to end up on
one line: 'Lord, we thank Thee we have not
been left to live by the dim light of natur'.'
'Lisha Cole, when he come home from Illinois,
walked over here to meetin', to surprise some
o' the folks. He waited in the entry to ketch

'em comin' out, an' the fust word he heard was,
'Lord, we thank Thee we have not been left
to live by the dim light of natur'.' 'Lisha said
he 'd had time to be shipwrecked (you know
he went to California fust an' made the v'yage),
an' be married twice, an' lay by enough to
keep him, and come home poor ; but when he
heard that, he felt as if the world had n't
moved sence he started."

Sally Ware dropped her mitten, to avoid
listening and the necessity of reply ; it was too
evident that the conversational tone was becoming profane. But Mrs. Page's eyes were
gleaming with pure dramatic joy, and she continued : —

"Well, a fortnight or so ago he went over
to see Isabel, an' Sadie an' her husband happened to be there. They were all settin' purrin'
in the dark, because they 'd forgot to send
for any kerosene. 'No light ?' says he, hittin'
his head ag'inst the chimbly-piece goin' in, —
'no light ?' 'No,' says Isabel, 'none but the
dim light of natur'.' "

There was a chime of delighted laughter in
many keys. The company felt the ease of un-
restricted speech. They wished the nooning
might be indefinitely prolonged.

"Sometimes I think she sets out to make
him believe she 's wuss 'n she is," remarked
Mrs. Cole. "Remember how she carried on
last Sabbath ?"

"I guess so!" returned Mrs. Page. "You
see, Tilly, he's kind o' pushin' her for'ard to
make her seem more suitable, — he'd like to
have her as old as the hills! — an' nothin'
would do but she must go into the Bible class.
Ain't a member that's under fifty, but there
that little young thing sets, cheeks red as a
beet, an' the elder asks her questions, when
he gits to her, as if he was coverin' on her
over with cotton wool. Well, last Sabbath old
Deacon Pitts — le's see, there ain't any o' his
folks present, be they? — well, he was late, an'
he had n't looked at his lesson besides. 'T was
the fust chapter in Ruth, where it begins, 'In
the days when the judges ruled.' You recollect Naomi told the two darters they'd got to
set sail, an' then the Bible says, 'they lifted up
their voice an' wept.' 'Who wept?' says the
parson to Deacon Pitts, afore he'd got fairly
se' down. The deacon he opened his Bible,
an' whirled over the leaves. 'Who wept,
Brother Pitts?' says the parson over ag'in.
Somebody found the deacon the place, an'
p'inted. He was growin' redder an' redder, an'
his spe'tacles kep' slippin' down, but he did
manage to see the chapter begun suthin'
about the judges. Well, by that time parson
spoke out sort o' sharp. 'Brother Pitts,' says
he, 'who wept?' The deacon see 't he'd
got to put some kind of a face on 't, an' he
looked up an' spoke out, as bold as brass.

'I conclude,' says he, —'I conclude 't was the judges!'"

Even Miss Ware smiled a little, and adjusted her gold beads. The others laughed out rich and free.

"Well, what 'd that have to do with Isabel?" asked Mrs. Ellison, who never forgot the main issue.

"Why, everybody else drawed down their faces, an' tried to keep 'em straight, but Isabel, she begun to laugh, an' she laughed till the tears streamed down her cheeks. Deacon Pitts was real put out, for him, an' the parson tried not to take no notice. But it went so fur he could n't help it, an' so he says, 'Miss Isabel, I 'm real pained,' says he. But 't was jest as you 'd cuff the kitten for snarlin' up your yarn."

"Well, what 's Isabel goin' to do?" asked Mrs. Ellison. "S'pose she 'll marry him?"

"Why, she won't unless he tells her to. If he does, I dunno but she 'll think she 's got to."

"I say it 's a shame," put in Mrs. Robbins incisively; "an' Isabel with everything all fixed complete so 't she could have a good time. Her sister 's well married, an' Isabel stays every night with her. Them two girls have been together ever sence their father died. An' here she 's got the school, an' she 's goin' to Sudleigh every Saturday to take lessons in readin', an' she'd be as happy as a cricket, if on'y he'd let her alone."

"She reads real well," said Mrs. Ellison. "She come over to our sociable an' read for us. She could turn herself into anybody she'd a mind to. Len wrote a notice of it for the 'Star.' That's the only time we've had oysters over our way."

"I'd let it be the last," piped up a thin old lady, with a long figured veil over her face. "It's my opinion oysters lead to dancin'."

"Well, let 'em lead," said optimistic Mrs. Page. "I guess we need n't foller."

"Them that have got rheumatism in their knees can stay behind," said the young married woman, drawn by the heat of the moment into a daring at once to be repented. "Mrs. Ellison, you're getting ahead of us over in your parish. They say you sing out of sheet music."

"Yes, they do say so," interrupted the old lady under the figured veil. "If there's any worship in sheet music, I'd like to know it!"

"Come, come!" said peace-loving Mrs. Page; "there's the men filin' in. We must n't let 'em see us squabblin'. They think we're a lot o' cacklin' hens anyway, tickled to death over a piece o' chalk. There's Isabel, now. She's goin' to look like her aunt Mary Ellen, over to Saltash."

Isabel preceded the men, who were pausing for a word at the door, and went down the aisle

to her pew. She bowed to one and another,
in passing, and her color rose. They could
not altogether restrain their guiltily curious
gaze, and Isabel knew she had been talked
over. She was a healthy-looking girl, with
clear blue eyes and a quantity of soft brown
hair. Her face was rather large-featured, and
one could see that, if the world went well with
her, she would be among those who develop
beauty in middle life.

The group of dames dispersed to their sev-
eral pews, and settled their faces into expres-
sions more becoming a Sunday mood. The
village folk, who had time for a hot dinner,
dropped in, one by one, and by and by the
parson came, — a gaunt man, with thick red-
brown hair streaked with dull gray, and red-
brown, sanguine eyes. He was much beloved,
but something impulsive and unevenly bal-
anced in his nature led even his people to
regard him with more or less patronage. He
kept his eyes rigorously averted from Isabel's
pew, in passing; but when he reached the
pulpit, and began unpinning his heavy gray
shawl, he did glance at her, and his face grew
warm. But Isabel did not look at him, and all
through the service she sat with a haughty
pose of the head, gazing down into her lap.
When it was over, she waited for no one, since
her sister was not at church, but sped away
down the snowy road.

The next day, Isabel stayed after school, and
so it was in the wintry twilight that she walked
home, guarded by the few among her flock who
had been kept to learn the inner significance
of common fractions. Approaching her own
house, she quickened her steps, for there before the gate (taken from its hinges and resting for the winter) stood a blue pung. The
horse was dozing, his Roman nose sunken
almost to the snow at his feet. He looked as
if he had come to stay. Isabel withdrew her
hand from the persistent little fingers clinging
to it.

"Good-night, children," said she. "I guess
I've got company. I must hurry in. Come
bright and early to-morrow."

The little group marched away, swathed in
comforters, each child carrying the dinner-pail
with an easy swing. Their reddened faces
lighted over the chorusing good-nights, and
they kept looking back, while Isabel ran up
the icy path to her own door. It was opened
from within, before she reached it, and a tall,
florid woman, with smoothly banded hair, stood
there to receive her. Though she had a powerful frame, she gave one at the outset an impression of weak gentleness, and the hands
she extended, albeit cordial, were somewhat
limp. She wore her bonnet still, though she
had untied the strings and thrown them back ;
and her ample figure was tightly laced under a
sontag.

"Why, aunt Luceba!" cried Isabel, radiant. "I'm as glad as I can be.   When did you rain down?"

"Be you glad?" returned aunt Luceba, her somewhat anxious look relaxing into a smile. "Well, I'm pleased if you be.   Fact is, I run away, an' I'm jest comin' to myself, an' wonderin' what under the sun set me out to do it."

"Run away!" repeated Isabel, drawing her in, and at once peeping into the stove.   "Oh, you fixed the fire, didn't you?   It keeps real well.   I put on coal in the morning, and then again at night."

"Isabel," began her aunt, standing by the stove, and drumming on it with agitated fingers, "I hate to have you live as you do.   Why under the sun can't you come over to Saltash, an' stay with us?"

Isabel had thrown off her shawl and hat, and was standing on the other side of the stove; she was tingling with cold and youthful spirits.

"I'm keeping school," said she.   "School can't keep without me.   And I'm going over to Sudleigh, every Saturday, to take elocution lessons.   I'm having my own way, and I'm happy as a clam.   Now, why can't you come and live with me?   You said you would, the very day aunt Eliza died."

"I know I did," owned the visitor, lowering her voice, and casting a glance over her shoulder.   "But I never had an idea then how Mary

Ellen 'd feel about it. She said she would n't live in this town, not if she was switched. I dunno why she 's so ag'in' it, but she seems to be, an' there 't is!"

"Why, aunt Luceba!" Isabel had left her position to draw forward a chair. "What 's that?" She pointed to the foot of the lounge, where, half hidden in shadow, stood a large, old-fashioned blue chest.

"'Sh! that 's it! that 's what I come for. It 's her chist."

"Whose?"

"Your aunt 'Liza's." She looked Isabel in the face with an absurd triumph and awe. She had done a brave deed, the nature of which was not at once apparent.

"What 's in it?" asked Isabel, walking over to it.

"Don't you touch it!" cried her aunt, in agitation. "I would n't have you meddle with it — But there! it 's locked. I al'ays forgit that. I feel as if the things could git out an' walk. Here! you let it alone, an' byme-by we 'll open it. Se' down here on the lounge. There, now! I guess I can tell ye. It was sister 'Liza's chist, an' she kep' it up attic. She begun it when we wa'n't more 'n girls goin' to Number Six, an' she 's been fillin' on 't ever sence."

"Begun it! You talk as if 't was a quilt!" Isabel began to laugh.

"Now don't!" said her aunt, in great distress. "Don't ye! I s'pose 't was because we was such little girls an' all when 'Liza started it, but it makes me as nervous as a witch, an' al'ays did. You see, 'Liza was a great hand for deaths an' buryin's; an' as for funerals, she 'd ruther go to 'em than eat. I 'd say that if she was here this minute, for more 'n once I said it to her face. Well, everybody 't died, she saved suthin' they wore or handled the last thing, an' laid it away in this chist; an' last time I see it opened, 't was full, an' she kind o' smacked her lips, an' said she should have to begin another. But the very next week she was took away."

"Aunt Luceba," said Isabel suddenly, "was aunt Eliza hard to live with? Did you and aunt Mary Ellen have to toe the mark?"

"Don't you say one word," answered her aunt hastily. "That 's all past an' gone. There ain't no way of settlin' old scores but buryin' of 'em. She was older 'n we were, an' on'y a step-sister, arter all. We must think o' that. Well, I must come to the end o' my story, an' then we 'll open the chist. Next day arter we laid her away, it come into my head, 'Now we can burn up them things.' It may ha' been wicked, but there 't was, an' the thought kep' arter me, till all I could think of was the chist; an' byme-by I says to Mary Ellen, one mornin', 'Le's open it to-day an'

make a burnfire!' An' Mary Ellen she turned
as white as a sheet, an' dropped her spoon into
her sasser, an' she says : 'Not yet ! Luceba,
don't you ask me to touch it yet.' An' I found
out, though she never'd say another word,
that it unset her more'n it did me. One day,
I come on her up attic stan'in' over it with the
key in her hand, an' she turned round as if I'd
ketched her stealin', an' slipped off downstairs.
An' this arternoon, she went into Tilly Ellison's with her work, an' it come to me all of a
sudden how I'd git Tim Yatter to harness an'
load the chist onto the pung, an' I'd bring it
over here, an' we'd look it over together ; an'
then, if there's nothin' in it but what I think,
I'd leave it behind, an' maybe you or Sadie'd
burn it. John Cole happened to ride by, and
he helped me in with it. I ain't a-goin' to
have Mary Ellen worried. She's different
from me. She went to school, same's you
have, an' she's different somehow. She's been
meddled with all her life, an' I'll be whipped
if she sha'n't make a new start. Should you
jest as lieves ask Sadie or John ?"

"Why, yes," said Isabel wonderingly ; "or
do it myself. I don't see why you care."

Aunt Luceba wiped her beaded face with a
large handkerchief.

"I dunno either," she owned, in an exhausted voice. "I guess it's al'ays little
things you can't stand. Big ones you can butt

ag'inst. There! I feel better, now I 've told ye. Here 's the key. Should you jest as soon open it?"

Isabel drew the chest forward with a vigorous pull of her sturdy arm. She knelt before it and inserted the key. Aunt Luceba rose and leaned over her shoulder, gazing with the fascination of horror. At the moment the lid was lifted, a curious odor filled the room.

"My soul!" exclaimed Aunt Luceba. "O my soul!" She seemed incapable of saying more; and Isabel, awed in spite of herself, asked, in a whisper : —

"What 's that smell? I know, but I can't think."

"You take out that parcel," said aunt Luceba, beginning to fan herself with her handkerchief. "That little one down there 't the end. It 's that. My soul! how things come back! Talk about spirits! There 's no need of 'em! *Things* are full bad enough!"

Isabel lifted out a small brown paper package, labeled in a cramped handwriting. She held it to the fading light. "'Slippery elm left by my dear father from his last illness,'" she read, with difficulty. "'The broken piece used by him on the day of his death.'"

"My land!" exclaimed aunt Luceba weakly. "Now what 'd she want to keep that for? He had it round all that winter, an' he used to give us a little mite, to please us. Oh, dear! it

smells like death. Well, le's lay it aside an'
git on. The light's goin', an' I must jog
along. Take out that dress. I guess I know
what 't is, though I can't hardly believe it."

Isabel took out a black dress, made with a
full, gathered skirt and an old-fashioned waist.
"'Dress made ready for aunt Mercy,'" she
read, "'before my dear uncle bought her a
robe.' But, auntie," she added, "there's no
back breadth !"

"I know it ! I know it ! She was so large
they had to cut it out, for fear 't would n't go
into the coffin ; an' Monroe Giles said she was
a real particular woman, an' he wondered how
she'd feel to have the back breadth of her
quilted petticoat showin' in heaven. I declare
I'm 'most sick ! What's in that pasteboard
box ?"

It was a shriveled object, black with long-
dried mould.

"'Lemon held by Timothy Marden in his
hand just before he died.' Aunt Luceba,"
said Isabel, turning with a swift impulse, "I
think aunt Eliza was a horror !"

"Don't you say it, if you do think it," said
her aunt, sinking into a chair and rocking
vigorously. "Le's git through with it as
quick 's we can. Ain't that a bandbox ? Yes,
that's great-aunt Isabel's leghorn bunnit. You
was named for her, you know. An' there's
cousin Hattie's cashmere shawl, an' Obed's

spe'tacles. An' if there ain't old Mis' Eaton's false front! Don't you read no more. I don't care what they're marked. Move that box a mite. My soul! There's ma'am's checked apron I bought her to the fair! Them are all her things down below." She got up and walked to the window, looking into the chestnut branches, with unseeing eyes. She turned about presently, and her cheeks were wet. "There!" she said; "I guess we need n't look no more. Should you jest as soon burn 'em?"

"Yes," answered Isabel. She was crying a little, too. "Of course I will, auntie. I'll put 'em back now. But when you're gone, I'll do it; perhaps not till Saturday, but I will then."

She folded the articles, and softly laid them away. They were no longer gruesome, since even a few of them could recall the beloved and still remembered dead. As she was gently closing the lid, she felt a hand on her shoulder. Aunt Luceba was standing there, trembling a little, though the tears had gone from her face.

"Isabel," said she, in a whisper, "you need n't burn the apron, when you do the rest. Save it careful. I should like to put it away among my things."

Isabel nodded. She remembered her grandmother, a placid, hopeful woman, whose every deed breathed the fragrance of godly living.

"There!" said her aunt, turning away with
the air of one who thrusts back the too insistent past, lest it dominate her quite. "It's
gittin' along towards dark, an' I must put for
home. I guess that hoss thinks he's goin' to
be froze to the ground. You wrop up my soap-
stone while I git on my shawl. Land! don't
it smell hot? I wisht I had n't been so spry
about puttin' on 't into the oven." She hurried
on her things ; and Isabel, her hair blowing
about her face, went out to uncover the horse
and speed the departure. The reins in her
hands, aunt Luceba bent forward once more
to add, "Isabel, if there's one thing left for
me to say, to tole you over to live with us, I
want to say it."

Isabel laughed. "I know it," she answered
brightly. "And if there's anything I can say
to make you and aunt Mary Ellen come over
here " —

Aunt Luceba shook her head ponderously,
and clucked at the horse. "Fur's I'm concerned, it's settled now. I'd come, an' be
glad. But there's Mary Ellen! Go 'long!"
She went jangling away along the country
road to the music of old-fashioned bells.

Isabel ran into the house, and, with one
look at the chest, set about preparing her supper. She was enjoying her life of perfect
freedom with a kind of bravado, inasmuch as it
seemed an innocent delight of which nobody

approved. If the two aunts would come to live with her, so much the better; but since they refused, she scorned the descent to any domestic expedient. Indeed, she would have been glad to sleep, as well as to eat, in the lonely house; but to that her sister would never consent, and though she had compromised by going to Sadie's for the night, she always returned before breakfast. She put up a leaf of the table standing by the wall, and arranged her simple supper there, uttering aloud as she did so fragments of her lesson, or dramatic sentences which had caught her fancy in reading or in speech. Finally, as she was dipping her cream toast, she caught herself saying, over and over, " My soul!" in the tremulous tone her aunt had used at that moment of warm emotion. She could not make it quite her own, and she tried again and again, like a faithful parrot. Then of a sudden the human power and pity of it flashed upon her, and she reddened, conscience-smitten, though no one was by to hear. She set her dish upon the table with indignant emphasis.

"I 'm ashamed of myself!" said Isabel, and she sat down to her delicate repast, and forced herself, while she ate with a cordial relish, to fix her mind on what seemed to her things common as compared with her beloved ambition. Isabel often felt that she was too much absorbed in reading, and that, somehow or other, God would come to that conclusion also, and take away her wicked facility.

The dark seemed to drift quickly down, that night, because her supper had been delayed, and she washed her dishes by lamplight. When she had quite finished, and taken off her apron, she stood a moment over the chest, before sitting down to her task of memorizing verse. She was wondering whether she might not burn a few of the smaller things to-night ; yet somehow, although she was quite free from aunt Luceba's awe of them, she did feel that the act must be undertaken with a certain degree of solemnity. It ought not to be accomplished over the remnants of a fire built for cooking; it should, moreover, be to the accompaniment of a serious mood in herself. She turned away, but at that instant there came a jingle of bells. It stopped at the gate. Isabel went into the dark entry, and pressed her face against the side-light. It was the parson. She knew him at once; no one in Tiverton could ever mistake that stooping figure, draped in a shawl. Isabel always hated him the more when she thought of his shawl. It flashed upon her then, as it often did when revulsion came over her, how much she had loved him until he had conceived this altogether horrible attachment for her. It was like a cherished friend who had begun to cut undignified capers. More than that, there

lurked a certain cruelty in it, because he
seemed to be trading on her inherited rever-
ence for his office. If he should ask her to
marry him, he was the minister, and how could
she refuse? Unless, indeed, there were somebody else in the room, to give her courage,
and that was hardly to be expected. Isabel
began casting wildly about her for help. Her
thoughts ran in a rushing current, and even in
the midst of her tragic despair some sense of
the foolishness of it smote her like a comic
note, and she could have laughed hysterically.

"But I can't help it," she said aloud, "I am
afraid. I can't put out the light. He's seen
it. I can't slip out the back door. He'd hear
me on the crust. He'll — ask me — to-night!
Oh, he will! he will! and I said to myself I'd
be cunning and never give him a chance. Oh,
why couldn't aunt Luceba have stayed? My
soul! my soul!" And then the dramatic fibre,
always awake in her, told her that she had
found the tone she sought.

He was blanketing his horse, and Isabel
had flown into the sitting-room. Her face was
alive with resolution and a kind of joy. She
had thought. She threw open the chest, with
a trembling hand, and pulled out the black
dress.

"I'm sorry," she said, as she slipped it on
over her head, and speaking as if she addressed
some unseen guardian, "but I can't help it.

If you don't want your things used, you keep him from coming in!"

The parson knocked at the door. Isabel took no notice. She was putting on the false front, the horn spectacles, the cashmere shawl, and the leghorn bonnet, with its long veil. She threw back the veil, and closed the chest. The parson knocked again. She heard him kicking the snow from his feet against the scraper. It might have betokened a decent care for her floors. It sounded to Isabel like a lover's haste, and smote her anew with that fear which is the forerunner of action. She blew out the lamp, and lighted a candle. Then she went to the door, schooling herself in desperation to remember this, to remember that, to remember, above all things, that her under dress was red and that her upper one had no back breadth. She threw open the door.

"Good-evening" — said the parson. He was about to add " Miss Isabel," but the words stuck in his throat.

"She ain't to home," answered Isabel. "My niece ain't to home."

The parson had bent forward, and was eyeing her curiously, yet with benevolence. He knew all the residents within a large radius, and he expected, at another word from the shadowy masker, to recognize her also. "Will she be away long?" he hesitated.

"I guess she will," answered Isabel promptly.

"She ain't to be relied on. I never found her so." Her spirits had risen. She knew how exactly she was imitating aunt Luceba's mode of speech. The tones were dramatically exact, albeit of a more resonant quality. "Auntie's voice is like suet," she thought. "Mine is vinegar. *But I've got it !*" A merry devil assailed her, the child of dramatic triumph. She spoke with decision : "Won't you come in ?"

The parson crossed the sill, and waited courteously for her to precede him ; but Isabel thought, in time, of her back breadth, and stood aside.

"You go fust," said she, "an' I'll shet the door."

He made his way into the ill-lighted sitting-room, and began to unpin his shawl.

"I ain't had my bunnit off sence I come," announced Isabel, entering with some bustle, and taking her stand, until he should be seated, within the darkest corner of the hearth. "I've had to turn to an' clear up, or I should n't ha' found a spot as big as a hin's egg to sleep in to-night. Maybe you don't know it, but my niece Isabel's got no more faculty about a house 'n I have for preachin' — not a mite."

The parson had seated himself by the stove, and was laboriously removing his arctics. Isabel's eyes danced behind her spectacles as she thought how large and ministerial they

were. She could not see them, for the spectacles dazzled her, but she remembered exactly
how they looked.   Everything about him filled
her with glee, now that she was safe, though
within his reach.   " 'Now, infidel,' " she said
noiselessly, " ' I have thee on the hip!' "

The parson had settled himself in his accustomed attitude when making parochial calls.
He put the tips of his fingers together, and
opened conversation in his tone of mild good-
will : —

" I don't seem to be able to place you.   A
relative of Miss Isabel's, did you say ? "

She laughed huskily.   She was absorbed in
putting more suet into her voice.

" You make me think of uncle Peter Nudd,"
she replied, " when he was took up into Bunker
Hill Monument.   Albert took him, one o' the
boys that lived in Boston.   Comin' down, they
met a woman Albert knew, an' he bowed.
Uncle Peter looked round arter her, an' then
he says to Albert, ' I dunno 's I rightly remember who that is !' "

The parson uncrossed his legs and crossed
them the other way.   The old lady began to
seem to him a thought too discursive, if not
hilarious.

" I know so many of the people in the various parishes " — he began, but he was interrupted without compunction.

" You never 'd know me.   I 'm from out

West.   Isabel's father's brother married my
uncle — no, I would say my step-niece.   An'
so I'm her aunt.   By adoption, 't ennyrate.
We al'ays call it so, leastways when we're
writin' back an' forth.   An' I've heard how
Isabel was goin' on, an' so I ketched up my
bunnit, an' put for Tiverton.   'If she ever
needed her own aunt,' says I — ' her aunt by
adoption — she needs her now.' "

Once or twice, during the progress of this
speech, the visitor had shifted his position,
as if ill at ease.   Now he bent forward, and
peered at his hostess.

"Isabel is well ? " he began tentatively.

"Well enough !   But, my sakes ! I'd ruther
she'd be sick abed or paraletic than carry on
as she does.   Slack ?   My soul !   I wisht you
could see her sink closet !   I wisht you could
take one look over the dirty dishes she leaves
round, not washed from one week's end to
another ! "

"But she's always neat.   She looks like an
— an angel ! "

Isabel could not at once suppress the grat-
ified note which crept of itself into her
voice.

"That's the outside o' the cup an' platter,"
she said knowingly.   "I thank my stars she
ain't likely to marry.   She'd turn any man's
house upside down inside of a week."

The parson made a deprecating noise in his

throat. He seemed about to say something,
and thought better of it.

"It may be," he hesitated, after a moment,
— "it may be her studies take up too much of
her time. I have always thought these elocution lessons" —

"Oh, my land!" cried Isabel, in passionate
haste. She leaned forward as if she would im-
plore him. "That's her only salvation. That's
the makin' of her. If you stop her off there,
I dunno but she'd jine a circus or take to
drink! Don't you dast to do it! I'm in the
family, an' I know."

The parson tried vainly to struggle out of
his bewilderment.

"But," said he, "may I ask how you heard
these reports? Living in Illinois, as you do —
did you say Illinois or Iowa?"

"Neither," answered Isabel desperately.
"'Way out on the plains. It's the last house
afore you come to the Rockies. Law! you
can't tell how a story gits started, nor how fast
it will travel. 'T ain't like a gale o' wind; the
weather bureau ain't been invented that can
cal'late it. I heard of a man once that told a
lie in California, an' 'fore the week was out it
broke up his engagement in New Hampshire.
There's the 'tater-bug — think how that trav-
els! So with this. The news broke out in
Missouri, an' here I be."

"I hope you will be able to remain."

"Only to-night," she said in haste. More and more nervous, she was losing hold on the sequence of her facts. "I'm like mortal life, here to-day an' there to-morrer. In the mornin' I sha'n't be found." ("But Isabel will," she thought, from a remorse which had come too late, "and she'll have to lie, or run away. Or cut a hole in the ice and drown herself!")

"I'm sorry to have her lose so much of your visit," began the parson courteously, but still perplexing himself over the whimsies of an old lady who flew on from the West, and made nothing of flying back. "If I could do anything towards finding her" —

"I know where she is," said Isabel unhappily. "She's as well on 't as she can be, under the circumstances. There's on'y one thing you could do. If you should be willin' to keep it dark 't you 've seen me, I should be real beholden to ye. You know there ain't no time to call in the neighborhood, an' such things make talk, an' all. An' if you don't speak out to Isabel, so much the better. Poor creatur', she's got enough to bear without that!" Her voice dropped meltingly in the keenness of her sympathy for the unfortunate girl who, embarrassed enough before, had deliberately set for herself another snare. "I feel for Isabel," she continued, in the hope of impressing him with the necessity for silence and inaction. " I do feel for her ! Oh, gracious me ! What 's that ? "

A decided rap had sounded at the front door. The parson rose also, amazed at her agitation.

" Somebody knocked," he said. " Shall I go to the door ? "

" Oh, not yet, not yet ! " cried Isabel, clasping her hands under her cashmere shawl. " Oh, what shall I do ? "

Her natural voice had asserted itself, but, strangely enough, the parson did not comprehend. The entire scene was too bewildering. There came a second knock. He stepped toward the door, but Isabel darted in front of him. She forgot her back breadth, and even through that dim twilight the scarlet of her gown shone ruddily out. She placed herself before the door.

" Don't you go ! " she entreated hoarsely. " Let me think what I can say."

Then the parson had his first inkling that the strange visitor must be mad. He wondered at himself for not thinking of it before, and the idea speedily coupled itself with Isabel's strange disappearance. He stepped forward and grasped her arm, trembling under the cashmere shawl.

" Woman," he demanded sternly, " what have you done with Isabel North ? "

Isabel was thinking ; but the question, twice

repeated, brought her to herself. She began to laugh, peal on peal of hysterical mirth ; and the parson, still holding her arm, grew compassionate.

"Poor soul!" said he soothingly. "Poor soul! sit down here by the stove and be calm — be calm!"

Isabel was overcome anew.

"Oh, it is n't so!" she gasped, finding breath. "I 'm not crazy. Just let me be!"

She started under his detaining hand, for the knock had come again. Wrenching herself free, she stepped into the entry. "Who 's there?" she called.

"It 's your aunt Mary Ellen," came a voice from the darkness. "Open the door."

"O my soul!" whispered Isabel to herself. "Wait a minute!" she continued. "Only a minute!"

She thrust the parson back into the sitting-room, and shut the door. The act relieved her. If she could push a minister, and he could obey in such awkward fashion, he was no longer to be feared. He was even to be refused. Isabel felt equal to doing it.

"Now, look here," said she rapidly ; "you stand right there while I take off these things. Don't you say a word. No, Mr. Bond, don't you speak!" Bonnet, false front, and spectacles were tossed in a tumultuous pile.

"Isabel!" gasped the parson.

"Keep still!" she commanded. "Here! fold this shawl!"

The parson folded it neatly, and meanwhile Isabel stepped out of the mutilated dress, and added that also to the heap. She opened the blue chest, and packed the articles hastily within. "Here!" said she; "toss me the shawl. Now if you say one word — Oh, parson, if you only will keep still, I'll tell you all about it! That is, I guess I can!" And leaving him standing in hopeless coma, she opened the door.

"Well," said aunt Mary Ellen, stepping in, "I'm afraid your hinges want greasing. How do you do, Isabel? How do you do?" She put up her face and kissed her niece. Aunt Mary Ellen was so pretty, so round, so small, that she always seemed timid, and did the commonest acts of life with a gentle grace. "I heard voices," she said, walking into the sitting-room. "Sadie here?"

The parson had stepped forward, more bent than usual, for he was peering down into her face.

"Mary Ellen!" he exclaimed.

The little woman looked up at him — very sadly, Isabel thought.

"Yes, William," she answered. But she was untying her bonnet, and she did not offer to shake hands.

Isabel stood by with downcast eyes, waiting

to take her things, and aunt Mary Ellen looked searchingly up at her as she laid her mittens on the pile. The girl, without a word, went into the bedroom, and her aunt followed her.

"Isabel," said she rapidly, "I saw the chest. Have you burnt the things?"

"No," answered Isabel in wonder. "No."

"Then don't you! don't you touch 'em for the world." She went back into the sitting-room, and Isabel followed. The candle was guttering, and aunt Mary Ellen pushed it toward her. "I don't know where the snuffers are," she said. "Lamp smoke?"

Isabel did not answer, but she lighted the lamp. She had never seen her aunt so full of decision, so charged with an unfamiliar power. She felt as if strange things were about to happen. The parson was standing awkwardly. He wondered whether he ought to go. Aunt Mary Ellen smoothed her brown hair with both hands, sat down, and pointed to his chair.

"Sit a spell," she said. "I guess I shall have something to talk over with you."

The parson sat down. He tried to put his fingers together, but they trembled, and he clasped his hands instead.

"It's a long time since we've seen you in Tiverton," he began.

"It would have been longer," she answered, "but I felt as if my niece needed me."

Here Isabel, to her own surprise, gave a little sob, and then another. She began crying angrily into her handkerchief.

"Isabel," said her aunt, "is there a fire in the kitchen?"

"Yes," sobbed the girl.

"Well, you go out there and lie down on the lounge till you feel better. Cover you over, and don't be cold. I'll call you when there's anything for you to do."

Tall Isabel rose and walked out, wiping her eyes. Her little aunt sat mistress of the field. For many minutes there was silence, and the clock ticked. The parson felt something rising in his throat. He blew his nose vigorously.

"Mary Ellen" — he began. "But I don't know as you want me to call you so!"

"You can call me anything you're a mind to," she answered calmly. She was nearsighted, and had always worn spectacles. She took them off and laid them on her knee. The parson moved involuntarily in his chair. He remembered how she had used to do that when they were talking intimately, so that his eager look might not embarrass her. "Nothing makes much difference when folks get to be as old as you and I are."

"I don't feel old," said the parson resentfully. "I do *not!* And you don't look so."

"Well, I am. We're past our youth.

We 've got to the point where the only way to renew it is to look out for the young ones."

The parson had always had with her a way of reading her thought and bursting out boyishly into betrayal of his own.

"Mary Ellen," he cried, "I never should have explained it so, but Isabel looks like you!"

She smiled sadly. "I guess men make themselves think 'most anything they want to," she answered. "There may be a family look, but I can't see it. She 's tall, too, and I was always a pint o' cider — so father said."

"She 's got the same look in her eyes," pursued the parson hotly. "I 've always thought so, ever since she was a little girl."

"If you begun to notice it then," she responded, with the same gentle calm, "you 'd better by half ha' been thinking of your own wife and her eyes. I believe they were black."

"Mary Ellen, how hard you are on me! You did n't use to be. You never were hard on anybody. You would n't have hurt a fly."

Her face contracted slightly. "Perhaps I would n't! perhaps I would n't! But I 've had a good deal to bear this afternoon, and maybe I do feel a little different towards you from what I ever have felt. I 've been hearing a loose-tongued woman tell how my own niece has been made town-talk because a man old enough to know better was running after her.

I said, years ago, I never would come into this
place while you was in it; but when I heard
that, I felt as if Providence had marked out
the way.   I knew I was the one to step into
the breach.   So I had Tim harness up and
bring me over, and here I am.   William, I don't
want you should make a mistake at your time
of life!"

The minister seemed already a younger man.
A strong color had risen in his face.   He felt
in her presence a fine exhilaration denied him
through all the years without her.   Who could
say whether it was the woman herself or the
resurrected spirit of their youth?   He did not
feel like answering her.   It was enough to
hear her voice.   He leaned forward, looking at
her with something piteous in his air.

"Mary Ellen," he ventured, "you might as
well say 'another mistake.'   I did make one.
You know it, and I know it."

She looked at him with a frank affection,
entirely maternal.   "Yes, William," she said,
with the same gentle firmness in her voice,
"we 've passed so far beyond those things that
we can speak out and feel no shame.   You did
make a mistake.   I don't know as 't would be
called so to break with me, but it was to marry
where you did.   You never cared about her.
You were good to her.   You always would
be, William; but 't was a shame to put her
there."

The parson had locked his hands upon his knees. He looked at them, and sad lines of recollection deepened in his face.

"I was desperate," he said at length, in a low tone. "I had lost you. Some men take to drink, but that never tempted me. Besides, I was a minister. I was just ordained. Mary Ellen, do you remember that day?"

"Yes," she answered softly, "I remember." She had leaned back in her chair, and her eyes were fixed upon vacancy with the suffused look of tears forbidden to fall.

"You wore a white dress," went on the parson, "and a bunch of Provence roses. It was June. Your sister always thought you dressed too gay, but you said to her, 'I guess I can wear what I want to, to-day of all times.'"

"We won't talk about her. Yes, I remember."

"And, as God is my witness, I couldn't feel solemn, I was so glad! I was a minister, and my girl — the girl that was going to marry me — sat down there where I could see her, dressed in white. I always thought of you afterwards with that white dress on. You've stayed with me all my life, just that way."

Mary Ellen put up her hand with a quick gesture to hide her middle-aged face. With a thought as quick, she folded it resolutely upon the other in her lap. "Yes, William,"

she said. "I was a girl then. I wore white
a good deal."

But the parson hardly heeded her. He was
far away. "Mary Ellen," he broke out suddenly, a smile running warmly over his face,
and creasing his dry, hollow cheeks, "do you
remember that other sermon, my trial one?
I read it to you, and then I read it to Parson Sibley. And do you remember what he
said?"

"Yes, I remember. I did n't suppose you
did." Her cheeks were pink. The corners
of her mouth grew exquisitely tender.

"You knew I did! 'Behold, thou art fair,
my love; behold, thou art fair; thou hast
doves' eyes.' I took that text because I
could n't think of anything else all summer. I
remember now it seemed to me as if I was in
a garden — always in a garden. The moon
was pretty bright, that summer. There were
more flowers blooming than common. It must
have been a good year. And I wrote my sermon lying out in the pine woods, down where
you used to sit hemming on your things. And
I thought it was the Church, but do all I
could, it was a girl — or an angel!"

"No, no!" cried Mary Ellen, in bitterness
of entreaty.

"And then I read the sermon to you under
the pines, and you stopped sewing, and looked
off into the trees; and you said 't was beauti-

ful. But I carried it to old Parson Sibley that
night, and I can see just how he looked sitting
there in his study, with his great spectacles
pushed up on his forehead, and his hand drumming on a book. He had the dictionary put
in a certain place on his table because he found
he'd got used to drumming on the Bible, and
he was a very particular man. And when I
got through reading the sermon, his face
wrinkled all up, though he did n't laugh out
loud, and he came over to me and put his hand
on my shoulder. 'William,' says he, 'you go
home and write a doctrinal sermon, the stiffest
you can. *This one's about a girl.* You might
give it to Mary Ellen North for a wedding-
present.'"

The parson had grown almost gay under
the vivifying influence of memory. But Mary
Ellen did not smile.

"Yes," she repeated softly, "I remember."

"And then I laughed a little, and got out
of the study the best way I could, and ran
over to you to tell you what he said. And I
left the sermon in your work-basket. I 've
often wished, in the light of what came afterwards — I 've often wished I 'd kept it. Somehow 't would have brought me nearer to
you."

It seemed as if she were about to rise from
her chair, but she quieted herself and dulled
the responsive look upon her face.

"Mary Ellen," the parson burst forth, "I
know how I took what came on us the very
next week, but I never knew how you took it.
Should you just as lieves tell me?"

She lifted her head until it held a noble
pose. Her eyes shone brilliantly, though indeed they were doves' eyes.

"I'll tell you," said she. "I could n't have
told you ten years ago, — no, nor five! but
now it's an old woman talking to an old man.
I was given to understand you were tired of
me, and too honorable to say so. I don't
know what tale was carried to you" —

"She said you'd say 'yes' to that rich fellow in Sudleigh, if I'd give you a chance!"

"I knew 't was something as shallow as
that. Well, I'll tell you how I took it. I
put up my head and laughed. I said, 'When
William Bond wants to break with me, he'll
say so.' And the next day you did say so."

The parson wrung his hands in an involuntary gesture of appeal.

"Minnie! Minnie!" he cried, "why did n't
you save me? What made you let me *be* a
fool?"

She met his gaze with a tenderness so great
that the words lost all their sting.

"You always were, William," she said
quietly. "Always rushing at things like Job's
charger, and having to rush back again. Never
once have I read that without thinking of you.

That's why you fixed up an angel out of poor little Isabel."

The parson made a fine gesture of dissent. He had forgotten Isabel.

"Do you want to know what else I did?" Her voice grew hard and unfamiliar. "I'll tell you. I went to my sister Eliza, and I said: 'Some way or another, you've spoilt my life. I'll forgive you just as soon as I can — maybe before you die, maybe not. You come with me!' and I went up garret, where she kept the chest with things in it that belonged to them that had died. There it sets now. I stood over it with her. 'I'm going to put my dead things in here,' I said. 'If you touch a finger to 'em, I'll get up in meeting and tell what you've done. I'm going to put in everything left from what you've murdered; and every time you come here, you'll remember you were a murderer.' I frightened her. I'm glad I did. She's dead and gone, and I've forgiven her; but I'm glad now!"

The parson looked at her with amazement. She seemed on fire. All the smouldering embers of a life denied had blazed at last. She put on her glasses and walked over to the chest.

"Here!" she continued; "let's uncover the dead. I've tried to do it ever since she died, so the other things could be burned; but my courage failed me. Could you turn these

screws, if I should get you a knife? They're
in tight. I put 'em in myself, and she stood
by."

The little lid of the till had been screwed
fast. The two middle-aged people bent over it
together, trying first the scissors and then the
broken blade of the parson's old knife. The
screws came slowly. When they were all out,
he stood back a pace and gazed at her. Mary
Ellen looked no longer alert and vivified. Her
face was haggard.

"I shut it," she said, in a whisper. "You
lift it up."

The parson lifted the lid. There they lay,
her poor little relics, — a folded manuscript, an
old-fashioned daguerreotype, and a tiny locket.
The parson could not see. His hand shook
as he took them solemnly out and gave them
to her. She bent over the picture, and looked
at it, as we search the faces of the dead. He
followed her to the light, and, wiping his
glasses, looked also.

"That was my picture," he said musingly.
"I never 've had one since. And that was
mother's locket. It had " — He paused and
looked at her.

"Yes," said Mary Ellen softly; "it 's got it
now." She opened the little trinket; a warm,
thick lock of hair lay within, and she touched
it gently with her finger. "Should you like
the locket, because 't was your mother's?"

She hesitated ; and though the parson's tone halted also, he answered at once : —

" No, Mary Ellen, not if you 'll keep it.   I should rather think 't was with you."

She put her two treasures in her pocket, and gave him the other.

" I guess that 's your share," she said, smiling faintly.   " Don't read it here.   Just take it away with you."

The manuscript had been written in the cramped and awkward hand of his youth, and the ink upon the paper was faded after many years.   He turned the pages, a smile coming now and then.

" ' Thou hast doves' eyes,' " he read, — " ' thou hast doves' eyes ! ' "   He murmured a sentence here and there.   " Mary Ellen," he said at last, shaking his head over the manuscript in a droll despair, " it is n't a sermon. Parson Sibley had the rights of it.   It 's a love-letter !"   And the two old people looked in each other's wet eyes and smiled.

The woman was the first to turn away.

" There!" said she, closing the lid of the chest ; " we 've said enough.   We 've wiped out old scores.   We 've talked more about ourselves than we ever shall again ; for if old age brings anything, it 's thinking of other people — them that have got life before 'em.   These your rubbers ? "

The parson put them on, with a dazed obe-

dience. His hand shook in buckling them.
Mary Ellen passed him his coat, but he noticed that she did not offer to hold it for him.
There was suddenly a fine remoteness in her
presence, as if a frosty air had come between
them. The parson put the sermon in his inner
pocket, and buttoned his coat tightly over it.
Then he pinned on his shawl. At the door he
turned.

"Mary Ellen," said he pleadingly, "don't
you ever want to see the sermon again?
Should n't you like to read it over?"

She hesitated. It seemed for a moment as
if she might not answer at all. Then she remembered that they were old folks, and need
not veil the truth.

"I guess I know it 'most all by heart," she
said quietly. "Besides, I took a copy before
I put it in there. Good-night!"

"Good-night!" answered the parson joyously. He closed the door behind him and
went crunching down the icy path. When he
had unfastened the horse and sat tucking the
buffalo-robe around him, the front door was
opened in haste, and a dark figure came flying
down the walk.

"Mr. Bond!" thrilled a voice.

"Whoa!" called the parson excitedly. He
was throwing back the robe to leap from the
sleigh when the figure reached him. "Oh!"
said he; "Isabel!"

She was breathing hard with excitement and
the determination grown up in her mind during that last half hour of her exile in the kitchen.

" Parson," — forgetting a more formal address, and laying her hand on his knee, — " I 've
got to say it ! Won't you please forgive me ?
Won't you, please ? I can't explain it " —

" Bless your heart, child ! " answered the
parson cordially ; " you need n't try to. I
guess I made you nervous."

" Yes," agreed Isabel, with a sigh of relief,
" I guess you did." And the parson drove
away.

Isabel ran, light of heart and foot, back into
the warm sitting-room, where aunt Mary Ellen
was standing just where he had left her. She
had her glasses off, and she looked at Isabel
with a smile so vivid that the girl caught her
breath, and wondered within herself how aunt
Mary Ellen had looked when she was young.

" Isabel," said she, " you come here and give
me a corner of your apron to wipe my glasses.
I guess it 's drier 'n my handkerchief."

HORN O' THE MOON

IF you drive along Tiverton Street, and then
turn to the left, down the Gully Road, you
journey, for the space of a mile or so, through
a bewildering succession of damp greenery,
with noisy brooks singing songs below you, on
either side, and the treetops on the level with
your horse's feet. Few among the older inhabitants ever take this drive, save from necessity, because it is conceded that the dampness
there is enough, even in summer, to "give you
your death o' cold;" and as for the young, to
them the place wears an eerie look, with its
miniature suggestion of impassable gulfs and
roaring torrents. Yet no youth reaches his
majority without exploring the Gully. He who
goes alone is the more a hero; but even he
had best leave two or three trusty comrades
reasonably near, not only to listen, should he
call, but to stand his witnesses when he afterwards declares where he has been. It is a
fearsome thing to explore that lower stratum
of this round world, so close to the rushing
brook that it drowns your thoughts, though not
your apprehensions, and to go slipping about
over wet boulders and among dripping ferns;

but your fears are fears of the spirit. They
are inherited qualms. You shiver because
your grandfathers and fathers and uncles have
shivered there before you. If you are very
brave indeed, and naught but the topmost
round of destiny will content you, possibly you
penetrate still further into green abysses, and
come upon the pool where, tradition says, an
ancient trout has his impregnable habitation.
Apparently, nobody questions that the life of
a trout may be indefinitely prolonged, under
the proper conditions of a retired dusk ; and
the same fish that served our grandfathers for
a legend now enlivens our childish days. When
you meet a youngster, ostentatiously setting
forth for the Gully Road, with bait-box and
pole, you need not ask where he is going ;
though if you have any human sympathy in
the pride of life, you will not deny him his
answer : —

" Down to have a try for the old trout ! "

The pool has been still for many years.
Not within the memory of aged men has the
trout turned fin or flashed a speckled side ; but
he is to this day an historical present. He
has lived, and therefore he lives always.

Those who do not pause upon the Gully
Road, but keep straight on into the open, will
come into the old highway leading up and
up to Horn o' the Moon. It is an unshaded,
gravelly track, pointing duly up-hill for three

long miles ; and it has become a sober way to most of us, in this generation : for we never take it unless we go on the solemn errand of getting Mary Dunbar, that famous nurse, to care for our sick or dead. There is a tradition that a summer visitor once hired a " shay," and drove, all by herself, up to Horn o' the Moon, drawn on by the elusive splendor of its name. But she met such a dissuading flood of comment by the way as to startle her into the state of mind commonly associated with the Gully Road. Farmers, haying in the field, came forward, to lean on the fence, and call excitedly, —

"Where ye goin' ? "

" Horn o' the Moon," replied she, having learned in Tiverton the value of succinct replies.

"Who 's sick ? "

" Nobody."

" Got any folks up there ? "

" No.   Going to see the place."

The effect of this varied. Some looked in amazement ; one ventured to say, " Well, that 's the beater ! " and another dropped into the cabalistic remark which cannot be defined, but which has its due significance, " Well, you *must* be sent for ! "   The result of all this running commentary was such that, when the visitor reached the top of the hill where Horn o' the Moon lies, encircled by other lesser

heights, she was stricken by its exceeding des-
olation, and had no heart to cast more than a
glance at the noble view below. She turned
her horse, and trotted, recklessly and with
many stumblings, down again into friendly
Tiverton.

Horn o' the Moon is unique in its melancholy. It has so few trees, and those of so
meagre and wind-swept a nature, that it might
as well be entirely bald. No apples grow
there; and in the autumn, the inhabitants make
a concerted sally down into Tiverton Street,
to purchase their winter stock, such of them
as can afford it. The poorer folk — and they
are all poor enough — buy windfalls, and string
them to dry; and so common is dried-apple-
pie among them that, when a Tivertonian finds
this makeshift appearing too frequently on his
table, he has only to remark, " I should think
this was Horn o' the Moon!" and it disappears,
to return no more until the slur is somewhat
outworn.

There is very little grass at the top of the
lonely height, and that of a husky, whispering
sort, in thin ribbons that flutter low little
songs in the breeze. They never cease; for,
at Horn o' the Moon, there is always a wind
blowing, differing in quality with the season.
Sometimes it is a sighing wind from other
heights, happier in that they are sweet with
firs. Sometimes it is exasperating enough to

make the March breezes below seem tender ;
then it tosses about in snatching gusts, buffet-
ing, and slapping, and excoriating him who
stands in its way.   Somehow, all the peculiar-
ities of Horn o' the Moon seem referable, in a
mysterious fashion, to the wind.   The people
speak in high, strenuous voices, striving to
hold their own against its wicked strength.
Most of them are deaf.   Is that because the
air beats ceaselessly against the porches of
their ears ?   They are a stunted race ; for they
have grown into the habit of holding the head
low, and plunging forward against that battling
element.   Even the fowl at Horn o' the Moon
are not of the ordinary sort.   Their feathers
grow the wrong way, standing up in a ragged
and disorderly fashion ; and they, too, have the
effect of having been blown about and disarranged, until nature yielded, and agreed to
their permanent roughness.

Moreover, all the people are old or middle-
aged ; and possibly that is why, again, the settlement is so desolate.   It is a disgrace for
us below to marry with Horn o' the Mooners,
though they are a sober folk ; and now it hap-
pens that everybody up there is the cousin of
everybody else.   The race is dying out, we
say, as if we considered it a distinct species ;
and we agree that it would have been wiped
away long ago, by weight of its own eccentricity, had not Mary Dunbar been the making

of it. She is the one righteous among many.
She is the good nurse whom we all go to seek,
in our times of trouble, and she perpetually
saves her city from the odium of the world.

Mary was born in Tiverton Street. We are
glad to remember that, we who condemn by
the wholesale, and are assured that no good
can come out of Nazareth. When she was a
girl of eighteen, her father and mother died ;
and she fell into a state of spiritual exaltation, wherein she dreamed dreams, and had
periods of retirement within her house, communing with other intelligences. We said
Mary had lost her mind ; but that was difficult
to believe, since no more wholesome type of
womanhood had ever walked our streets. She
was very tall, built on the lines of a beauty tran-
scending our meagre strain. Nobody approved
of those broad shoulders and magnificent arms.
We said it was a shame for any girl to be
so overgrown ; yet our eyes followed her, delighted by the harmony of line and action.
Then we whispered that she was as big as a
moose, and that, if we had such arms, we
never 'd go out without a shawl. Her "mit-
tins" must be wide enough for any man !

Mary did everything perfectly. She walked
as if she went to meet the morning, and must
salute it worthily. She carried a weight as a
goddess might bear the infant Bacchus ; and
her small head, poised upon that round throat,

wore the crown of simplicity, and not of pride.
But we only told how strong she was, and how
much she could lift. We loved Mary, but
sensibility had to shrink from those great proportions and that elemental strength.

One snowy morning, Mary's spiritual vision
called her out of our midst, to which she
never came back save as we needed her. The
world was very white that day, when she rose,
in her still house, dressed herself hastily, and
roused a neighbor, begging him to harness,
and drive her up to Horn o' the Moon. Folks
were sick there, with nobody to take care of
them. The neighbor reasoned, and then refused, as one might deny a person, however
beloved, who lives by the intuitions of an unseen world. Mary went home again, and, as
he believed, to stay. But she had not hesitated in her allegiance to the heavenly voice.
Somehow, through the blinding snow and
unbroken road, she ploughed her way up to
Horn o' the Moon, where she found an epidemic of diphtheria ; and there she stayed.
We marveled over her guessing how keenly
she was needed ; but since she never explained,
it began to be noised abroad that some wandering peddler told her. That accounted for everything ; and Mary had no time for talk. She
was too busy, watching with the sick, and
going about from house to house, cooking delicate gruels and broiling chicken for those who

were getting well. It is said that she even did the barn work, and milked the cows, during that tragic time. We were not surprised. Mary was a great worker, and she was fond of " creatur's."

Whether she came to care for these stolid people on the height, or whether the vision counseled her, Mary gave up her house in the village, and bought a little old dwelling under an overhanging hillside, at Horn o' the Moon. It was a nest built into the rock, its back sitting snugly there. The dark came down upon it quickly. In winter, the sun was gone from the little parlor as early as three o'clock ; but Mary did not mind. That house was her temporary shell ; she only slept in it in the intervals of hurrying away, with blessed feet, to tend the sick, and hold the dying in untiring arms. I shall never forget how, one morning, I saw her come out of the door, and stand silent, looking toward the rosy east. There was the dawn, and there was she, its priestess, while all around her slept. I should not have been surprised had her lips, parted already in a mysterious smile, opened still further in a prophetic chanting to the sun. But Mary saw me, and the alert, answering look of one who is a messenger flashed swiftly over her face. She advanced like the leader of a triumphal procession.

"Anybody want me ?" she called. "I'll get my bunnit."

It was when she was twenty, and not more than settled in the little house at Horn o' the Moon, that her story came to her. The Veaseys were her neighbors, perhaps five doors away; and one summer morning, Johnnie Veasey came home from sea. He brought no money, no coral from foreign parts, nor news of grapes in Eshcol. He simply came empty-handed, as he always did, bearing only, to vouch for his wanderings, a tanned face, and the bright, red-brown eyes that had surely looked on things we never saw. Adam Veasey, his brother, had been paralyzed for years. He sat all day in the chimney corner, looking at his shaking hands, and telling how wide a swathe he could cut before he was afflicted. Mattie, Adam's wife, had long dealt with the problem of an unsupported existence. She had turned into a flitting little creature with eager eyes, who made it her business to prey upon a more prosperous world. Mattie never went about without a large extra pocket attached to her waist; into this, she could slip a few carrots, a couple of doughnuts, or even a loaf of bread. She laid a lenient tax upon the neighbors and the town below. Was there a frying of doughnuts at Horn o' the Moon? No sooner had the odor risen upon the air, than Mattie stood on the spot, dumbly insistent on her toll. Her very clothes smelled of food; and it was said that, in fly-time, it was a sight to see her walk

abroad, because of the hordes of insects settling here and there on her odoriferous gown.
When Johnnie Veasey appeared, Mattie's soul
rose in arms. Their golden chance had come
at last.

"You got paid off?" she asked him, three
minutes after his arrival, and Johnnie owned,
with the cheerfulness of those rich only in
hope, that he did get paid, and lost it all, the
first night on shore. He got into the wrong
boarding-house, he said. It was the old number, but new folks.

Mattie acquiesced, with a sigh. He would
make his visit and go again, and, that time,
perhaps fortune might attend him. So she
went over to old Mrs. Hardy's, to borrow a
"riz loaf," and the wanderer was feasted, according to her little best.

Johnnie stayed, and Horn o' the Moon roused
itself, finding that he had brought the anti-
podes with him. He was the teller of tales.
He described what he had seen, and then, by
easy transitions, what others had known and
he had only heard, until the intelligence of
these stunted, wind-blown creatures, on their
island hill, took fire; and every man vowed he
wished he had gone to sea, before it was too
late, or even to California, when the gold craze
was on. Johnnie had the tongue of the impro-
visator, and he loved a listener. He liked to
sit out on a log, in the sparse shadow of the

one little grove the hill possessed, and, with
the whispering leaves above him tattling un-
comprehended sayings brought them by the
wind, gather the old men about him, and talk
them blind.   As he sat there, Mary came
walking swiftly by, a basket in her hand.
Johnnie came bolt upright, and took off his
cap.   He looked amazingly young and fine,
and Mary blushed as she went by.

"Who's that?" asked Johnnie of the village
fathers.

"That's only Mary Dunbar.   Guess you
ain't been here sence she moved up."

Johnnie watched her walking away, for the
rhythm of her motion attracted him.   He did
not think her pretty; no one ever thought that.

It happened, then, that he spent two or
three evenings at the Hardys', where Mary
went, every night, to rub grandmother and put
her to bed; and while she sat there in the
darkened room, soothing the old woman for
her dreary vigil, she heard his golden tales of
people in strange lands.   It seemed very wonderful to Mary.   She had not dreamed there
were such lands in all the world; and when
she hurried home, it was to hunt out her old
geography, and read it until after midnight.
She followed rivers to their sources, and dwelt
upon mountains with amazing names.   She
was seeing the earth and its fullness, and her
heart beat fast.

Next day she went away for a long case,
giving only one little sigh in the going, to the
certainty that, when she came back, Johnnie
Veasey would be off on another voyage to
lands beyond the sea. Mary was not of the sort
who cry for the moon just because they have
seen it. She had simply begun to read a fairy
tale, and somebody had taken it away from her
and put it high on the shelf. But on the very
first morning after her return, when she rose
early, longing for the blissful air of her own
bleak solitude, Mattie Veasey stood there at
her door. Mary had but one first question for
every comer : —

"Anybody sick?"

"You let me step in," answered Mattie, a
determined foot on the sill. "I want to tell
you how things stand."

It was evident that Mattie was going on a
journey. She was an exposition of the domestic resources of Horn o' the Moon. Her dress
came to the tops of her boots. It was the
plaid belonging to Stella Hardy, who had died
in her teens. It hooked behind; but that was
no matter, for the enveloping shawl, belonging to old Mrs. Titcomb, concealed that youthful eccentricity. Her shoes — congress, with
world-weary elastics at the side — were her
own, inherited from an aunt; and her bonnet
was a rusty black, with a mourning veil.
There was, at that time, but one new bonnet

at Horn o' the Moon, and its owner had sighed,
when Mattie proposed for it, brazenly saying
that she guessed nobody'd want anything that
set so fur back. Whereupon the suppliant
sought out Mrs. Pillsbury, whose mourning
headgear, bought in a brief season of prosperity, nine years before, had become, in a manner, village property. It was as duly in public
requisition as the hearse; and its owner cherished a melancholy pride in this official state.
She never felt as if she owned it, — only that
she was the keeper of a sacred trust; and
Mattie, in asking for it, knew that she demanded no more than her due, as a citizen
should. It was an impersonal matter between
her and the bonnet; and though she should
wear it on a secular errand, the veil did not
signify. She knew everybody else knew whose
bonnet it was; and that if anybody supposed
she had met with a loss, they had only to ask,
and she to answer. So, in the consciousness
of an armor calculated to meet the world,
she skillfully brought her congress boots into
Mary's kitchen, and sat down, her worn little
hands clasped under the shawl.

"You've just got home," said she. "I
s'pose you ain't heard what's happened to
Johnnie?"

Mary rose, a hand upon her chair.

"No! no! He don't want no nussin'. You
set down. I can't talk so — ready to jump an'
run. My! how good that tea does smell!"

Mary brought a cup, and placed it at her
hand, with the deft manner of those who have
learned to serve.   Mattie sugared it, and
tasted, and sugared again.

"My! how good that is!" she repeated.
"You don't steep it to rags, as some folks do.
I have to, we're so nigh the wind.   Well, you
had n't been gone long before Johnnie had a
kind of a fall.   'T wa'n't much of a one, neither,
— down the ledge.   I dunno how he done it
— he climbs like a cat — seems as if the Old
Boy was in it — but half his body he can't
move.   Palsy, I s'pose; numb, not shakin',
like Adam's."

Mary listened gravely, her hands on her
knees.

"How long 's he been so?"

"Nigh on to five weeks."

"Had the doctor?"

"Yes, we called in that herb-man over to
Saltash, an' he says there ain't no chance for
him.   He 's goin' to be like Adam, only wuss.
An' I 've been down to the Poor Farm, to tell
'em they 've got to take him in."   Her little
hands worked; her eager eyes ate their way
into the heart.   Mary could see exactly how
she had had her way with the selectmen.   "I
told 'em they 'd got to," she repeated.   "He
ain't got no money, an' we ain't got nuthin',
an' have two paraletics on my hands I can't.
So they told me they 'd give me word to-day;

an' I 'm goin' down to settle it. I 'm in hopes they 'll bring me back, an' take him along down."

"Yes," answered Mary gravely. "Yes."

"Well, now I 've come to the beginnin' o' my story." Mattie took that last delicious sip of tea at the bottom of the cup. " He 's layin' in bed, an' Adam 's settin' by the stove ; an' I wanted to know if you would n't run in, long towards noon, an' warm up suthin' for 'em."

"Yes, indeed," said Mary Dunbar. " I 'll be there."

She rose, and Mattie, albeit she dearly loved to gossip, felt that she must rise, too, and be on her way. She tried to amplify on what she had already said, but Mary did not seem to be listening ; so, treading carefully, lest the dust and dew beset her precious shoes, she took her way down the hill, like a busy little ant, born to scurry and gather.

Mary looked hastily about the room, to see if its perfect order needed a farewell touch ; and then she drank her cup of tea, and stepped out into the morning. The air was fresh and sweet. She wore no shawl, and the wind lifted the little brown rings on her forehead, and curled them closer. Mary held a hand upon them, and hurried on. She had no more thought of appearances than a woman in a desert land, or in the desert made by lack of praise ; for she knew no one looked at her.

To be clean and swift was all her life demanded.

Adam sat by the stove, where the ashes were still warm. It was not a day for fires, but he loved his accustomed corner. He was a middle-aged man, old with the suffering which is not of years, and the pathos of his stricken state hung about him, from his unkempt beard to the dusty black clothing which had been the Tiverton minister's outworn suit. One would have said he belonged to the generation before his brother.

"That you, Mary?" he asked, in his shaking voice. "Now, ain't that good? Come to set a spell?"

"Where is he?" responded Mary, in a swift breathlessness quite new to her.

"In there. We put up a bed in the clock-room."

It was the unfinished part of the house. The Veaseys had always meant to plaster, but that consummation was still afar. The laths showed meagrely; it was a skeleton of a room, — and, sunken in the high feather-bed between the two windows, lay Johnnie Veasey, his buoyancy all gone, his face quite piteous to see, now that its tan had faded. Mary went up to the bedside, and laid one cool, strong hand upon his wrist. His eyes sought her with a wild entreaty; but she knew, although he seemed to suffer, that this was the misery of delirium, and

not the conscious mind. Adam had come
trembling to the door, and stood there, one
hand beating its perpetual tattoo upon the
wall. Mary looked up at him with that ab-
stracted gaze with which we weigh and judge.

"He's feverish," said she. "Mattie didn't
tell me that. How long's he been so?"

"I dunno. I guess a matter o' two days."

"Two days?"

"Well, it might be off an' on ever sence he
fell." Adam was helpless. He depended upon
Mattie, and Mattie was not there.

"What did the doctor leave?"

Adam looked about him. "'Twas the herb
doctor," he said. "He had her steep some
trade in a bowl."

Mary Dunbar drew her hand away, and
walked two or three times up and down the
bare, bleak room. The seeking eyes were following her. She knew how little their dis-
tended agony might mean; but nevertheless
they carried an entreaty. They leaned upon
her, as the world, her sick world, was wont to
lean. Mary was, in many things, a child; but
her attitude had grown to be maternal. Suddenly she turned to Adam, where he stood,
shaking and hesitating, in the doorway.

"You goin' to send him off?"

"'Pears as if that's the only way," shuffled
Adam.

"To-day?"

"Well, I dunno's they'll come" —

Mary walked past him, her mind assured.

"There, that'll do," said she. "You set down in your corner. I'll be back byme-by."

She hurried out into the bleak world which was her home, and, at that moment, it looked very fair and new. The birds were singing, loudly as they ever sang up here where there were few leaves to nest in. Mary stopped an instant to listen, and lifted her face wordlessly to the clear blue sky. It seemed as if she had been given a gift. There, before one of the houses, she called aloud, with a long, lingering note, "Jacob!" and Jacob Pease rose from his milking-stool, and came forward. Jacob was tall and snuff-colored, a widower of three years' standing. There was a theory that he wanted Mary, and lacked the courage to ask her.

"That you, Mary Dunbar?" said he. "Anything on hand?"

"I want you to come and help me lift," answered Mary.

Jacob set down his milk pail, and followed her into the Veaseys' kitchen. She drew out the tin basin, and filled it at the sink.

"Wash your hands," said she. "Adam, you set where you generally do. You'll be in the way."

Jacob followed her into the sick-room, and Adam weakly shuffled in behind.

"For the land's sake!" he began, but Mary was at the head of the bed, and Jacob at the foot.

"I'll carry his shoulders," she said, in the voice that admits no demur. "You take his feet and legs. Sort o' fold the feather-bed up round him, or we never shall get him through the door."

"Which way?" asked Jacob, still entirely at rest on a greater mind.

"Out!" commanded Mary, — "out the front door."

Adam, in describing that dramatic moment, always declared that nobody but Mary Dunbar could have engineered a feather-bed through the narrow passage, without sticking midway. He recalled an incident of his boyhood when, in the Titcomb fire, the whole family had spent every available instant before the falling of the roof, in trying to push the second-best bed through the attic window, only to leave it there to burn. But Mary Dunbar took her patient through the doorway as Napoleon marched over the Alps; she went with him down the road toward her own little house under the hill. Only then did Adam, still shuffling on behind, collect his intelligence sufficiently to shout after her, —

"Mary, what under the sun be you doin' of? What you want me to tell Mattie? S'pose she brings the selec'men, Mary Dunbar!"

She made no reply, even by a glance. She
walked straight on, as if her burden lightened,
and into her own cave-like house and her little
neat bedroom.

"Lay him down jest as he is," she said to
Jacob. "We won't try to shift him to-day.
Let him get over this."

Jacob stretched himself, after his load, put
his hands in his pockets, and made up his
mouth into a soundless whistle.

"Yes! well!" said he. "Guess I better
finish milkin'."

Mary put her patient "to-rights," and set
some herb drink on the back of the stove.
Presently the little room was filled with the
steamy odor of a bitter healing, and she was
on the battlefield where she loved to conquer.
In spite of her heaven-born instinct, she knew
very little about doctors and their ways of cure.
Earth secrets were hers, some of them inherited
and some guessed at, and luckily she had never
been involved in those greater issues to be
dealt with only by an exalted science. Later
in her life, she was to get acquainted with the
young doctor, down in Tiverton Street, and
hear from him what things were doing in his
world. She was to learn that a hospital is not
a slaughter house incarnadined with writhing
victims, as some of us had thought. She was
even to witness the magic of a great surgeon;
though that was in her old age, when her atti-

tude toward medicine had become one of humble thankfulness that, in all her daring, she had done no harm. To-day, she thought she could set a bone or break up a fever; and there was no doubt in her mind that, if other deeds were demanded of her, she should be led in the one true way. So she sat down by her patient, and was watching there, hopeful of moisture on his palm, when Mattie broke into the front room, impetuous as the wind. Mary rose and stepped out to meet her, shutting the door as she went. Passing the window, she saw the selectmen, in the vehicle known as a long-reach, waiting at the gate.

"Hush, Mattie!" said she, "you'll wake him."

Mattie, in her ill-assorted respectabilities of dress, seemed to have been involved but recently in some bacchanalian orgie. Her shawl was dragged to one side, and her bonnet sat rakishly. She was intoxicated with her own surprise.

"Mary Dunbar!" cried she, "I'd like to know the meanin' of all this go-round!"

"There!" answered Mary, with a quietude like that of the sea at ebb, "I can't stop to talk. I'll settle it with the selec'men. You come, too."

Mattie's eyes were seeking the bedroom. Leave her alone, and her feet would follow. "You come along," repeated Mary, and Mattie came.

When the three selectmen saw Mary Dunbar stepping down the little slope, they gathered about them all their official dignity. Ebenezer Tolman sat a little straighter than usual, and uttered a portentous cough. Lothrop Wilson, mild by nature, and rather prone to whiffling in times of difficulty, frowned, with conscious effort; but that was only because he knew, in his own soul, how loyally he loved the under-dog, let justice go as it might. Then there was Eli Pike, occupying himself in pulling a rein from beneath the horse's tail. These two hated warfare, and were nervously conscious that, should they fail in firmness, Ebenezer would deal with them. Mary went swiftly up to the wagon, and laid one hand upon the wheel.

"I've got John Veasey in my house," she began rapidly. "I can't stop to talk. He's pretty sick."

Ebenezer cleared his throat again.

"We understood his folks had put him on the town," said he.

Mattie made a little eager sound, and then stopped.

"He ain't on the town yet," said Mary. "He's in my bedroom. An' there he's goin' to stay. I've took this job." She turned away from them, erect in her decision, and went up the path. Eli Pike looked after her, with an understanding sympathy. He was the man who had walked two miles, one night, to shoot a fox, trapped, and left there helpless with a broken leg. Lothrop gazed straight ahead, and said nothing.

"Look here!" called Ebenezer. "Mary! Mary! you look here!"

Mary turned about at the door. She was magnificent in her height and dignity. Even Ebenezer felt almost ashamed of what he had to say; but still the public purse must be regarded.

"You can't bring in a bill for services," he announced. "If he's on the town, he'll have to go right into the Poorhouse with the rest."

Mary made no answer. She stood there a second, looking at him, and he remarked to Eli, "I guess you might drive on."

But Mattie, following Mary up to the house, to talk it over, tried the door in vain.

"My land!" she ejaculated, "if she ain't bolted it!" So the nurse and her patient were left to themselves.

As to the rest of the story, I tell it as we hear it still in Tiverton. At first, it was reckoned among the miracles; but when the new doctor came, he explained that it accorded quite honestly with the course of violated nature, and that, with some slight pruning here and there, the case might figure in his books. What science would say about it, I do not know; tradition was quite voluble.

It proved a very long time before Johnnie grew better, and in all those days Mary Dunbar was a happy woman. She stepped about the house, setting it in order, watching her charge, and making delicate possets for him to take. When the "herb-man" came, she turned him away from the door with a regal courtesy. It was not so much that she despised his knowledge, as that he knew no more than she, and this was her patient. The young doctor in Tiverton told her afterwards that she had done a dangerous thing in not calling in some accredited wearer of the cloth; but Mary did not think of that. She went on her way of innocence, delightfully content. And all those days, Johnnie Veasey, as soon as he came out of his fever, lay there and watched her with eyes full of a listless wonder. He was still in that borderland of helplessness where the unusual seems only a part of the new condition of things. Neighbors called, and Mary refused them entrance, with a finality which admitted no appeal.

"I've got sickness here," she would say, standing in the doorway confronting them. "He's too weak to see anybody. I guess I won't ask you in."

But one day, the minister appeared, his fat gray horse climbing painfully up from the Gully Road. It was a warm afternoon; and as soon as Mary saw him, she went out of her

house, and closed the door behind her. When
he had tied his horse, he came toward her,
brushing the dust of the road from his irre-
proachable black. He was a new minister, and
very particular. Mary shook hands with him,
and then seated herself on the step.

"Won't you set down here?" she asked.
"I 've got sickness, an' I can't have talkin' any
nearer. I 'm glad it 's a warm day."

The minister looked at the step, and then
at Mary. He felt as if his dignity had been
mildly assaulted, and he preferred to stand.

"I should like to offer prayer for the young
man," he said. "I had hoped to see him."

Mary smiled at him in that impersonal way
of hers.

"I don't let anybody see him," said she. "I
guess we shall all have to pray by ourselves."

The minister was somewhat nettled. He
was young enough to feel the slight to his
official position; and moreover, there were
things which his rigid young wife, primed by
the wonder of the town, had enjoined upon
him to say. He flushed to the roots of his
smooth brown hair.

"I suppose you know," said he, "that you 're
taking a very peculiar stand."

Mary turned her head, to listen. She
thought she heard her patient breathing, and
her mind was with him.

"You seem," said the minister, "to have

taken in a man who has no claim on you, instead of letting him stay with his people. If you are going to marry him, let me advise you to do it now, and not wait for him to get well. The opinion of the world is, in a measure, to be respected, — though only in a measure."

Mary had risen to go in, but now she turned upon him.

"Married!" she repeated ; and then again, in a hushed voice, — "married !"

" Yes," replied the minister testily, standing by his guns, "married."

Mary looked at him a moment, and then again she moved away. She glanced round at him, as she entered the door, and said very gently, "I guess you better go now. Goodday."

She closed the door, and the minister heard her bolt it. He told his wife briefly, on reaching home, that there was n't much chance to talk with Mary, and perhaps the less there was said about it the better.

But as Mary sat down by her patient's bed, her face settled into sadness, because she was thinking about the world. It had not, heretofore, been one of her recognized planets ; now that it had swung her way, she marveled at it.

The very next night, while she was eating her supper in the kitchen, the door opened, and Mattie walked in. Mattie had been washing late that afternoon. She always washed at odd

times, and often in dull weather her undried
clothes hung for days upon the line.   She was
" all beat out," for she had begun at three, and
steamed through her work, to have an early
supper at five.

"There, Mary Dunbar!" cried she; "I said
I 'd do it, an' I have.   There ain't a neighbor
got into this house for weeks, an' folks that
want you to go nussin' have been turned away.
I says to Adam, this very afternoon, ' I 'll be
whipped if I don't git in an' see what 's goin'
on !'   There 's some will have it Johnnie 's got
well, an' drove away without saying good-by
to his own folks, an' some say he ain't likely
to live, an' there he lays without a last word to
his own brother !   As for the childern, they 've
got an idea suthin' 's been done to uncle
Johnnie, an' you can't mention him but they
cry."

Mary rose calmly and began clearing her
table.   "I guess I would n't mention him,
then," said she.

A muffled sound came from the bedroom.
It might have been laughter.   Then there was
a little crack, and Mary involuntarily looked
at the lamp chimney.   She hurried into the
bedroom, and stopped short at sight of her
patient, lying there in the light of the flickering fire.   His face had flushed, and his eyes
were streaming.

"I laughed so," he said chokingly.   "She

always makes me. And something snapped into place in my neck. I don't know what it was, — but *I can move !*"

He held out his hand to her. Mary did not touch it ; she only stood looking at him with a wonderful gaze of pride and recognition, and yet a strange timidity. She, too, flushed, and tears stood in her eyes.

" I 'll go and tell Mattie," said she, turning toward the door. " You want to see her ? "

"For God's sake, no! not till I'm on my feet." He was still laughing. " I guess I can get up to-morrow."

Mary went swiftly out, and shut the door behind her.

"I guess you better not see him to-night," she said. " You can come in to-morrer. I should n't wonder if he 'd be up then."

"I told Adam " — began Mattie, but Mary put a hand on her thin little arm, and held it there.

"I 'd rather talk to-morrer," said she gently. " Don't you come in before 'leven ; but you come. Tell Adam to, if he wants. I guess your brother 'll be gettin' away before long." She opened the outer door, and Mattie had no volition but to go. " It 's a nice night, ain't it ? " called Mary cheerfully, after her. " Seems as if there never was so many stars."

Then she went back into the kitchen, and with the old thrift and exactitude prepared her

patient's supper.   He was sitting upright,
bolstered against the head of the bed ; and he
looked like a great mischievous boy, who had,
in some way, gained a long-desired prize.

"See here !" he called.   "Tell me I can't
get up to-morrow ?   Why, I could walk !"

They had a very merry time while he ate.
Mary remembered that afterwards, with a
bruised wonder that laughter comes so cheap.
Johnnie talked incessantly, not any more of
the wonders of the deep, but what he meant
to do when he got into the world again.

"How'd I come here in your house, any
way ?" he asked.   "Mattie and Adam put me
here to get rid of me ?   Tell me all over again."

"I take care of folks, you know," answered
Mary briefly.   "I have, for more 'n two years.
It 's my business."

Johnnie looked at her a moment, crimsoning
as he tried to speak.

"What you goin' to ask ?"

Mary started.   Then she answered steadily, —

"That 's all right.   I don't ask much, anyway ; but when folks don't have ready money,
I never ask anything.   There, you must n't
talk no more, even if you are well.   I 've got
to wash these dishes."

She left him to his meditations, and only once
more that evening did they speak together.
When she came to the door, to say good-night,

he was flat among his pillows, listening for
her.

"Say!" he called, "you come in. No, you
need n't unless you want to ; but if ever I earn
another cent of money, you 'll see. And I
ain't the only friend you 've got. There 's a
girl down in Southport would do anything in
the world for you, if she only knew."

Next morning, Johnnie walked weakly out
of doors, despite his nurse's cautions ; for, not
knowing what had happened to him, she was
in a wearying dark as to whether it might not
happen again. After his breakfast, he got a
ride with Jacob Pease, who was going down
Sudleigh way, and Jacob came back without
him. He bore a message, full of gratitude, to
Mary. At Sudleigh, Johnnie had telegraphed,
to find out whether the ship Firewing was still
in port ; and he had heard that he must lose
no time in joining her. He should never forget what Mary had done for him. So Jacob
said ; but he was a man of tepid words, and
perhaps he remembered the message too
coldly.

When Mattie came over, that afternoon, to
make her call, she found the house closed.
Mary had gone on foot down into Tiverton,
where old Mrs. Lamson, who was sick with a
fever, lay still in need. It was many weeks
before she came home again to Horn o' the
Moon ; and then Grandfather Sinclair had

broken his leg, so that interest in her miracle became temporarily inactive.

Two years had gone when there came to her a little package, through the Tiverton mail. It was tied with the greatest caution, and directed in a straggling hand. Mary opened it just as she struck into the Gully Road, on her way home. Inside was a little purse, and three gold pieces. She paused there, under the branches, the purse in one hand, and the gold lying within her other palm. For a long time she stood looking at them, her face set in that patient sadness seen in those whose only holding is the past. It was all over and done, and yet it had never been at all. She thought a little about herself, and that was very rare, for Mary. She was not the poorer for what her soul desired ; she was infinitely the richer, and she remembered the girl at Southport, not with the pang that once afflicted her heart, but with a warm, outrushing sense of womanly sympathy. If he had money, perhaps he could marry. Perhaps he was married now. Coming out of the Gully Road, she opened the purse again, and the sun struck richly upon the gold within. Mary smiled a little, wanly, but still with a sense of the good, human kinship in life.

"I won't ever spend 'em," she said to herself. "I 'll keep 'em to bury me."

A STOLEN FESTIVAL

DAVID MACY's house stood on the spur of a
breezy upland at the end of a road. The far-
away neighbors, who lived on the main highway and could see the passin', often thanked
their stars that they had been called to no
such isolation ; you might, said they, as well
be set down in the middle of a pastur'. They
wondered how David's Letty could stand it.
She had been married 'most a year, and before
that she was forever on the go. But there !
if David Macy had told her the sun rose in
the west, she 'd ha' looked out for it there
every identical mornin'.

The last proposition had some color in it ;
for Letty was very much in love. To an im-
partial view, David was a stalwart fellow with
clear gray eyes and square shoulders, a prosperous yeoman of the fibre to which America
owes her being. But according to Letty he
was something superhuman in poise and charm.
David had no conception of his heroic respon-
sibilities ; nothing could have puzzled him more
than to guess how the ideal of him grew and
strengthened in her maiden mind, and how her
after-worship exalted it into something thrilling

and passionate, not to be described even by
a tongue more facile than hers. Letty had a
vivid nature, capable of responding to those
delicate influences which move to spiritual
issues. There were throes of love within her,
of aspiration, of an ineffable delight in being.
She never tried to understand them, nor did
she talk about them ; but then, she never tried
to paint the sky or copy the robin's song.
Life was very mysterious ; but one thing was
quite as mysterious as another. She did sometimes brood for a moment over the troubled
sense that, in some fashion, she spoke in another key from "other folks," who did not appear to know that joy is not altogether joy,
but three-quarters pain, and who had never
learned how it brings its own aching sense of
incompleteness ; but that only seemed to her
a part of the general wonder of things. There
had been one strange May morning in her
life when she went with her husband into the
woods, to hunt up a wild steer. She knew
every foot of the place, and yet one turn of the
path brought them into the heart of a picture
thrillingly new with the unfamiliarity of pure
and living beauty. The evergreens enfolded
them in a palpable dusk; but entrancingly
near, shimmering under a sunny gleam, stood
a company of birches in their first spring wear.
They were trembling, not so much under the
breeze as from the hurrying rhythm of the

year. Their green was vivid enough to lave
the vision in light ; and Letty looked beyond
it to a brighter vista still. There, in an opening, lay a bank of violets, springing in the
sun. Their blue was a challenge to the skyey
blue above ; it pierced the sight, awaking new
longings and strange memories. It seemed
to Letty as if some invisible finger touched
her on the heart and made her pause. Then
David turned, smiling kindly upon her, and
she ran to him with a little cry, and put her
arms about his neck.

"What is it ? " he asked, stroking her hair
with a gentle hand. " What is it, little child ? "

" Oh, it 's nothin' ! " said Letty chokingly.
" It 's only — I like you so ! "

The halting thought had no purple wherein
to clothe itself; but it meant as much as if she
had read the poets until great words had become familiar, and she could say "love." He
was the spring day, the sun, the blue of the
sky, the quiver of leaves ; and she felt it, and
had a pain at her heart.

Now, on an autumn morning, David was
standing within the great space in front of
the barn, greasing the wheels preliminary to a
drive to market ; and Letty stood beside him,
bareheaded, her breakfast dishes forgotten.
She was a round thing, with quick movements
not ordinarily belonging to one so plump ; her
black hair was short, and curled roughly, and

there were freckles on her little snub nose.
David looked up at her red cheeks and the
merry shine of her eyes, and smiled upon her.

"You look pretty nice this mornin'," he
remarked.

Letty gave a little dancing step and laughed.
The sun was bright; there was a purple haze
over the hills, and the nearer woods were yel-
low. The world was a jewel newly set for
her.

"I *am* nice!" said she. "David, do you
know our anniversary 's comin' on? It 's 'most
a year since we were married, — a year the
fifteenth."

David loosened the last wheel, and rose to
look at her.

"Sho!" said he, with great interest. "Is
that so? Well, 't was a good bargain. Best
trade I ever made in *my* life!"

"And we 've got to celebrate," said Letty
masterfully. "I 'll tell you how. I 've had it all
planned for a month. We 'll get up at four,
have our breakfast, ride over to Star Pond, and
picnic all day long. We 'll take a boat and go
out rowin', and we 'll eat our dinner on the
water!"

David smiled back at her, and then, with a
sudden recollection, pursed his lips.

"I 'm awful sorry, Letty," he said honestly,
"but I 've got to go over to Long Pastur' an'
do that fencin', or I can't put the cattle in

there before we turn 'em into the shack. You
know that fence was all done up in the spring,
but that cussed breachy cow o' Tolman's
hooked it down; an' if I wait for him to do
it — well, you know what he is!"

"Oh, you can put off your fencin'!" cried
Letty. "Only one day! Oh, you can!"

"I could 'most any other time," said David,
with reason, "but here it is 'most Saturday,
an' next week the thrashin'-machine 's comin'.
I'm awful sorry, Letty. I am, honest!"

Letty turned half round like a troubled child,
and began grinding one heel into the turf.
She was conscious of an odd mortification. It
was not, said her heart, that the thing itself was
so dear to her; it was only that David ought
to want immeasurably to do it. She always
put great stress upon the visible signs of an invisible bond, and she would be long in getting
over her demand for the unreason of love.

David threw down the monkey-wrench, and
put an arm about her waist.

"Come, now, you don't care, do you?" he
asked lovingly. "One day 's the same as another, now ain't it?"

"Is it?" said Letty, a smile running over
her face and into her wet eyes. "Well, then,
le's have Fourth o' July fireworks next Sunday
mornin'!"

David looked a little hurt; but that was
only because he was puzzled. His sense of

humor wore a different complexion from Letty's.
He liked a joke, and he could tell a good story,
but they must lie within the logic of fun.
Letty could put her own interpretation on her
griefs, and twist them into shapes calculated
to send her into hysterical mirth.

"You see," said David soothingly, "we 're
goin' to be together as long as we live. It
ain't as if we 'd got to rake an' scrape an' plan
to git a minute alone, as it used to be, now is
it? An' after the fencin' 's done, an' the
thrashin', an' we 've got nothin' on our minds,
we 'll take both horses an' go to Star Pond.
Come, now! Be a good girl!"

The world seemed very quiet because Letty
was holding silence, and he looked anxiously
down at the top of her head. Then she re-
lented a little and turned her face up to his —
her rebellious eyes and unsteady mouth. But
meeting the loving honesty of his look, her
heart gave a great bound of allegiance, and
she laughed aloud.

"There!" she said. "Have it so. I won't
say another word. _I_ don't care!"

These were David's unconscious victories,
born, not of his strength or tyranny, but out
of the woman's maternal comprehension, her
lavish concession of all the small things of life
to the one great code. She had taken him for
granted, and thenceforth judged him by the
intention and not the act.

David was bending to kiss her, but he stopped midway, and his arm fell.

"There's Debby Low," said he. "By jinks! I ain't more 'n half a man when she's round, she makes me feel so sheepish. I guess it's that eye o' her'n. It goes through ye like a needle."

Letty laughed light-heartedly, and looked down the path across the lot. Debby, a little, bent old woman, was toiling slowly along, a large carpet-bag swinging from one hand. Letty drew a long breath and tried to feel resigned.

"She's got on her black alpaca," said she. "She's comin' to spend the day!"

David answered her look with one of commiseration, and, gathering up his wrench and oil, "put for" the barn.

"I'd stay, if I could do any good," he said hastily, "but I can't. I might as well stan' from under."

Debby threw her empty carpet-bag over the stone wall, and followed it, clambering slowly and painfully. Her large feet were clad in congress boots; and when she had alighted, she regarded them with deep affection, and slowly wiped them upon either ankle, a stork-like process at which David, safe in the barn, could afford to smile.

"If it don't rain soon," she called fretfully, "I guess you'll find yourselves alone an' forsaken, like pelicans in the wilderness. Anybody

must want to see ye to traipse up through that
lot as I've been doin', an' git their best clo'es
all over dirt."

"You could ha' come in the road," said
Letty, smiling. Letty had a very sweet temper, and she had early learned that it takes all
sorts o' folks to make a world. It was a part of
her leisurely and generous scheme of life to
live and let live.

"Ain't the road dustier 'n the path?" inquired Debby contradictorily. "My stars! I
guess 't is. Well, now, what do you s'pose
brought me up here this mornin'?"

Letty's eyes involuntarily sought the bag,
whose concave sides flapped hungrily together;
but she told her lie with cheerfulness. "I
don't know."

"I guess ye don't. No, I ain't comin' in.
I'm goin' over to Mis' Tolman's, to spend the
day. I'm in hopes she's got b'iled dish. You
look here!" She opened the bag, and searched
portentously, the while Letty, in some un-
worthy interest, regarded the smooth, thick
hair under her large poke-bonnet. Debby had
an original fashion of coloring it; and this no
one had suspected until her little grandson innocently revealed the secret. She rubbed it
with a candle, in unconscious imitation of an
actor's make-up, and then powdered it with
soot from the kettle. "I believe to my soul
she does!" said Letty to herself.

But Debby, breathing hard, had taken something from the bag, and was holding it out on the end of a knotted finger.

"There!" she said, "ain't that your'n? Vianna said 't was your engagement ring."

Letty flushed scarlet, and snatched the ring tremblingly. She gave an involuntary look at the barn, where David was whistling a merry stave.

"Oh, my!" she breathed. "Where'd you find it?"

"Well, that's the question!" returned Debby triumphantly. "Where'd ye lose it?"

But Letty had no mind to tell. She slipped the ring on her finger, and looked obstinate.

"Can't I get you somethin' to put in your bag?" she asked cannily. Debby was diverted, though only for the moment.

"I should like a mite o' pork," she answered, lowering her voice and giving a glance, in her turn, at the barn. "I s'pose ye don't want *him* to know of it?"

"I should like to be told why!" flamed Letty, in an indignation disproportioned to its cause. Debby had unconsciously hit the raw. "Do you s'pose I'd do anything David can't hear?"

"Law, I did n't know," said Debby, as if the matter were of very little consequence. "Mis' Peleg Chase, she gi'n me a beef-bone, t' other day, an' she says, 'Don't ye tell *him*!' An'

Mis' Squire Hill gi'n me a pail o' lard ; but she
hid it underneath the fence, an' made me come
for 't after dark.   I dunno how you 're goin' to
git along with men-folks, if ye offer 'em the
whip-hand.   They 'll take it, anyways.   Well,
don't you want to know where I come on this
ring ? "

Letty had taken a few hasty steps toward
the house.   "Yes, I do," owned she, turning
about.   " Where was it ? "

" Well, Sammy was in swimmin', an' he dove
into the Old Hole, to see 'f 't had any bottom
to 't.   Vianna made him vow he would n't go
in whilst he had that rash ; but he come home
with his shirt wrong side out, an' she made him
own up.   But he 'd ha' told anyway, he was so
possessed to show that ring.   He see suthin'
gleamin' on a willer root nigh the bank, an' he
dove, an' there 't was.   I told Sammy mebbe
you 'd give him suthin' for 't, an' he said there
wa'n't nothin' in the world he wanted but a
mite o' David's solder, out in the shed-cham-
ber."

" He shall have it," said Letty hastily.
" I 'll get it now.   Don't you say anything ! "
And then she knew she had used the formula
she detested, and that she was no better than
Mrs. Peleg Chase, or the wife of Squire Hill.

She ran frowning into the house, and down
and up from kitchen to cellar.   Presently she
reappeared, panting, with a great tin pan borne

before her like a laden salver. She set it down
at Debby's feet, and began packing its contents
into the yawning bag.

"There!" she said, working with haste.
"There's the solder, all of it. And here's
some of our sweet corn. We planted late."

Debby took an ear from the pan, and, tearing open the husk, tried a kernel with a critical thumb.

"Tough, ain't it?" she remarked, disparagingly. "Likely to be, this time o' year. Is
that the pork?"

It was a generous cube, swathed in a fresh
white cloth.

"Yes, it is," said Letty breathlessly, thrust-
ing it in and shutting the bag. "There!"

"Streak o' fat an' streak o' lean?" inquired
Debby remorselessly.

"It's the best we've got; that's all I can
say. Now I've got to speak to David before
he harnesses. Good-by!"

In a fever of impatience, she fled away to the
barn.

"Well, if ever!" ejaculated Debby, lifting the bag and turning slowly about, to take
her homeward path. "Great doin's, *I* say!"
And she made no reply when Letty, prompted
by a tardy conscience, stopped in the barn
doorway and called to her, "Tell Sammy I'm
much obliged. Tell him I shall make turn-
overs to-morrow." Debby was thinking of the

pork, and the likelihood of its being properly diversified.

Letty swept into the barn like a hurrying wind. The horses backed, and laid their ears flat, and David, grooming one of them, gentled him and inquired of him confidentially what was the matter.

"Oh, David, come out here! please come out!" called Letty breathlessly. "I've got to see you."

David appeared, with some wonderment on his face, and Letty precipitated herself upon him, mindless of curry-comb and horse-hairs and the fact that she was presently to do butter. "David," she cried, "I can't stand it. I've got to tell you. You know this ring?"

David looked at it, interested and yet perplexed.

"Seems if I'd seen you wear it," said he.

Letty gave way, and laughed hysterically.

"Seems if you had!" she repeated. "I've wore it over a year. There ain't a girl in town but knows it. I showed it to 'em all. I told 'em 't was my engagement ring."

David looked at it, and then at her. She seemed to him a little mad. He could quiet the horses, but not a woman, in so vague an exigency.

"What made you tell 'em that?" he asked, at a venture.

"Don't you see? There wasn't one of 'em

that was engaged but had a ring — and presents, David — and they knew I never had anything, or I 'd have showed 'em."

David was not a dull man ; he had very sound views on the tariff, and, though social questions might thrive outside his world, the town blessed him for an able citizen. But he felt troubled ; he was condemned, and it was the world's voice which had condemned him.

"I don't know 's I ever did give you anything, Letty," he said, with a new pain stirring in his face. "I don't b'lieve I ever thought of it. It was n't that I begrudged anything."

"Oh, my soul, no ! " cried Letty, in an agony of her own. "I knew how 't was. It wa'n't your way, but they did n't know that. And I could n't have 'em thinkin' what they did think, now could I ? So I bought me — David, I bought me that high comb I used to wear, and — and a blue handkerchief — and a thimble — and — and — this ring. And I said you give 'em to me. And I trusted to chance for your never findin' it out. But I always hated the things ; and as soon as we were married, I broke the comb, and burnt up the handkerchief, and hammered the thimble into a little wad, and buried it. But I did n't dare to stop wearin' the ring, for fear folks would notice. Then t' other day I felt so about it I knew the time had come, and I went down to the Old Hole and threw it in. And now that hateful

Sammy's found it and brought it back, and
I've sent him your solder, and Debby's promised me she would n't tell you about the pork,
and I — I'm no better than the rest of 'em
that lie and lie and don't let their men-folks
know!" Letty was sobbing bitterly, and David drew her into his arms and laid his cheek
down on her hair. His heart was aching too.
They had all the passionate sorrow of children
over some grief not understood.

"Why did n't you tell me?" he asked at
length.

"When?" said Letty chokingly.

"Then — when folks expected things —
before we were married."

"Oh, David, I could n't!"

"No," said David sadly, "I s'pose you
could n't."

Letty had been holding one hand very
tightly clenched. It was a plump hand, with
deep dimples and firm, short fingers. She
unclasped it, and stretched out toward him a
wet, pink palm.

"There!" she said despairingly. "There's
the ring."

Again David felt his inadequacy to the situation. "Don't you want to wear it?" he
hesitated. "It's real pretty. What's that red
stone?"

"I hate it!" cried Letty viciously. "It's
a garnet. Oh, David, don't you ever let me
set eyes on it again!"

David took it slowly from her hand. He drew out his pocket - book, opened it, and dropped the ring inside. "There!" he said, "I guess 't won't do me no hurt to come acrost it once in a while." Then they kissed each other again, like two children; Letty's tears wet his face, and he felt them bitterer than if they had been his own.

But for Letty the air had cleared. Now, she felt, there was no trouble in her path. She had all the irresponsible joy of one who has had a secret, and feels the burden roll away. She was like Christian without his pack. She put her hands on David's shoulders, and looked at him radiantly.

"Oh, I'm so glad!" she cried. "I'm just as wicked as I was before; but it don't seem to make any difference, now you know it!"

Though David also smiled, he was regarding her with a troubled wonder. He never expected to follow these varying moods. They were like swallow-flights, and he was content to see the sun upon their wings. So he drove thoughtfully off, and Letty went back to her work with a singing heart. She was not quite sure that it was right to be happy again, all at once, but she could not still her blood. To be forgiven, to find herself free from the haunting consciousness that she could deceive the creature to whom she held such passionate allegiance — this was enough to shape a new heaven

and a new earth.   Her simple household duties
took on the significance of noble ceremonies.
She sang as she went about them, and the
words were those of a joyous hymn.   She
seemed to be serving in a temple, making it
clean and fragrant in the name of love.

Saturday was a day born of heavenly intentions.   Letty ran out behind the house, where
the ground rose abruptly, and looked off, en-
tranced, into the blue distance.   It was the
stillest day of all the fall.   Not a breath stirred
about her ; but in the maple grove at the side
of the house, where the trees had turned early
under the chill of an unseasonable night, yel-
low leaves were sifting down without a sound.
Goldenrod was growing dull, clematis had ripened into feathery spray, and she knew how
the closed gentians were painting great purple
dashes by the side of the road.   "Oh !" she
cried aloud, in rapture.   It was her wedding
day ; a year ago the sun had shone as warmly
and benignantly as he was shining now, and the
same haze had risen, like an exhalation, from
the hills.   She saw a special omen in it, and
felt herself the child of happy fortune, to be so
mothered by the great blue sky.   Then she ran
in to give David his breakfast, and tell him, as
they sat down, that it was their wedding morning.   As she went, she tore a spray of blood-
red woodbine from the wall, and bound it
round her waist.

But David was not ready for breakfast; he
was talking with a man at the barn, and half
an hour later came hurrying in to his retarded
meal.

"I've got to eat an' run," said he; "Job
Fisher kep' me. It's about that ma'sh. But
the time wa'n't wasted. He'll sell ten acres
for twenty dollars less 'n he said last week.
Too bad to keep you waitin'! You'd ought
to eat yours while 't was hot."

Letty, with a little smile all to herself, sat
demurely down and poured coffee; this was
no time to talk of anniversaries. David ate in
haste, and said good-by.

"I'm goin' down the lot to get my withes,"
said he. "Whilst I'm gone, you put me up a
mite o' luncheon. I sha'n't lay off to come
home till night."

"Oh, David!" said Letty, with a little cry.
Then the same knowing smile crept over her
face. "No, I sha'n't," added she willfully.
"I'm goin' to bring it to you."

"Fetch me my dinner? Why, it's a mile
and a half 'cross lots! I guess you won't!"

"You go right along, David," said Letty de-
cisively. "I don't want to hear another word.
I ain't seen the Long Pastur' this summer,
and I'm comin'. Good-by!" She disappeared
down the cellar stairs with the butter-plate
poised on a pyramid of dishes, and David, having no time to argue, went off to his work.

About ten o'clock Letty took her way down to the Long Pasture ; she was a very happy woman, and she could hold her happiness before her face, regarding it frankly and with a full delight. The material joys of life might seem to escape her ; but she could have them, after all. The great universe, warm with sun and warm with love, was on her side. Even the day seemed something tangible in gracious being ; and as Letty trudged along, her basket on her arm, she reasoned upon her own riches and owned she had enough. David was not like anybody else ; but he was better than anybody else, and he was hers. Even his faults were dearer than other men's virtues. She heard the sound of his axe upon the stakes, breaking the lovely stillness with a significance lovelier still.

"David !" she called, long before reaching the little brook that runs beneath the bank, and he leaped the fence and came to meet her. "David !" she repeated, and looked up in his face with eyes so solemn and so full of light that he held her still a moment to look at her.

"Letty," he said, "you 're real pretty !" And then they both laughed, and walked on together through the shade.

The day knit up its sweet, long minutes full of the serious beauty of the woods. David worked hard, and for a time Letty lingered near him ; then she strayed away, and came

back to him, from moment to moment, with
wonderful treasures. Now it was cress from
the spring, now a palm-full of partridge ber-
ries, or a cluster of checkerberry leaves for a
"cud," or a bit of wood-sorrel. By and by the
fall stillness gave out a breath of heat, and the
sun stood high overhead. Letty spread out
her dinner, and David made her a fire among
the rocks. The smoke rose in a blue efflo-
rescence ; and with the sweet tang of burning
wood yet in the air, they sat down side by side,
drinking from one cup, and smiling over the
foolish nothings of familiar talk. At the end
of the meal, Letty took a parcel from the basket, something wrapped in a very fine white
napkin. She flushed a little, unrolling it, and
her eyes deepened.

"What's all this ?" asked David, sniffing
the air. "Fruit-cake ?"

Letty nodded without looking at him ; there
was a telltale quivering in her face. She divided the cake carefully, and gave her husband
half. David had lain back on a piny bank ;
and as he ate, his eyes followed the treetops,
swaying a little now in a rhythmic wind. But
Letty ate her piece as if it were sacramental
bread. She put out her hand to him, and he
stroked the short, faithful fingers, and then
held them close. He smiled at her ; and for a
moment he mused again over that starry light
in her eyes. Then his lids fell, and he had a

little nap, while Letty sat and dreamed back over the hours, a year and more ago, when her mother's house smelled of spices, and this cake was baked for her wedding day.

When they went home again, side by side, the fencing was all done, and David had an after-consciousness of happy playtime. He carried the basket, with his axe, and Letty, like an untired little dog, took brief excursions of discovery here and there, and came back to his side with her weedy treasures. Once — was it something in the air? — he called to her : —

"Say, Letty, wa'n't it about this kind o' weather the day we were married?"

But Letty gave a little cry, and pointed out a frail white butterfly on a mullein leaf. "See there, David! how cold he looks! I'd like to take him along. He'll freeze to-night." David forgot his question, and she was glad. Some inner voice was at her heart, warning her to leave the day unspoiled. Her joy lay in re-membering; it seemed a small thing to her that he should forget.

"We've had a real good time," he said, as he gave her the basket at the kitchen door. "Now, as soon as thrashin' 's done, we'll go to Star Pond."

After supper they covered up the squashes, for fear of a frost; and then they stood for a moment in the field, and looked at the harvest moon, risen in a great effrontery of splendor.

"Letty," asked David suddenly, "should n't you like to put on your little ring? It 's right here in my pocket."

"No! no!" said Letty hastily. "I never want to set eyes on it again."

"I guess I 'll get you another one 't you could wear. I looked t' other day when I went to market; but there was so many I did n't das't to make a choice unless you was with me."

Letty clung to him passionately. "Oh, David," she cried, with a break in her voice, "I don't want any rings. I want just you."

David put out one hand and softly touched the little blue kerchief about her head. "Anyway," he said, "we won't have any more secrets from one another, will we?"

Letty gave a little start, and she caught her breath before answering :—

"No, we won't — not unless they 're nice ones !"

A LAST ASSEMBLING

THIS happened in what Dilly Joyce, in deference to a form of speech, was accustomed to call her young days; though really her spirit seemed to renew itself with every step, and her body was to the last a willing instrument. She lived in a happy completeness which allowed her to carry on the joys of youth into the maturity of years. But things did happen to her from twenty to thirty-five which could never happen again. When Dilly was a girl, she fell in love, and was very heartily and honestly loved back again. She had been born into such willing harmony with natural laws, that this in itself seemed to belong to her life. It partook rather of the faithfulness of the seasons than of human tragedy or strenuous overthrow. Even so early she felt great delight in natural things; and when her heart turned to Jethro Moore, she had no doubt whatever of the straightness of its path. She trusted all the primal instincts without knowing she trusted them. She was thirsty; here was water, and she drank. Jethro was a little older than she, the son of a minister in a neighboring town. His father had marked out

his plan of life ; but Jethro had had enough to
do with the church on hot summer Sundays,
when "fourthly" and "sixthly" lulled him into
a pleasing coma, and when even the shimmer
of Mrs. Chase's shot silk failed to awaken his
deep eyes to their accustomed delight in fabric
and color.   To him, the church was a concrete
and very dull institution : to his father, it was
a city set on a hill, whence a shining path led
direct to God's New Jerusalem.   Therefore it
was easy enough for the boy to say he preferred business, and that he wanted uncle
Silas to take him into his upholstery shop ;
and he never, so long as he lived, understood
his father's tragic silence over the choice.   He
had broken the succession in a line of priests ;
but it seemed to him that he had simply told
what he wanted to do for a living.   So he
went away to the city, and news came flying
back of his wonderful fitness for the trade.
He understood colors, fabrics, design ; he had
been sent abroad for ideas, and finally he was
dispatched to the Chicago house, to oversee
the business there.   Thus it was many years
before Dilly met him again ; but they remained
honestly faithful, each from a lovely simplicity of nature, but a simplicity quite different
in kind.   Jethro did not grow rich very fast
(uncle Silas saw to that), but he did prosper ;
and he was ready to marry his girl long before
she owned herself ready to marry him.   She

took care of a succession of aged relatives, all
afflicted by a strange and interesting diversity
of trying diseases ; and then, after the last
death, she settled down, quite poor, in a little
house on the Tiverton Road, and "went out
nussin'," the profession for which her previous
life had fitted her. With a careless generosity,
she made over to her brother the old farm-
house where they were born, because he had a
family and needed it. But he died, and was
soon followed by his wife and child ; and now
Dilly was quite alone with the house and
the family debts. The time had come, wrote
Jethro, for them to marry. She was free, at
last, and he had enough. Would she take
him, now ? Dilly answered quite frankly and
from a serenity born of faith in the path before
her and a certainty that no feet need slip. She
was ready, she wrote. She hoped he was willing she should sell the old place, to pay Tom's
debts. That would leave her without a cent ;
but since he was coming for her, and she
need n't go to Chicago alone, she did n't know
that there was anything to worry about. He
would buy her ticket. There was an ineffable
simplicity about Dilly. She had no respect
whatever for money, save as a puzzling means
to a few necessary ends. And now the place
had been sold, and Jethro was coming in a
month. Meanwhile Dilly was to pack up the
few family effects she could afford to keep,
and the rest would go by auction.

Little as she was accustomed to dread experiences which came in the inevitable order of nature, she did think of the last day and night in the old house as something of an ordeal. People felt that the human meant very little to Dilly; but that was not true. It was only true that she held herself remote from personal intimacies; but all the fine, invisible bonds of race and family took hold of her like irresistible factors, and welded her to the universe anew.

As she started out from her little house, this summer morning, and began her three-mile walk to the old homestead, she felt as if some solemn event in her life were about to happen; her heart beat higher, and brought about the suffocating feeling of a hand laid upon the throat. She was a slight creature, with a delicate face and fine black hair. Her slender body seemed all made for action, and the poise of an assured motion dwelt in it and wrapped about its angularity like a gracious charm. She was walking down a lane, her short skirts brushed by the morning dew. She chose to go 'cross lots, not because in this case it was nearer than the road, but because it seemed impossible to go another way. Yet never in her life had she seen less of the outward garment of things than she was seeing this morning. A flouting bobolink flew from stake to stake in front of her, and bub-

bled out in melody. She heard a scythe
swishing in a neighboring field, and the musical call of the mowing-machine afar, and she
did not look up. Dumb to the beautiful outer
world, she was broad awake to human souls:
the souls of the Joyces, alive so long before
her and stretching back into an unknown past.
They had lived, one after another, in the old
house, since colonial times; and now, after
this quiet act of a concluding drama, Dilly was
going to lower the curtain, and sweep them
from the stage.

Her mind was peopled with figures. She
thought of Jethro, too. He seemed to be
coming ever nearer and nearer. She could
hear his tread marching into her life, and could
see his face. It was very moving, as she remembered it. A long line of scholarly forbears had dowered him with a refinement and
grace quite startling in this unornamented spot,
and some old Acadian ancestor had lent him
beauty. His eyes were dark, and they held an
unfathomable melancholy. The line of his
forehead and nose ran haughtily and yet delicate; and even after years of absence, Dilly
sometimes caught her breath when she thought
of the way his head was set upon his shoulders. She had never in her life seen a man
or woman who was entirely beautiful, and he
saturated her longing like a prodigal stream.

She was a little dazed when she climbed the

low stone wall, crossed the road, and came into
the grassy wilderness of the Joyce back yard.
Nature had triumphed riotously, as she will
when niggardly thrift is away. The grass lay
rich and shining, lodged by last night's shower,
and gate and cellar-case were choked by it.
The cinnamon roses bloomed in a spicy har-
diness of pink, and the gnarled apple-trees had
shed their broken branches, and were covered
with little green buttons of fruit. Dilly stopped
to look about her, and her eyes filled. The
tears were hot; they hurt her, and so recalled
her to the needs of life.

"There!" she said, "I mustn't do so!" —
and she walked straight forward through the
open shed, and fitted her key in the lock. The
door sagged; but she pushed it open and
stepped in. The deserted kitchen lay there in
desolate order, and the old Willard clock slept
upon the wall. Dilly hastily pushed a chair
before it (this was the only chair old Daniel
Joyce would allow the children to climb in)
and wound the clock. It began ticking slowly,
with the old, remembered sound. Somehow
it seemed beautiful to Dilly that the clock
should speak with the voice of all those years
agone; it was a kind of loyalty which appealed
to the soul like a piercing miracle. Then she
ran through to the sitting-room, and started
the old eight-day in the corner; and the house
breathed and was alive again. She threw open

the windows, all save those on the Dilloway
side (lest kindly neighbors should discover she
was at home), and the soft rose-scented air
flooded the rooms like an invisible presence,
and bore out the smell of age upon gracious
wings. Now, Dilly worked fast and steadily,
lest some human thing should come upon her.
She tied up bedclothes, and opened long-closed
cupboards. She made careful piles of clothing
from the attic; and finally, her mind a little
tired, she sat down on the floor and began
looking over papers and daguerreotypes from
her father's desk.   Just as she had lost herself
in the ancient history of which they were the
signs, there came a knock at the back door.
So assured had become her idea of a continued
housekeeping, that the summons did not seem
in the least strange.   The house lived again;
it had thrown open its arms to human kind.

"Come in!" she called; and a light step
sounded in the kitchen and crossed the sill.
It was a man, dark-eyed and very handsome.
"Oh!" murmured Dilly, catching her breath
and holding both hands clasped upon the
papers in her lap.   "Jethro!"

The stranger was much moved, and his
black eyes deepened. He looked at her kindly,
perhaps lovingly, too.   "Yes," he said, at last.
"So you'd know me?"

Dilly got lightly up, and the papers fell
about her in a shower; yet she made no motion

toward him. "Oh, yes," she said softly, "I should know you. You ain't changed at all."

That was not true. He looked ten years older than his real age; yet time had only dowered him with a finer grace and charm. All the lines in his face were those of gentleness and truth. His mouth had the old delicate curves. One meeting him that day might have said, with a throb of involuntary homage, "How beautiful he must have been when he was young!" But to Dilly he bore even a more subtile distinction than in that far-away time; he had ripened into something harmonizing with her own years. He came forward a little, and held out both hands; but Dilly did not take them, and he dropped the left one. Then she laid her fingers lightly in his, and they greeted each other like old acquaintances. A flush rose in her smooth brown cheek. Her eyes grew bright with that startled questioning which is of the woods. He looked at her the more intently, and his breath quickened. She had none of the blossomy charm of more robust womanhood; but he recognized the old gypsy element which had once bewitched him, and felt he loved her still.

"Well," he said, and his voice shook a little, "are you glad to see me?"

Dilly moved back, and sat down in her mother's little sewing-chair by the desk. "I don't know as I can tell," she answered. "This is a strange day."

Jethro nodded. "I meant to surprise you," he said. "So I never wrote I was coming on so soon. I was real disappointed to find your house shut up; but the neighbors told me where you'd gone, and what you'd gone for. Then I walked over here."

Dilly's face brightened all over with a responsive smile. "Did you come through the woods?" she asked. "What made you?"

"Why, I knew you'd go that way," he answered. "I thought you'd get wool-gathering over some weed or another, and maybe I'd overtake you."

They both laughed, and the ice was broken. Dilly got briskly up and gathered a drawer-full of papers into her apron.

"I can't stop workin'," she said. "I want to fix it so's not to stay here more 'n one night. Now you talk! I know what these are. I can run 'em over an' listen too."

"I think 't was real good of you to turn in the place to Tom's folks," said Jethro, also seating himself, and, as Dilly saw with a start, as if it were an omen, in her father's great chair. "Not that you'll ever need it, Dilly. You won't want for a thing. I've done real well."

Dilly's long fingers assorted papers and laid them at either side, with a neat precision. She looked up at him then, and her eyes had again the quick, inquiring glance of some wild creature in a situation foreign to its habits.

"Well," she said, "well! I guess I don't resk
anything.   An' if I did — why, I'd resk it!"

Jethro bent forward a little.   He was smiling, and Dilly met the glance, half fascinated.
She wondered that she could forget his smile;
and yet she had forgotten it.   Like running
water, it was never twice the same.

"Dilly," said he, much moved, "you'll have
a good time from this out, if ever a woman did.
You'll keep house in a brick block, where the
cars run by your door, and you can hire two
girls."

"Oh, my!" breathed Dilly.   A quick look
of trouble darkened her face, as a shadow
sweeps across the field.

"What is it?" asked Jethro, in some alarm.
"Don't you like what I said?"

Dilly smiled, though her eyes were still
apprehensive.

"It ain't that," she answered slowly, striving
in her turn to be kind.   "Only I guess I never
happened to think before just how 't would be.
I never spec'lated much on keepin' house."

"But somebody'd have to keep it," said
Jethro good-naturedly, smiling on her.   "We
can get good help.   You'll like to have a real
home table, and you can invite company every
day, if you say so.   I never was close, Dilly, —
you know that.   I sha'n't make you account
for things."

Dilly got up, and, still holding her papers

in her apron, walked swiftly to the window.
There she stood, a moment, looking out into
the orchard, where the grass lay tangled under
the neglected, happy trees. Her eyes traveled
mechanically from one to another. She knew
them all. That was the "sopsyvine," its red
fruitage fast coming on ; there was the Porter
she had seen her father graft ; and down in
the corner grew the August sweet. Life out
there looked so still and sane and homely.
She knew no city streets, — yet the thought
of them sounded like a pursuit. She turned
about, and came back to her chair.

"I guess I never dreamt how you lived,
Jethro," she said gently. "But it don't make
no matter. You 're contented with it."

"I ain't a rich man," said Jethro, with some
quiet pride ; "but I 've got enough. Yes, I
like my business ; and city life suits me.
You 'll fall in with it, too."

Then silence settled between them ; but
that never troubled Dilly. She was used to
long musings on her walks to and from her
patients, and in her watching beside their beds.
Conversation seemed to her a very spurious
thing when there is nothing to say.

"What you thinking about?" he asked suddenly.

Dilly looked up at him with her bright, truth-
telling glance. "I was thinkin'," she answered,
with a clarity never ruthless, because it was

so sweet, — "I was thinkin' you make me homesick, somehow or another."

Jethro looked at her doubtfully, and then, as she smiled at him, he smiled also.

"I don't believe it's me," he said, confidently. "It's because you're going over things here. It's the old house."

"Maybe," said Dilly, nodding and tying her last bundle of papers. "But I don't know. I never had quite such feelin's before. It's the nearest to bein' afraid of anything I've come acrost. I guess I shall have to run out into the lot an' take my bearin's."

Jethro got up, put his hands in his pockets, and walked about the room. He was very gentle, but he did at heart cherish the masculine theory that the unusual in woman is never to be judged by rules.

"But it is a queer kind of a day," owned Dilly, pushing in the last drawer. "Why, Jethro!" She faced him, and her voice broke in excitement. "You don't know, I ain't begun to tell you, how queer it seems to me. Why, I've dreaded this day for weeks! but when it come nigh, it begun to seem to me like a joyful thing. I felt as if they all knew of it: them that was gone. It seemed as if they stood 'round me, ready to uphold me in what I was doin'. I shouldn't be surprised if they were all here now. I don't feel a mite alone."

Her voice shook with excitement; her eyes were big and black. Jethro came up to her, and laid a kindly hand on her shoulder. It was a fine hand, long and shapely, and Dilly, looking down at it, remembered, with a strange regretfulness, how she had once loved its lines.

"There, poor girl!" he said, "you're tired thinking about it. No wonder you've got fancies. I guess the ghosts won't trouble us. There's nothing here worse than ourselves." And again, in spite of the Joyces, Dilly felt homesick and alone.

There came a soft thudding sound upon the kitchen floor, and she turned, alert, to listen. This was Mrs. Eli Pike in her carpet slippers; she had stood so much over soap-making that week that her feet had taken to swelling. She was no older than Dilly, but she had seemed matronly in her teens. She looked very large, as she padded forward through the doorway, and her pink face and double chin seemed to exude kindliness as she came.

"There, Dilly Joyce! if this ain't jest like you!" she exclaimed. "Creep in here an' not let anybody know! Why, Jethro, that you? Recognize you! Well, I guess I should!"

She included them both in a neighborly glance, and Dilly was very grateful. Yet it seemed to her that now, at last, she might break down and cry. The tone of olden friendliness was hard to bear, when no other voices answered. She could endure the silent house, but not the intercourse of a life so sadly changed.

"There!" continued Mrs. Pike, with a nod, "I guess I know! You're tired to pieces with this pickin' and sortin', an' you're comin' over to dinner, both on ye. Eli's dressed a hin. I had to wring her neck. *He* wouldn't ha' done it; you know that, Dilly! An' I've been beatin' up eggs. Now don't you say one word. You be there by twelve. Jethro, you got a watch? You see 't she starts, now!" And Mrs. Pike marched away victorious, her apron over her head, and waving one hand before her as she went. She had once been stung by bees, on just such a morning as this, and she had a set theory that they infested all strange dooryards.

Dilly felt as if even the Joyces could not save her day in its solemn significance unless, indeed, they should appear in their proper persons. She thought of her bread and butter and boiled eggs, lying in her little bundle, and the simple meal seemed as unattainable as if it were some banquet dreamed of in delirium. It was of one piece with cars going by the house, and two maid-servants to correct. To Dilly, a car meant a shrieking monster propelled by steam: yet not even that drove her to such insanity of revulsion as the two servants. They alone made her coming life seem like one eternal school, with the committee ever on the platform, and no recess. But she worked very meekly and soberly, and Jethro took off his coat and helped her; then, just before twelve, they washed their hands and went across the orchard to Mrs. Pike's.

The rest of the day seemed to Dilly like a confused though not an unfamiliar dream. She knew that the dinner was very good, and that it choked her, so that Mrs. Pike, alert in her first pride of housekeeping, was quite cordially harsh with her for not eating more; and that Jethro talked about Chicago; and Eli Pike, older than his wife and graver, said "Do tell!" now and again, and seemed to picture in his mind the outlines of city living. She escaped from the table as soon as possible, under pretext of the work to be done, and slipped back to the empty house; and there Jethro found her, and began helping her again.

The still afternoon settled down in its grooves of beauty, and its very loveliness gave Dilly a pain at the heart. She remembered that this was the hour when her mother used to yawn over her long seam, or her knitting, and fall asleep by the window, while the bees droned outside in the jessamine, and a humming-bird — there had always been one, year after year, and Dilly could never get over the impression that it was the same bird — hovered on his invisible perch and thrilled his wings

divinely. Then the day slipped over an unseen height, and fell into a sheltered calm.
The work was not done, and they had to go
over to Mrs. Pike's again to supper, and to
spend the night. Dilly longed to stretch herself on the old kitchen lounge in her own
home ; but Mrs. Pike told her plainly that she
was crazy, and Jethro, with a kindly authority,
bade her yield. And because words were like
weapons that returned upon her to hurt her
anew, she did yield, and talked patiently to
one and another neighbor as they came in
to see Jethro, and to inquire when he meant
to be married.

"Soon," said Jethro, with assurance. "As
soon as Dilly makes up her mind."

All that evening, Eli Pike sat on the steps,
where he could hear the talk in the sitting-
room without losing the whippoorwill's song
from the Joyce orchard, and Dilly longed to
slip out and sit quietly beside him. He would
know. But she could only be civil and grateful, and when half past eight came, take her
lamp and go up to bed. Jethro was given the
best chamber, because he had succeeded and
came from Chicago ; but Dilly had a little
room that looked straight out across the treetops down to her own home.

At first, after closing the door behind her,
she felt only the great blessedness of being
alone. She put out the light and threw her-

self, as she was, face downwards on the bed.
There she lay for long moments, suffering;
and this was one of the few times in her life
when she was forced to feel that human pain
which is like a stab in the heart. For she was
one of those wise creatures who give themselves long spaces of silence, and so heal them
quickly of their wounds, like the sage little
animals that slip away from combat, to cure
their hurt with leaves. Presently, a great
sense of rest enfolded her, a rest ineffably
precious because it was so soon to be over. It
was like great riches lent only for a time.
Outside this familiar quiet was the world,
thrilled by a terrifying life pressing upon her
and calling. She longed to put her hands before her eyes, and shut out the possibility of
meeting its garish glory; she did cover her
ears, lest its cry should pierce them and she
could not resist. And so she lay there shivering, until a strange inviting that was peace
and not commotion seemed to approach her
from another side, and her inner self became
conscious of unheard voices. They were not
clamorous, but sweet, and they drowned her
will, and drew her to themselves. She got
softly up, and, going to the darkened window,
looked out across the orchard. There, in the
greenness, lay the old house. It called on her
to come. It seemed to Dilly that she could
not make haste enough to be there. She

slipped softly down the narrow stairway, and across the kitchen, where the shadows of the moonlit windows lay upon the floor. A great excitement thrilled her blood; and though quite safe from discovery, she was not wholly at ease until she had entered the orchard path, and knew her feet were wet with dew, and heard the whippoorwill, so near now that she might have startled him from his neighboring tree. No other bird note could have fitted her mood so well. The wild melancholy of his tone, his home in the night, and the omens blended with his song seemed to remove him from the world as she herself was removed; and she hastened on with a fine exaltation, fitted her key again in the lock, and shut the door behind her.

As soon as Dilly had entered the sitting-room, where the old desk stood in its place, and the clock was ticking, she felt as if all her confusion and trouble were over. She smiled to herself in the darkness. She had come home, and it was very good. They had begun with the attic, in their rearranging, and this room remained unchanged. It had been her wish to keep it, in its sweet familiarity, un-altered till the last. She drew forward her father's chair, and sat down in it, with luxu-rious abandonment, to rest. Her mother's little cricket was by her side, and she put her feet on it and exhaled a long sigh of content.

Her eyes rested on the dark cavern which was
the fireplace ; and there fell upon her a sweet
sense of completed bliss, as if it were alight
and she could watch the dancing flames. And
suddenly Dilly was aware that the Joyces were
all about her.

She had been sure, in her coming through
the woods, that they knew and cared ; now
she was certain that, in some fashion, they
recognized their bondage and loyalty to the
place, as she recognized her own, and that they
upheld her to her task. She thought them
over, as she sat there, and saw their souls more
keenly than if she had met them, men and
women, face to face. There was the shoemaker among them, who, generations back,
was sitting on his bench when news came of
the battle of Lexington, and who threw down
hammer and last, and ran wildly out into the
woods, where he stayed three days and nights,
calling with a loud voice upon Almighty God
to save him from ill-doing. Then he had
drowned himself in a little brook too shallow
for the death of any but a desperate man. He
had been the disgrace of the Joyces ; they
dared not think of him, and they know, even to
this day, that he is remembered among their
townsmen as the Joyce who was a coward, and
killed himself rather than go to war. But here
he stood — was it the man, or some secret intelligence of him ? — and Dilly, out of all his

race, was the one to comprehend him. She
saw, with a thrill of passionate sympathy, how
he had believed with all his soul in the wicked-
ness of war, and how the wound to his country
so roused in him the desire of blood that he
fled away and prayed his God to save him from
mortal guilt, — and how, finding that he saw
with an overwhelming delight the red of anticipated slaughter, and knew his traitorous feet
were bearing him to the ranks, he chose the
death of the body rather than sin against the
soul. And Dilly was glad; the blood in her
own veins ran purer for his sake.

There was old Delilah Joyce, who went into
a decline for love, and wasted quite away. She
had been one of those tragic fugitives on the
island of being, driven out into the storm of
public sympathy to be beaten and undone; for
she was left on her wedding day by her lover,
who vowed he loved her no more. But now
Dilly saw her without the pathetic bravery of
her silken gown which was never worn, and knew
her for a woman serene and glad. That very
day she had unfolded the gown in the attic,
where it had lain, year upon year, wrapped
about by the poignant sympathy of her kin, a
perpetual reminder of the hurts and faithlessness of life. It had become a relic, set aside
from modern use. She felt now as if she could
even wear it herself, though silk was not for
her, or deck some little child in its shot and

shimmering gayety. For it came to her, with
a glad rush of acquiescent joy, that all his life,
the man, though blinded by illusion, had been
true to her whom he had left; and that, instead of being poor, she was very rich. It was
from that moment that Dilly began to understand that the soul does not altogether weld its
own bonds, but that they lie in the secret core
of things, as the planet rushes on its appointed
way.

There was Annette Joyce, who married a
Stackpole, and, to the disgust of her kin, clung
to him through one debauch after another,
until the world found out that Annette
"could n't have much sense of decency herself,
or she would n't put up with such things." But
on this one night Dilly found out that Annette's
life had been a continual laying hold of Eternal
Being, not for herself, but for the creature she
loved; that she had shown the insolence and
audacity of a thousand spirits in one, besieging
high heaven and crying in the ear of God: " I
demand of Thee this soul that Thou hast made."
And somehow Dilly knew now that she was of
those who overcome.

So the line stretched on, until she was aware
of souls of which she had never heard; and
she knew that, faulty as their deeds might be,
they had striven, and the strife was not in vain.
She felt herself to be one drop in a mighty
river, flowing into the water which is the sum

of life; and she was content to be absorbed in that great stream. There was human comfort in the moment, too; for all about her were those whom she had seen with her bodily eyes, and their presence brought an infinite cheer and rest. Dilly felt the safety of the universe; she smiled lovingly over the preciousness of all its homely ways. She thought of the twilights when she had sat on the doorstone, eating huckleberries and milk, and seeing the sun drop down the west; she remembered one night when her little cat came home, after it had been lost, and felt the warm touch of its fur against her hand. She saw how the great chain of things is held by such slender links, and how there is nothing that is not most sacred and most good. The hum of summer life outside the window seemed to her the life in her own veins, and she knew that nothing dwells apart from anything else, and that, whether we wot of it or not, we are of one blood.

The night went on to that solemn hush that comes before the dawn. Dilly felt the presence of the day, and what it would demand of her; but now she did not fear. For Jethro, too, had been with her; and at last she understood his power over her and could lay it away like a jewel in a case, a precious thing, and yet not to be worn. She saw him, also, in his stream of being, as she was swept along through hers, and knew how that old race had given him a beauty which was not his, but theirs, — and how, in the melancholy of his eyes, she loved a soul long passed, and in the wonder of his hand the tender lines of other hands, waving to fiery action. He was an inheritor; and she had loved, not him, but his inheritance.

Now it was the later dusk of night, and the cocks crowed loudly in a clear diminuendo, dying far away. Dilly pressed her hands upon her eyes, and came awake to the outer world. She looked about the room with a warm smile, and reviewed, in feeling, her happy night. It was no longer hard to dismantle the place. The room, the house, the race were hers forever; she had learned the abidingness of what is real. When she closed the door behind her, she touched the casing as if she loved it, and, crossing the orchard, she felt as if all the trees could say: "We know, you and we!"

As she entered the Pike farmyard, Eli was just going to milking, with clusters of shining pails.

"You're up early," said he. "Well, there's nothin' like the mornin'!"

"No," answered Dilly, smiling at him with the radiance of one who carries good news, "except night-time! There's a good deal in that!" And while Eli went gravely on, pondering according to his wont, she ran up to smooth her tumbled bed.

After breakfast, while Mrs. Pike was carrying

away the dishes, Dilly called Jethro softly to
one side.

"You come out in the orchard. I want to
speak to you."

Her voice thrilled with something like the
gladness of confidence, and Jethro's own face
brightened. Dilly read that vivid anticipation,
and caught her breath. Though she knew it
now, the old charm would never be quite gone.
She took his hand and drew him forward. She
seemed like a child, unaffected and not afraid.
Out in the path, under the oldest tree of all,
she dropped his hand and faced him.

"Jethro," she said, "we can't do it. We
can't get married."

He looked at her amazed. She seemed to be
telling good news instead of bad. She gazed
up at him smilingly. He could not understand.

"Don't you care about me?" he asked at
length, haltingly; and again Dilly smiled at him
in the same warm confidence.

"Oh, yes," she said eagerly. "I do care,
ever and ever so much. But it's your folks
I care about. It ain't you. I've found it all
out, Jethro. Things don't al'ays belong to us.
Sometimes they belong to them that have gone
before; an' half the time we don't know it."

Jethro laid a gentle hand upon her arm.
"You're all tired out," he said soothingly.
"Now you give up picking over things, and let
me hire somebody. I'll be glad to."

But Dilly withdrew a little from his touch. "You're real good, Jethro," she answered steadily. She had put aside her exaltation, and was her old self, full of common-sense and kindly strength. " But I don't feel tired, an' I ain't a mite crazed. All you can do is to ride over to town with Eli — he's goin' after he feeds the pigs — an' take the cars from there. It's all over, Jethro. It is, truly. I ain't so sorry as I might be; for it's borne in on me you won't care this way long. An' you need n't, dear ; for nothin' between us is changed a mite. The only trouble is, it ain't the kind of thing we thought."

She looked in his eyes with a long, bright farewell glance, and turned away. She had left behind her something which was very fine and beautiful; but she could not mourn. And all that morning, about the house, she sang little snatches of song, and was content. The Joyces had done their work, and she was doing hers.

THE WAY OF PEACE

IT was two weeks after her mother's funeral when Lucy Ann Cummings sat down and considered. The web of a lifelong service and devotion still clung about her, but she was bereft of the creature for whom it had been spun. Now she was quite alone, save for her two brothers and the cousins who lived in other townships, and they all had homes of their own. Lucy Ann sat still, and thought about her life. Brother Ezra and brother John would be good to her. They always had been. Their solicitude redoubled with her need, and they had even insisted on leaving Annabel, John's daughter, to keep her company after the funeral. Lucy Ann thought longingly of the healing which lay in the very loneliness of her little house; but she yielded, with a patient sigh. John and Ezra were men-folks, and doubtless they knew best.

A little more than a week had gone when school " took up," rather earlier than had been intended, and Annabel went away in haste, to teach. Then Lucy Ann drew her first long breath. She had resisted many a kindly office from her niece, with the crafty innocence of the gentle who can only parry and never thrust. When Annabel wanted to help in packing away grandma's things, aunt Lucy agreed, half-heartedly, and then deferred the task from day to day. In reality, Lucy Ann never meant to pack them away at all. She could not imagine her home without them; but that, Annabel would not understand, and her aunt pushed aside the moment, reasoning that something is pretty sure to happen if you put things off long enough. And something did; Annabel went away. It was then that Lucy Ann took a brief draught of the cup of peace.

Long before her mother's death, when they both knew how inevitably it was coming, Lucy Ann had, one day, a little shock of surprise. She was standing before the glass, coiling her crisp gray hair, and thinking over and over the words the doctor had used, the night before, when he told her how near the end might be. Her delicate face fell into deeper lines. Her mouth dropped a little at the corners; her faded brown eyes were hot with tears, and stopping to wipe them, she caught sight of herself in the glass.

"Why," she said aloud, "I look jest like mother!"

And so she did, save that it was the mother of five years ago, before disease had corroded the dear face, and patience wrought its tracery there.

"Well," she continued, smiling a little at the poverty of her state, "I shall be a real comfort to me when mother's gone!"

Now that her moment of solitude had struck, grief came also. It glided in, and sat down by her, to go forth no more, save perhaps under its other guise of a patient hope. She rocked back and forth in her chair, and moaned a little to herself.

"Oh, I never can bear it!" she said pathetically, under her breath. "I never can bear it in the world!"

The tokens of illness were all put away. Her mother's bedroom lay cold in an unsmiling order. The ticking of the clock emphasized the inexorable silence of the house. Once Lucy Ann thought she heard a little rustle and stir. It seemed the most natural thing in the world, coming from the bedroom, where one movement of the clothes had always been enough to summon her with flying feet. She caught her breath, and held it, to listen. She was ready, undisturbed, for any sign. But a great fly buzzed drowsily on the pane, and the fire crackled with accentuated life. She was quite alone. She put her hand to her heart, in that gesture of grief which is so entirely natural when we feel the stab of destiny; and then she went wanly into the sitting-room, looking about her for some pretense of duty to solace her poor mind. There again she caught sight of herself in the glass.

"Oh, my!" breathed Lucy Ann. Low as they were, the words held a fullness of joy.

Her face had been aging through these days of grief; it had grown more and more like her mother's. She felt as if a hand had been stretched out to her, holding a gift, and at that moment something told her how to make the gift enduring. Running over to the little table where her mother's work-basket stood, as it had been, undisturbed, she took out a pair of scissors, and went back to the glass. There she let down her thick gray hair, parted it carefully on the sides, and cut off lock after lock about her face. She looked a caricature of her sober self. But she was well used to curling hair like this, drawing its crisp silver into shining rings; and she stood patiently before the glass and coaxed her own locks into just such fashion as had framed the older face. It was done, and Lucy Ann looked at herself with a smile all suffused by love and longing. She was not herself any more; she had gone back a generation, and chosen a warmer niche. She could have kissed her face in the glass, it was so like that other dearer one. She did finger the little curls, with a reminiscent passion, not daring to think of the darkness where the others had been shut; and, at that instant, she felt very rich. The change suggested a more faithful portraiture, and she went up into the spare room and looked through the closet where her

mother's clothes had been hanging so long, untouched. Selecting a purple thibet, with a little white sprig, she slipped off her own dress,
and stepped into it. She crossed a muslin
kerchief on her breast, and pinned it with the
cameo her mother had been used to wear. It
was impossible to look at herself in the doing ;
but when the deed was over, she went again to
the glass and stood there, held by a wonder
beyond her will. She had resurrected the creature she loved ; this was an enduring portrait,
perpetuating, in her own life, another life as
well.

"I 'll pack away my own clo'es to-morrer,"
said Lucy Ann to herself. "Them are the
ones to be put aside."

She went downstairs, hushed and tremulous,
and seated herself again, her thin hands crossed
upon her lap ; and there she stayed, in a pleasant dream, not of the future, and not even of
the past, but face to face with a recognition of
wonderful possibilities. She had dreaded her
loneliness with the ache that is despair ; but
she was not lonely any more. She had been
allowed to set up a little model of the taber-
nacle where she had worshiped ; and, having
that, she ceased to be afraid. To sit there,
clothed in such sweet familiarity of line and
likeness, had tightened her grasp upon the
things that are. She did not seem to herself
altogether alive, nor was her mother dead.

They had been fused, by some wonderful
alchemy; and instead of being worlds apart,
they were at one. So, John Cummings, her
brother, stepping briskly in, after tying his
horse at the gate, came upon her unawares, and
started, with a hoarse, thick cry. It was in the
dusk of evening; and, seeing her outline against
the window, he stepped back against the wall
and leaned there a moment, grasping at the
casing with one hand. "Good God!" he
breathed, at last, "I thought 't was mother!"

Lucy Ann rose, and went forward to meet
him.

"Then it's true," said she. "I'm so pleased.
Seems as if I could git along, if I could look a
little mite like her."

John stood staring at her, frowning in his
bewilderment.

"What have you done to yourself?" he
asked. "Put on her clo'es?"

"Yes," said Lucy Ann, "but that ain't all.
I guess I do resemble mother, though we ain't
any of us had much time to think about it.
Well, I *am* pleased. I took out that daguerreotype she had, down Saltash way, though it
don't favor her as she was at the end. But if I
can take a glimpse of myself in the glass, now
and then, mebbe I can git along."

They sat down together in the dark, and
mused over old memories. John had always
understood Lucy Ann better than the rest.

When she gave up Simeon Bascom to stay at home with her mother, he never pitied her much; he knew she had chosen the path she loved. The other day, even, some one had wondered that she could have heard the funeral service so unmoved; but he, seeing how her face had seemed to fade and wither at every word, guessed what pain was at her heart. So, though his wife had sent him over to ask how Lucy Ann was getting on, he really found out very little, and felt how painfully dumb he must be when he got home. Lucy Ann was pretty well, he thought he might say. She'd got to looking a good deal like mother.

They took their "blindman's holiday," Lucy Ann once in a while putting a stick on the leaping blaze, and, when John questioned her, giving a low-toned reply. Even her voice had changed. It might have come from that bed-room, in one of the pauses between hours of pain, and neither would have been surprised.

"What makes you burn beech?" asked John, when a shower of sparks came crackling at them.

"I don't know," she answered. "Seems kind o' nat'ral. Some of it got into the last cord we bought, an' one night it snapped out, an' most burnt up mother's nightgown an' cap while I was warmin' 'em. We had a real time of it. She scolded me, an' then she laughed, an' I laughed — an' so, when I see a stick or two o' beech to-day, I kind o' picked it out a-purpose."

John's horse stamped impatiently from the gate, and John, too, knew it was time to go. His errand was not done, and he balked at it.

"Lucy Ann," said he, with the bluntness of resolve, "what you goin' to do?"

Lucy Ann looked sweetly at him through the dark. She had expected that. She smoothed her mother's dress with one hand, and it gave her courage.

"Do?" said she; "why, I ain't goin' to do nothin'. I 've got enough to pull through on."

"Yes, but where you goin' to live?"

"Here."

"Alone?"

"I don't feel so very much alone," said she, smiling to herself. At that moment she did not. All sorts of sweet possibilities had made themselves real. They comforted her, like the presence of love.

John felt himself a messenger. He was speaking for others that with which his soul did not accord.

"The fact is," said he, "they 're all terrible set ag'inst it. They say you 're gittin' along in years. So you be. So are we all. But they will have it, it ain't right for you to live on here alone. Mary says she should be scairt to death. She wants you should come an' make it your home with us."

"Yes, I dunno but Mary would be scairt," said Lucy Ann placidly. "But I ain't. She's real good to ask me; but I can't do it, no more 'n she could leave you an' the children an' come over here to stay with me. Why, John, this is my home!"

Her voice sank upon a note of passion. It trembled with memories of dewy mornings and golden eves. She had not grown here, through all her youth and middle life, like moss upon a rock, without fitting into the hollows and softening the angles of her poor habitation. She had drunk the sunlight and the rains of one small spot, and she knew how both would fall. The place, its sky and clouds and breezes, belonged to her : but she belonged to it as well.

John stood between two wills, his own and that of those who had sent him. Left to himself, he would not have harassed her. To him, also, wedded to a hearth where he found warmth and peace, it would have been sweet to live there always, though alone, and die by the light of its dying fire. But Mary thought otherwise, and in matters of worldly judgment he could only yield.

"I don't want you should make a mistake," said he. "Mebbe you an' I don't look for'ard enough. They say you'll repent it if you stay, an' there'll be a hurrah-boys all round. What say to makin' us a visit? That'll kind o' stave it off, an' then we can see what's best to be done."

Lucy Ann put her hands to her delicate throat, where her mother's gold beads lay lightly, with a significant touch. She, like John, had an innate gentleness of disposition. She distrusted her own power to judge.

"Maybe I might," said she faintly. "Oh, John, do you think I 've got to?"

"It need n't be for long," answered John briefly, though he felt his eyes moist with pity of her. "Mebbe you could stay a month?"

"Oh, I could n't do that!" cried Lucy Ann, in wild denial. "I never could in the world. If you 'll make it a fortnight, an' harness up yourself, an' bring me home, mebbe I might."

John gave his word, but when he took his leave of her, she leaned forward into the dark, where the impatient horse was fretting, and made her last condition.

"You 'll let me turn the key on things here jest as they be? You won't ask me to break up nuthin'?"

"Break up!" repeated John, with the intensity of an oath. "I guess you need n't. If anybody puts that on you, you send 'em to me."

So Lucy Ann packed her mother's dresses into a little hair trunk that had stood in the attic unused for many years, and went away to make her visit. When she drove up to the house, sitting erect and slender in her mother's cashmere shawl and black bonnet, Mary, watching from the window, gave a little cry, as at the

risen dead. John had told her about Lucy
Ann's transformation, but she put it all aside as
a crazy notion, not likely to last : now it seemed
less a pathetic masquerade than a strange by-
path taken by nature itself.

The children regarded it with awe, and half
the time called Lucy Ann "grandma." That
delighted her. Whenever they did it, she
looked up to say, with her happiest smile, —

"There! that's complete. You'll remember
grandma, won't you ? We must n't ever forget
her."

Here, in this warm-hearted household, anxious to do her service in a way that was not her
own, she had some happiness, of a tremulous
kind ; but it was all built up of her trust in a
speedy escape. She knit mittens, and sewed
long seams ; and every day her desire to fill the
time was irradiated by the certainty that twelve
hours more were gone. A few more patient
intervals, and she should be at home. Sometimes, as the end of her visit drew nearer, she
woke early in the morning with a sensation of
irresponsible joy, and wondered, for an instant,
what had happened to her. Then it always
came back, with an inward flooding she had
scarcely felt even in her placid youth. At
home there would be so many things to do,
and, above all, such munificent leisure ! For
there she would feel no need of feverish action
to pass the time. The hours would take care

of themselves ; they would fleet by, while she sat, her hands folded, communing with old memories.

The day came, and the end of her probation. She trembled a good deal, packing her trunk in secret, to escape Mary's remonstrances ; but John stood by her, and she was allowed to go. "You'll get sick of it," called Mary after them. " I guess you'll be glad enough to see the children again, an' they will you. Mind, you've got to come back an' spend the winter."

Lucy Ann nodded happily. She could agree to anything sufficiently remote ; and the winter was not yet here.

The first day in the old house seemed to her like new birth in Paradise. She wandered about, touching chairs and tables and curtains, the manifest symbols of an undying past. There were loving duties to be done, but she could not do them yet. She had to look her pleasure in the face, and learn its lineaments.

Next morning came brother Ezra, and Lucy Ann hurried to meet him with an exaggerated welcome. Life was never very friendly to Ezra, and those who belonged to him had to be doubly kind. They could not change his luck, but they might sweeten it. They said the world had not gone well with him ; though sometimes it was hinted that Ezra, being out of gear, could not go with the world. All the rivers ran away from him, and went to turn some other mill.

He was ungrudging of John's prosperity, but still he looked at it in some disparagement, and shook his head. His cheeks were channeled long before youth was over ; his feet were weary with honest serving, and his hands grown hard with toil. Yet he had not arrived, and John was at the goal before him.

"We heard you 'd been stayin' with John's folks," said he to Lucy Ann. "Leastways, Abby did, an' she thinks mebbe you 've got a little time for us now, though we ain't nothin' to offer compared to what you 're used to over there."

"I 'll come," said Lucy Ann promptly. "Yes, I 'll come, an' be glad to."

It was part of her allegiance to the one who had gone.

"Ezra needs bracin'," she heard her mother say, in many a sick-room gossip. "He 's got to be flattered up, an' have some grit put into him."

It was many weeks before Lucy Ann came home again. Cousin Rebecca, in Saltash, sent her a cordial letter of invitation for just as long as she felt like staying ; and the moneyed cousin at the Ridge wrote in like manner, following her note by a telegram, intimating that she would not take no for an answer. Lucy Ann frowned in alarm when the first letter came, and studied it by daylight and in her musings at night, as if some comfort might lurk between

the lines.   She was tempted to throw it in the
fire, not answered at all.   Still, there was a
reason for going.   This cousin had a broken
hip, she needed company, and the flavor of
old times.   The other had married a " drinkin'
man," and might feel hurt at being refused.
So, fortifying herself with some inner resolution she never confessed, Lucy Ann set her
teeth and started out on a visiting campaign.
John was amazed.   He drove over to see her
while she was spending a few days with an
aunt in Sudleigh.

"When you been home last, Lucy Ann?"
asked he.

A little flush came into her face, and she
winked bravely.

"I ain't been home at all," said she, in a low
tone.   "Not sence August."

John groped vainly in mental depths for
other experiences likely to illuminate this.   He
concluded that he had not quite understood
Lucy Ann and her feeling about home; but
that was neither here nor there.

"Well," he remarked, rising to go, "you're
gittin' to be quite a visitor."

"I'm tryin' to learn how," said Lucy Ann,
almost gayly.   "I've been a-cousinin' so long,
I sha'n't know how to do anything else."

But now the middle of November had come,
and she was again in her own house.   Cousin
Titcomb had brought her there and driven

away, concerned that he must leave her in a
cold kitchen, and only deterred by a looming
horse-trade from staying to build a fire. Lucy
Ann bade him good-by, with a gratitude which
was not for her visit, but all for getting home;
and when he uttered that terrifying valedictory
known as " coming again," she could meet it
cheerfully. She even stood in the door, watching him away; and not until the rattle of his
wheels had ceased on the frozen road, did she
return to her kitchen and stretch her shawled
arms pathetically upward.

"I thank my heavenly Father!" said Lucy
Ann, with the fervency of a great experience.

She built her fire, and then unpacked her
little trunk, and hung up the things in the
bedroom where her mother's presence seemed
still to cling.

"I'll sleep here now," she said to herself.
" I won't go out of this no more."

Then all the little homely duties of the hour
cried out upon her, like children long neglected;
and, with the luxurious leisure of those who
may prolong a pleasant task, she set her house
in order. She laid out a programme to occupy
her days. The attic should be cleaned to-morrow. In one day? Nay, why not three, to hold
Time still, and make him wait her pleasure?
Then there were the chambers, and the living-
rooms below. She felt all the excited joy of
youth; she was tasting anticipation at its best.

"It'll take me a week," said she. "That will be grand." She could hardly wait even for the morrow's sun; and that night she slept like those of whom much is to be required, and who must wake in season. Morning came, and mid-forenoon, and while she stepped about under the roof where dust had gathered and bitter herbs told tales of summers past, John drove into the yard. Lucy Ann threw up the attic window and leaned out.

"You put your horse up, an' I'll be through here in a second," she called. "The barn's open."

John was in a hurry.

"I've got to go over to Sudleigh, to meet the twelve o'clock," said he. "Harold's comin'. I only wanted to say I'll be over after you the night before Thanksgivin'. Mary wants you should be sure to be there to breakfast. You all right? Cephas said you seemed to have a proper good time with them."

John turned skillfully on the little green and drove away. Lucy Ann stayed at the window watching him, the breeze lifting her gray curls, and the sun smiling at her. She withdrew slowly into the attic, and sank down upon the floor, close by the window. She sat there and thought, and the wind still struck upon her unheeded. Was she always to be subject to the tyranny of those who had set up their hearthstones in a more enduring form? Was her

home not a home merely because there were
no men and children in it? She drew her
breath sharply, and confronted certain problems
of the greater world, not knowing what they
were. To Lucy Ann they did not seem problems at all. They were simply touches on the
individual nerve, and she felt the pain. Her
own inner self throbbed in revolt, but she never
guessed that any other part of nature was
throbbing with it. Then she went about her
work, with the patience of habit. It was well
that the attic should be cleaned, though the
savor of the task was gone.

Next day, she walked to Sudleigh, with a
basket on her arm. Often she sent her little
errands by the neighbors; but to-day she was
uneasy, and it seemed as if the walk might do
her good. She wanted some soda and some
needles and thread. She tried to think they
were very important, though some sense of
humor told her grimly that household goods
are of slight use to one who goes a-cousining.
Her day at John's would be prolonged to seven;
nay, why not a month, when the winter itself
was not too great a tax for them to lay upon
her? In her deserted house, soda would lose
its strength, and even cloves decay. Lucy Ann
felt her will growing very weak within her;
indeed, at that time, she was hardly conscious
of having any will at all.

It was Saturday, and John and Ezra were

almost sure to be in town. She thought of that, and how pleasant it would be to hear from the folks : so much pleasanter than to be always facing them on their own ground, and never on hers. At the grocery she came upon Ezra, mounted on a wagon-load of meal-bags, and just gathering up the reins.

"Hullo!" he called. "You did n't walk?"

"Oh, I jest clipped it over," returned Lucy Ann carelessly. "I 'm goin' to git a ride home. I see Marden's wagon when I come by the post-office."

"Well, I had n't any expectation o' your bein' here," said Ezra. "I meant to ride round to-morrer. We want you to spend Thanksgivin' Day with us. I 'll come over arter you."

"Oh, Ezra!" said Lucy Ann, quite sincerely, with her concession to his lower fortunes, "why did n't you say so! John 's asked me."

"The dogs!" said Ezra. It was his deepest oath. Then he drew a sigh. "Well," he concluded, "that 's our luck. We al'ays come out the leetle end o' the horn. Abby 'll be real put out. She 'lotted on it. Well, John 's inside there. He 's buyin' up 'bout everything there is. You 'll git more 'n you would with us."

He drove gloomily away, and Lucy Ann stepped into the store, musing. She was rather sorry not to go to Ezra's, if he cared.

It almost seemed as if she might ask John
to let her take the plainer way. John would
understand. She saw him at once where he
stood, prosperous and hale, in his great-coat,
reading items from a long memorandum, while
Jonathan Stevens weighed and measured. The
store smelled of spice, and the clerk that minute
spilled some cinnamon. Its fragrance struck
upon Lucy Ann like a call from some far-off
garden, to be entered if she willed. She laid a
hand on her brother's arm, and her lips opened
to words she had not chosen : —

"John, you should n't ha' drove away so
quick, t' other day. You jest flung out your
invitation an' run. You never give me no time
to answer. Ezra 's asked me to go there."

"Well, if that ain't smart ! " returned John.
" Put in ahead, did he ? Well, I guess it 's
the fust time he ever got round. I 'm terrible
sorry, Lucy. The children won't think it 's any
kind of a Thanksgivin' without you. Somehow
they 've got it into their heads it 's grandma
comin'. They can't seem to understand the
difference."

"Well, you tell 'em I guess grandma 's kind
o' pleased for me to plan it as I have," said
Lucy Ann, almost gayly. Her face wore a
strange, excited look. She breathed a little
faster. She saw a pleasant way before her,
and her feet seemed to be tending toward it
without her own volition. " You give my love

to 'em.   I guess they'll have a proper nice
time."

She lingered about the store until John had
gone, and then went forward to the counter.
The storekeeper looked at her respectfully.
Everybody had a great liking for Lucy Ann.
She had been a faithful daughter, and now that
she seemed, in so mysterious a way, to be
growing like her mother, even men of her own
age regarded her with deference.

"Mr. Stevens," said she, "I did n't bring so
much money with me as I might if I 'd had my
wits about me.   Should you jest as soon trust
me for some Thanksgivin' things?"

"Certain," replied Jonathan.   "Clean out
the store, if you want.   Your credit 's good."
He, too, felt the beguilement of the time.

"I want some things," repeated Lucy Ann,
with determination.   "Some cinnamon an' some
mace — there! I 'll tell you, while you weigh."

It seemed to her that she was buying the
spice islands of the world; and though the
money lay at home in her drawer, honestly
ready to pay, the recklessness of credit gave
her an added joy.   The store had its market,
also, at Thanksgiving time, and she bargained
for a turkey.   It could be sent her, the day
before, by some of the neighbors.   When she
left the counter, her arms and her little basket
were filled with bundles.   Joshua Marden was
glad to take them.

"No, I won't ride," said Lucy Ann. "Much obliged to *you*. Jest leave the things inside the fence. I'd ruther walk. I don't git out any too often."

She took her way home along the brown road, stepping lightly and swiftly, and full of busy thoughts. Flocks of birds went whirring by over the yellowed fields. Lucy Ann could have called out to them, in joyous understanding, they looked so free. She, too, seemed to be flying on the wings of a fortunate wind.

All that week she scrubbed and regulated, and took a thousand capable steps as briskly as those who work for the home-coming of those they love. The neighbors dropped in, one after another, to ask where she was going to spend Thanksgiving. Some of them said, "Won't you pass the day with us?" but Lucy Ann replied blithely : —

"Oh, John's invited me there!"

All that week, too, she answered letters, in her cramped and careful hand ; for cousins had bidden her to the feast. Over the letters she had many a troubled pause, for one cousin lived near Ezra, and had to be told that John had invited her ; and to three others, dangerously within hail of each, she made her excuse a turncoat, to fit the time. Duplicity in black and white did hurt her a good deal, and she sometimes stopped, in the midst of her slow transcription, to look up piteously and say aloud : —

"I hope I shall be forgiven!" But by the time the stamp was on, and the pencil ruling erased, her heart was light again. If she had sinned, she was finding the path intoxicatingly pleasant.

Through all the days before the festival, no house exhaled a sweeter savor than this little one on the green. Lucy Ann did her miniature cooking with great seriousness and care. She seemed to be dwelling in a sacred isolation, yet not altogether alone, but with her mother and all their bygone years. Standing at her table, mixing and tasting, she recalled stories her mother had told her, until, at moments, it seemed as if she not only lived her own life, but some previous one, through that being whose blood ran with hers. She was realizing that ineffable sense of possession born out of knowledge that the enduring part of a personality is ours forever, and that love is an unquenched fire, fed by memory as well as hope.

On Thanksgiving morning, Lucy Ann lay in bed a little later, because that had been the family custom. Then she rose to her exquisite house, and got breakfast ready, according to the unswerving programme of the day. Fried chicken and mince pie : she had had them as a child, and now they were scrupulously prepared. After breakfast, she sat down in the sunshine, and watched the people go by to service in Tiverton Church. Lucy Ann would have liked going, too; but there would be inconvenient questioning, as there always must be when we meet our kind. She would stay undisturbed in her seclusion, keeping her festival alone. The morning was still young when she put her turkey in the oven, and made the vegetables ready. Lucy Ann was not very fond of vegetables, but there had to be just so many — onions, turnips, and squash baked with molasses — for her mother was a Cape woman, preserving the traditions of dear Cape dishes. All that forenoon, the little house throbbed with a curious sense of expectancy. Lucy Ann was preparing so many things that it seemed as if somebody must surely keep her company; but when dinner-time struck, and she was still alone, there came no lull in her anticipation. Peace abode with her, and wrought its own fair work. She ate her dinner slowly, with meditation and a thankful heart. She did not need to hear the minister's careful catalogue of mercies received. She was at home ; that was enough.

After dinner, when she had done up the work, and left the kitchen without spot or stain, she went upstairs, and took out her mother's beautiful silk poplin, the one saved for great occasions, and only left behind because she had chosen to be buried in her wedding gown. Lucy Ann put it on with careful hands, and then laid about her neck the wrought collar she had selected the day before. She looked at

herself in the glass, and arranged a gray curl
with anxious scrutiny. No girl adorning for
her bridal could have examined every fold and
line with a more tender care. She stood there
a long, long moment, and approved herself.

"It's a wonder," she said reverently. "It's
the greatest mercy anybody ever had."

The afternoon waned, though not swiftly;
for Time does not always gallop when happiness pursues. Lucy Ann could almost hear
the gliding of his rhythmic feet. She did the
things set aside for festivals, or the days when
we have company. She looked over the pho-
tograph album, and turned the pages of the
"Ladies' Wreath." When she opened the case
containing that old daguerreotype, she scanned
it with a little distasteful smile, and then glanced
up at her own image in the glass, nodding her
head in thankful peace. She was the enduring
portrait. In herself, she might even see her
mother grow very old. So the hours slipped
on into dusk, and she sat there with her dream,
knowing, though it was only a dream, how sane
it was, and good. When wheels came rattling
into the yard, she awoke with a start, and
John's voice, calling to her in an inexplicable
alarm, did not disturb her. She had had her
day. Not all the family fates could take it
from her now. John kept calling, even while
his wife and children were climbing down,
unaided, from the great carryall. His voice

proclaimed its own story, and Lucy Ann heard
it with surprise.

"Lucy! Lucy Ann!" he cried. "You here?
You show yourself, if you're all right."

Before they reached the front door, Lucy
Ann had opened it and stood there, gently
welcoming.

"Yes, here I be," said she. "Come right
in, all of ye. Why, if that ain't Ezra, too, an'
his folks, turnin' into the lane. When'd you
plan it?"

"Plan it! we didn't plan it!" said Mary
testily. She put her hand on Lucy Ann's
shoulder, to give her a little shake; but, feeling
mother's poplin, she forbore.

Lucy Ann retreated before them into the
house, and they all trooped in after her.
Ezra's family, too, were crowding in at the
doorway; and the brothers, who had paused
only to hitch the horses, filled up the way behind. Mary, by a just self-election, was always
the one to speak.

"I declare, Lucy!" cried she, "if ever I
could be tried with you, I should be now.
Here we thought you was at Ezra's, an' Ezra's
folks thought you was with us; an' if we had n't
harnessed up, an' drove over there in the afternoon, for a kind of a surprise party, we should
ha' gone to bed thinkin' you was somewhere,
safe an' sound. An' here you've been, all day
long, in this lonesome house!"

"You let me git a light," said Lucy Ann
calmly. "You be takin' off your things, an' se'
down." She began lighting the tall astral lamp
on the table, and its prisms danced and swung.
Lucy Ann's delicate hand did not tremble;
and when the flame burned up through the
shining chimney, more than one started, at
seeing how exactly she resembled grandma, in
the days when old Mrs. Cummings had ruled
her own house. Perhaps it was the royalty of
the poplin that enwrapped her; but Lucy Ann
looked very capable of holding her own. She
was facing them all, one hand resting on the
table, and a little smile flickering over her face.

"I s'pose I was a poor miserable creatur' to
git out of it that way," said she. "If I'd felt
as I do now, I need n't ha' done it. I could ha'
spoke up. But then it seemed as if there wa'n't
no other way. I jest wanted my Thanksgivin'
in my own home, an' so I throwed you off the
track the best way I could. I dunno 's I lied.
I dunno whether I did or not; but I guess,
anyway, I shall be forgiven for it."

Ezra spoke first: "Well, if you did n't want
to come" —

"Want to come!" broke in John. "Of
course she don't want to come! She wants to
stay in her own home, an' call her soul her own
— don't you, Lucy?"

Lucy Ann glanced at him with her quick,
grateful smile.

"I'm goin' to, now," she said gently, and they knew she meant it.

But, looking about among them, Lucy Ann was conscious of a little hurt unhealed; she had thrown their kindness back.

"I guess I can't tell exactly how it is," she began hesitatingly; "but you see my home's my own, jest as yours is. You couldn't any of you go round cousinin', without feelin' you was tore up by the roots. You've all been real good to me, wantin' me to come, an' I s'pose I should make an awful towse if I never was asked; but now I've got all my visitin' done up, cousins an' all, an' I'm goin' to be to home a spell. An' I do admire to have company," added Lucy Ann, a bright smile breaking over her face. "Mother did, you know, an' I guess I take arter her. Now you lay off your things, an' I'll put the kettle on. I've got more pies 'n you could shake a stick at, an' there's a whole loaf o' fruit-cake, a year old."

Mary, taking off her shawl, wiped her eyes surreptitiously on a corner of it, and Abby whispered to her husband, "Dear creatur'!" John and Ezra turned, by one consent, to put the horses in the barn; and the children, conscious that some mysterious affair had been settled, threw themselves into the occasion with an irresponsible delight. The room became at once vocal with talk and laughter, and Lucy Ann felt, with a swelling heart, what a happy universe it is where so many bridges lie between this world and that unknown state we call the next. But no moment of that evening was half so sweet to her as the one when little John, the youngest child of all, crept up to her and pulled at her poplin skirt, until she bent down to hear.

"Grandma," said he, "when 'd you get well ? "

THE EXPERIENCE OF HANNAH PRIME

TIVERTON HOLLOW had occasionally an
evening meeting; this came about naturally
whenever religious zeal burned high, or when
the congregation felt, with some uneasiness,
that it had remained too long aloof from spiritual things.   To-night, the schoolhouse had
been designated for an assembling place, and
the neighborhood trooped thither, animated by
an excited importance, and doing justice to the
greatness of the occasion by " dressing up."
Farmers had laid aside their ordinary mood,
with overalls and jumpers, and donned an uncomfortable solemnity, an enforced attitude of
theological reflection, with their stocks. Wives
had urged their patient fingers into cotton
gloves, and in cashmere shawls, and bonnets
retrimmed with reference to this year's style,
pressed into the uncomfortable chairs, and folded
their hands upon the desks before them in
a sweet seriousness not unmingled with the desire of thriftily completing a duty no less exi-
gent than pickle-making, or the work of spring
and fall.   Last came the boys, clattering with
awkward haste over the dusty floor which had

known the touch of their bare feet on other
days. They looked about the room with some
awe and a puzzled acceptance of its being the
same, yet not the same. It was their own.
There were the maps of North and South
America; the yellowed evergreens, relic of "Last
Day," still festooned the windows, and an in-
tricate "sum," there explained to the uncom-
prehending admiration of the village fathers,
still adorned the blackboard. Yet the room
had strangely transformed itself into an alien
temple, invaded by theology and the breath of
an unknown world. But though sobered, they
were not cast down; for the occasion was en-
livened, in their case, by a heaven-defying pro-
fligacy of intent. Every one of them knew
that Sammy Forbes had in his pocket a pack of
cards, which he meant to drop, by wicked but
careless design, just when Deacon Pitts led in
prayer, and that Tom Drake was master of a
concealed pea-shooter, which he had sworn,
with all the asseverations held sacred by boys,
to use at some dramatic moment. All the
band were aware that neither of these daring
deeds would be done. The prospective actors
themselves knew it; but it was a darling joy
to contemplate the remote possibility thereof.

Deacon Pitts opened the meeting, reminding
his neighbors how precious a privilege it is for
two or three to be gathered together. His
companion had not been able to come. (The

entire neighborhood knew that Mrs. Pitts had been laid low by an attack of erysipelas, and that she was, at the moment, in a dark bedroom at home, helpless under elderblow.)

"She lays there on a bed of pain," said the deacon. "But she says to me, 'You go. Better the house o' mournin' than the house o' feastin',' she says. Oh, my friends! what can be more blessed than the counsel of an aged and feeble companion?"

The deacon sat down, and Tom Drake, his finger on the pea-shooter, assured himself, in acute mental triumph, that he had almost done it that time.

Then followed certain incidents eminently pleasing to the boys. To their unbounded relief, Sarah Frances Giles rose to speak, weeping as she began. She always wept at prayer meeting, though at the very moment of asserting her joy that she cherished a hope, and her gratitude that she was so nearly at an end of this earthly pilgrimage and ready to take her stand on the sea of glass mingled with fire. The boys reveled in her testimony. They were in a state of bitter uneasiness before she rose, and gnawed with a consuming impatience until she began to cry. Then they wondered if she could possibly leave out the sea of glass; and when it duly came, they gave a sigh of satiated bliss and sank into acquiescence in whatever might happen. This was a rich occasion to

their souls, for Silas Marden, who was seldom
moved by the spirit, fell upon his knees to
pray; but at the same unlucky instant, his
sister-in-law, for whom he cherished an unbounded scorn, rose (being "nigh-eyed" and
ignorant of his priority) and began to speak.
For a moment, the two held on together, "neck
and neck," as the happy boys afterward remembered, and then Silas got up, dusted his
knees, and sat down, not to rise again at any
spiritual call. "An' a madder man you never
see," cried all the Hollow next day, in shocked
but gleeful memory.

Taking it all in all, the meeting had thus far
mirrored others of its class. If the droning
experiences were devoid of all human passion,
it was chiefly because they had to be expressed
in the phrases of strict theological usage. There
was an unspoken agreement that feelings of
this sort should be described in a certain way.
They were not the affairs of the hearth and
market; they were matters pertaining to that
awful entity called the soul, and must be dressed
in the fine linen which she had herself elected
to wear.

Suddenly, in a wearisome pause, when minds
had begun to stray toward the hayfield and to-
morrow's churning, the door was pushed open,
and the Widow Prime walked in. She was
quite unused to seeking her kind, and the little
assembly at once awoke, under the stimulus of

surprise. They knew quite well where she
had been walking : to Sudleigh Jail, to visit her
only son, lying there for the third time, not, as
usual, for drunkenness, but for house-breaking.
She was a wiry woman, a mass of muscles animated by an eager energy. Her very hands
seemed knotted with clenching themselves in
nervous spasms. Her eyes were black, seeking,
and passionate, and her face had been scored
by fine wrinkles, the marks of anxiety and
grief. Her chocolate calico was very clean, and
her palm-leaf shawl and black bonnet were decent in their poverty. The vague excitement
created by her coming continued in a rustling
like that of leaves. The troubles of Hannah
Prime's life had been very bitter — so bitter
that she had, as Deacon Pitts once said, after
undertaking her conversion, turned from " me
and the house of God." A quickening thought
sprang up now in the little assembly that she
was " under conviction," and that it had become
the present duty of every professor to lead her
to the throne of grace. This was an exigency
for which none were prepared. At so strenuous a challenge, the old conventional ways of
speech fell down and collapsed before them, like
creatures filled with air. Who should minister
to one set outside their own comfortable lives
by bitter sorrow and wounded pride ? What
could they offer a woman who had, in one way
or another, sworn to curse God and die ? It

was Deacon Pitts who spoke, but in a tone hushed to the key of the unexpected.

"Has any one an experience to offer? Will any brother or sister lead in prayer?"

The silence was growing into a thing to be recognized and conquered, when, to the wonder of her neighbors, Hannah Prime herself rose. She looked slowly about the room, gazing into every face as if to challenge an honest understanding. Then she began speaking in a low voice thrilled by an emotion not yet explained. Unused to expressing herself in public, she seemed to be feeling her way. The silence, pride, endurance, which had been her armor for many years, were no longer apparent; she had thrown down all her defenses with a grave composure, as if life suddenly summoned her to higher issues.

"I dunno 's I 've got an experience to offer," she said. "I dunno 's it 's religion. I dunno what 't is. Mebbe you 'd say it don't belong to a meetin'. But when I come by an' see you all settin' here, it come over me I 'd like to tell somebody. Two weeks ago I was most crazy"— She paused of necessity, for something broke in her voice.

"That 's the afternoon Jim was took," whispered a woman to her neighbor. Hannah Prime went on.

"I jest as soon tell it now. I can tell ye all together what I could n't say to one on ye alone;

an' if anybody speaks to me about it arterwards, they'll wish they had n't. I was all by myself in the house. I set down in my clock-room, about three in the arternoon, an' there I set. I did n't git no supper. I could n't. I set there an' heard the clock tick. Byme-by it struck seven, an' that waked me up. I thought I'd gone crazy. The figgers on the wall-paper provoked me most to death; an' that red-an'-white tidy I made, the winter I was laid up, seemed to be talkin' out loud. I got up an' run outdoor jest as fast as I could go. I run out behind the house an' down the cart-path to that pile o' rocks that overlooks the lake; an' there I got out o' breath an' dropped down on a big rock. An' there I set, jest as still as I'd been settin' when I was in the house."

Here a little girl stirred in her seat, and her mother leaned forward and shook her, with alarming energy. "I never was so hard with Mary L. afore," she explained the next day, "but I was as nervous as a witch. I thought, if I heard a pin drop, I should scream."

"I dunno how long I set there," went on Hannah Prime, "but byme-by it begun to come over me how still the lake was. 'T was like glass; an' way over where it runs in 'tween them islands, it burnt like fire. Then I looked up a little further, to see what kind of a sky there was. 'T was light green, with clouds in it, all fire, an' it begun to seem to me as if it

was a kind o' land an' water up there — like
our'n, on'y not solid.   I set there an' looked
at it ; an' I picked out islands, an' ma'sh-land,
an' p'ints running out into the yeller-green sea.
An' everything grew stiller an' stiller.   The
loons struck up, down on the lake, with that
kind of a lonesome whinner ; but that on'y
made the rest of it seem quieter.   An' it begun
to grow dark all 'round me.   I dunno 's I ever
noticed before jest how the dark comes.   It
sifted down like snow, on'y you could n't see it.
Well, I set there, an' I tried to keep stiller an'
stiller, like everything else.   Seemed as if I
must.   An' pretty soon I knew suthin' was
walkin' towards me over the lot.   I kep' my eyes
on the sky ; for I knew 't would break suthin'
if I turned my head, an' I felt as if I could n't
bear to.   An' It come walkin', walkin', without takin' any steps or makin' any noise, till
It come right up 'side o' me an' stood still.
I did n't turn round.   I knew I must n't.   I
dunno whether It touched me ; I dunno whether
It said anything — but I know It made me a
new creatur'.   I knew then I should n't be
afraid o' things no more — nor sorry.   I found
out 't was all right.   'I 'm glad I 'm alive,' I
said.   'I 'm thankful !'   Seemed to me I 'd
been dead for the last twenty year.   I 'd come
alive.

"An' so I set there an' held my breath, for
fear 't would go.   I dunno how long, but the

moon riz up over my left shoulder, an' the sky begun to fade. An' then it come over me 't was goin'. I knew 't was terrible tender of me, an' sorry, an' lovin', an' so I says, 'Don't you mind; I won't forgit!' An' then It went. But that broke suthin', an' I turned an' see my own shadder on the grass; an' I thought I see another, 'side of it. Somehow that scairt me, an' I jumped up an' whipped it home without lookin' behind me. Now that's my experience," said Hannah Prime, looking her neighbors again in the face, with dauntless eyes. "I dunno what 't was, but it's goin' to last. I ain't afraid no more, an' I ain't goin' to be. There ain't nuthin' to worry about. Everything's bigger'n we think." She folded her shawl more closely about her and moved toward the door. There she again turned to her neighbors.

"Good-night!" she said, and was gone.

They sat quite still until the tread of her feet had ceased its beating on the dusty road. Then, by one consent, they rose and moved slowly out. There was no prayer that night, and "Lord dismiss us" was not sung.

HONEY AND MYRRH

THE neighborhood, the township, and the world had been snowed in. Snow drifted the road in hills and hollows, and hung in little eddying wreaths, where the wind took it, on the pasture slopes. It made solid banks in the dooryards, and buried the stone walls out of sight. The lacework of its fantasy became daintily apparent in the conceits with which it broidered over all the common objects familiar in homely lives. The pump, in yards where that had supplanted the old-fashioned curb, wore a heavy mob-cap. The vane on the barn was delicately sifted over, and the top of every picket in the high front-yard fence had a fluffy peak. But it was chiefly in the woods that the rapture and flavor of the time ran riot in making beauty. There every fir branch swayed under a tuft of white, and the brown refuse of the year was all hidden away.

That morning, no one in Tiverton Hollow had gone out of the house, save to shovel paths and do the necessary chores. The road lay untouched until ten o'clock, when a selectman gave notice that it was an occasion for "breakin' out," by starting with his team, and gathering oxen by the way until a conquering procession ground through the drifts, the men shoveling at intervals where the snow lay deepest, the oxen walking swayingly, head to the earth, and the faint wreath of their breath ascending and cooling on the air. It was "high times" in Tiverton Hollow when a road needed opening; some idea of the old primitive way of battling with the untouched forces of nature roused the people to an exhilaration dashed by no uncertainty of victory.

By afternoon, the excitement had quieted. The men had come in, reddened by cold, and eaten their noon dinner in high spirits, retailing to the less fortunate women-folk the stories swapped on the march. Then, as one man, they succumbed to the drowsiness induced by a morning of wind in the face, and sat by the stove under some pretense of reading the county paper, but really to nod and doze, waking only to put another stick of wood on the fire. So passed all the day before Christmas, and in the evening the shining lamps were lighted (each with a strip of red flannel in the oil, to give color), and the neighborhood rested in the tranquil certainty that something had really come to pass, and that their communication with the world was reëstablished.

Susan Peavey sat by the fire, knitting on a red mitten, and the young schoolmaster presided over the other hearth corner, reading

very hard, at intervals, and again sinking into
a drowsy study of the flames. There was an
impression abroad in Tiverton that the schoolmaster was going to be somebody, some time.
He wrote for the papers. He was always
receiving through the mail envelopes marked
"author's proofs," which, the postmistress said,
indicated that he was an author, whatever proofs
might be. She had an idea they might have
something to do with photographs ; perhaps
his picture was going into a book. It was very
well understood that teaching school at the
Hollow, at seven dollars a week, was an inter-
lude in the life of one who would some day
write a spelling-book, or exercise senatorial
rights at Washington. He was a long-legged,
pleasant looking youth, with a pale cheek, dark
eyes, and thick black hair, one lock of which,
hanging low over his forehead, he twisted
while he read. He kept glancing up at Miss
Susan and smiling at her, whenever he could
look away from his book and the fire, and she
smiled back. At last, after many such word-
less messages, he spoke.

"What lots of red mittens you do knit! Do
you send them all away to that society?"

Miss Susan's needles clicked.

"Every one," said she.

She was a tall, large woman, well-knit, with
no superfluous flesh. Her head was finely set,
and she carried it with a simple unconscious-

ness better than dignity. Everybody in Tiverton thought it had been a great cross to Susan Peavey to be so overgrown. They conceded that it was a mystery she had not turned out "gormin'." But that was because Susan had left her vanity behind with early youth, in the days when, all legs and arms, she had given up the idea of beauty. Her face was strong-featured, overspread by a healthy color, and her eyes looked frankly out, as if assured of finding a very pleasant world. The sick always delighted in Susan's nearness ; her magnificent health and presence were like a supporting tide, and she seemed to carry outdoor air in her very garments. The schoolmaster still watched her. She rested and fascinated him at once by her strength and homely charm.

"I shall call you the Orphans' Friend," said he.

She laid down her work.

"Don't you say one word," she answered, with an air of abject confession. "It don't interest me a mite! I give because it's my bounden duty, but I'll be whipped if I want to knit warm mittens all my life, an' fill poor barrels. Sometimes I wisht I could git a chance to provide folks with what they don't need ruther'n what they do."

"I don't see what you mean," said the schoolmaster. "Tell me."

Miss Susan was looking at the hearth. A

warmer flush than that of firelight alone lay on her cheek. She bent forward and threw on a pine knot. It blazed richly. Then she drew the cricket more securely under her feet, and settled herself to gossip.

"Anybody 'd think I 'd most talked myself out sence you come here to board," said she, "but you 're the beatemest for tolin' anybody on. I never knew I had so much to say. But there! I guess we all have, if there 's anybody 't wants to listen. I never 've said this to a livin' soul, an' I guess it 's sort o' heathenish to think, but I 'm tired to death o' fightin' ag'inst poverty, poverty! I s'pose it 's there, fast enough, though we 're all so well on 't we don't realize it ; an' I 'm goin' to do my part, an' be glad to, while I 'm above ground. But I guess heaven 'll be a spot where we don't give folks what they need, but what they don't."

"There is something in your Bible," began the schoolmaster hesitatingly, "about a box of precious ointment." He always said "your Bible," as if church members held a proprietary right.

"That 's it!" replied Miss Susan, brightening. "That 's what I al'ays thought. Spill it all out, I say, an' make the world smell as sweet as honey. My! but I do have great projicks settin' here by the fire alone! Great projicks!"

"Tell me some!"

"Well, I dunno 's I can, all of a piece, so to

speak; but when it gits along towards eight o'clock, an' the room's all simmerin', an' the moon lays out on the snow, it does seem as if we made a pretty poor spec' out o' life. We don't seem to have no color in it. Why, don't you remember 'Solomon in all his glory'? I guess 't would n't ha' been put in jest that way if there wa'n't somethin' in it. I s'pose he had crowns an' rings an' purple velvet coats an' brocade satin weskits, an' all manner o' things. Sometimes seems as I could see him walkin' straight in through that door there." She was running a knitting needle back and forth through her ball of yarn as she spoke, without noticing that some one had been stamping the snow from his feet on the doorstone outside. The door, after making some bluster of refusal, was pushed open, and on the heels of her speech a man walked in.

"My land!" cried Miss Susan, aghast. Then she and the schoolmaster, by one accord, began to laugh.

But the man did not look at them until he had scrupulously wiped his feet on the husk mat, and stamped them anew. Then he turned down the legs of his trousers, and carefully examined the lank green carpet-bag he had been carrying.

"I guess I trailed it through some o' the drifts," he remarked. "The road's pretty narrer, this season o' the year."

"You give us a real start," said Susan. "We thought be sure 't was Solomon, an' mebbe the Queen o' Sheba follerin' arter. Why, Solon Slade, you ain't walked way over to Tiverton Street!"

"Yes, I have," asserted Solon. He was a slender, sad-colored man, possibly of her own age, and he spoke in a very soft voice. He was Susan's widowed brother-in-law, and the neighbors said he was clever, but had n't no more spunk 'n a wet rag.

Susan had risen and laid down her knitting. She approached the table and rested one hand on it, a hawk-like brightness in her eyes.

"What you got in that bag?" asked she.

Solon was enjoying his certainty that he held the key to the situation.

"I got a mite o' cheese," he answered, approaching the fire and spreading his hands to the blaze.

"You got anything else? Now, Solon, don't you keep me here on tenter-hooks! You got a letter?"

"Well," said Solon, "I thought I might as well look into the post-office an' see."

"You thought so! You went a-purpose! An' you walked because you al'ays was half shackled about takin' horses out in bad goin'. You hand me over that letter!"

Solon approached the table, a furtive twinkle in his blue eyes. He lifted the bag and opened it slowly.   First, he took out a wedge-shaped package.

"That's the cheese," said he.   "Herb."

"My land!" ejaculated Miss Susan, while the schoolmaster looked on and smiled.   "You better ha' come to me for cheese.   I've got a plenty, tansy an' sage, an' you know it.   I see it!   There!   you gi' me holt on 't!"   It was a fugitive white gleam in the bottom of the bag; she pounced upon it and brought up a letter.   Midway in the act of tearing it open, she paused and looked at Solon with droll entreaty.   "It's your letter, by rights!" she added tentatively.

"Law!" said he, "I dunno who it's directed to, but I guess it's as much your'n as anybody's."

Miss Susan spread open the sheets with an air of breathless delight.   She bent nearer the lamp.   "'Dear father and auntie,'" she began.

"There!" remarked Solon, in quiet satisfaction, still warming his hands at the blaze.   "There!   you see 't is to both."

"My!   how she does run the words together! Here!"   Miss Susan passed it to the schoolmaster.   "You read it.   It's from Jenny.   You know she's away to school, an' we did n't think best for her to come home Christmas.   I knew she'd write for Christmas.   Solon, I told you so!"

The schoolmaster took the letter, and read it

aloud. It was a simple little message, full of
contentment and love and a girl's new delight
in life. When he had finished, the two older
people busied themselves a moment without
speaking, Solon in picking up a chip from the
hearth, and Susan in mechanically smoothing
the mammoth roses on the side of the carpet-
bag.

"Well, I 'most wish we 'd had her come
home," said he at last, clearing his throat.

"No, you don't either," answered Miss
Susan promptly. "Not with this snow, an'
comin' out of a house where it 's het up, into
cold beds an' all. Now I 'm goin' to git you a
mite o' pie an' some hot tea."

She set forth a prodigal supper on a leaf of
the table, and Solon silently worked his will
upon it, the schoolmaster eating a bit for company. Then Solon took his way home to the
house across the yard, and she watched at the
window till she saw the light blaze up through
his panes. That accomplished, she turned back
with a long breath and began clearing up.

"I 'm worried to death to have him over
there all by himself," said she. "S'pose he
should be sick in the night!"

"You 'd go over," answered the schoolmaster easily.

"Well, s'pose he could n't git me no word?"

"Oh, you 'd know it! You 're that sort."

Miss Susan laughed softly, and so seemed

to put away her recurrent anxiety. She came back to her knitting.

"How long has his wife been dead?" asked the schoolmaster.

"Two year. He an' Jenny got along real well together, but sence September, when she went away, I guess he's found it pretty dull pickin'. I do all I can, but land! 't ain't like havin' a woman in the house from sunrise to set."

"There's nothing like that," agreed the wise young schoolmaster. "Now let's play some more. Let's plan what we'd like to do to-morrow for all the folks we know, and let's not give them a thing they need, but just the ones they'd like."

Miss Susan put down her knitting again. She never could talk to the schoolmaster and keep at work. It made her dreamy, exactly as it did to sit in the hot summer sunshine, with the droning of bees in the air.

"Well," said she, "there's old Ann Wheeler that lives over on the turnpike. She don't want for nothin', but she keeps her things packed away up garret, an' lives like a pig."

"'Sold her bed and lay in the straw.'"

"That's it, on'y she won't sell nuthin'. I'd give her a house all winders, so 't she could n't help lookin' out, an' velvet carpets 't she'd got to walk on."

"Well, there's Cap'n Ben. The boys say

he's out of his head a good deal now; he fancies himself at sea and in foreign countries."

"Yes, so they say. Well, I'd let him set down a spell in Solomon's temple an' look round him. My sake! do you remember about the temple? Why, the nails was all gold. Don't you wish we'd lived in them times? Jest think about the wood they had — cedars o' Lebanon an' fir-trees. You know how he set folks to workin' in the mountains. I've al'ays thought I'd like to ben up on them mountains an' heard the axes ringin' an' listened to the talk. An' then there was pomegranates an' cherubim, an' as for silver an' gold, they were as common as dirt. When I was a little girl, I learnt them chapters, an' sometimes now, when I'm settin' by the fire, I say over that verse about the 'man of Tyre, skillful to work in gold, and in silver, in brass, in iron, in stone, and in timber, in purple, in blue, and in fine linen, and in crimson.' My! ain't it rich?"

She drew a long breath of surfeited enjoyment. The schoolmaster's eyes burned under his heavy brows.

"Then things smelt so good in them days," continued Miss Susan. "They had myrrh an' frankincense, an' I dunno what all. I never make my mincemeat 'thout snuffin' at the spicebox to freshen up my mind. No matter where I start, some way or another I al'ays git back to Solomon. Well, if Cap'n Ben wants to see

foreign countries, I guess he 'd be glad to set
a spell in the temple. Le's have on another
stick — that big one there by you. My! it 's
the night afore Christmas, ain't it ? Seems if
I could n't git a big enough blaze. Pile it on.
I guess I 'd as soon set the chimbly afire as
not ! "

There was something overflowing and heady
in her enjoyment. It exhilarated the schoolmaster, and he lavished stick after stick on the
ravening flames. The maple hardened into
coals brighter than its own panoply of autumn ;
the delicate bark of the birch flared up and
perished.

"Miss Susan," said he, " don't you want to
see all the people in the world ? "

" Oh, I dunno ! I 'd full as lieves set here an'
think about 'em. I can fix 'em up full as well
in my mind, an' perhaps they suit me better 'n
if I could see 'em. Sometimes I set 'em walkin'
through this kitchen, kings an' queens an' all.
My! how they do shine, all over precious
stones. I never see a di'mond, but I guess I
know pretty well how 't would look."

" Suppose we could give a Christmas dinner,
— what should we have ? "

" We 'd have oxen roasted whole, an' honey
— an' — but that 's as fur as I can git."

The schoolmaster had a treasury of which
she had never learned, and he said music-
ally : —

. . . "'a heap
Of candied apple, quince, and plum, and gourd;
With jellies soother than the creamy curd,
And lucid syrops, tinct with cinnamon;
Manna and dates, in argosy transferr'd
From Fez; and spicéd dainties, every one,
From silken Samarcand to cedar'd Lebanon.'"

"Yes, that has a real nice sound. It ain't like the Bible, but it's nice."

They sat and dreamed and the fire flared up into living arabesques and burnt blue in corners. A stick parted and fell into ash, and Miss Susan came awake. She had the air of rousing herself with vigor.

"There!" said she, "sometimes I think it's most sinful to make believe, it's so hard to wake yourself up. Arter all this, I dunno but when Solon comes for the pigs' kittle to-morrer, I shall ketch myself sayin', 'Here's the frankincense!'"

They laughed together, and the schoolmaster rose to light his lamp. He paused on his way to the stairs, and came back to set it down again.

"There are lots of people we haven't provided for," he said. "We haven't even thought what we'd give Jenny."

"I guess Jenny's got her heart's desire." Miss Susan nodded sagely. "I've sent her a box, with a fruit-cake an' pickles and cheese. She's all fixed out."

The schoolmaster hesitated, and turned the

lamp-wick up and down. Then he spoke, somewhat timidly, "What should you like to give
her father?"

Miss Susan's face clouded with that dreamy
look which sometimes settled upon her eyes
like haze.

"Well," said she, "I guess whatever I should
give him 'd only make him laugh."

"Flowers — and velvet — and honey — and
myrrh?"

"Yes," answered Miss Susan with gravity.
"Perhaps it 's jest as well some things ain't to
be had at the shops."

The schoolmaster took up his lamp again and
walked to the door.

"We never can tell," he said. "It may be
people want things awfully without knowing it.
And suppose they do laugh! They 'd better
laugh than cry. *I* should give all I could.
Good-night."

Miss Susan banked up the fire and set her
rising of dough on the hearth, after a discrim-
inating peep to see whether it was getting on
too fast. After that, she covered her plants by
the window and blew out the light, so that the
moon should have its way. She lingered for
a moment, looking out into a glittering world.
Not a breath stirred. The visible universe lay
asleep, and only beauty waked. She was aching
with a tumultuous emotion — the sense that life
might be very fair and shining, if we only dared

to shape it as it seems to us in dreams. The loveliness and repose of the earth appealed to her like a challenge; they alone made it seem possible for her also to dare.

Next morning, she rose earlier than usual, while the schoolmaster was still fast bound in sleep. She stayed only to start her kitchen fire, and then stood motionless a moment for a last decision. The great white day was beginning outside with slow, unconscious royalty. The pale winter dawn yielded to a flush of rose; nothing in the aspect of the heavens contradicted the promise of the night before. It seemed to her a wonderful day, dramatic, visible in peace, because, on that morning, all the world was thinking of the world and not of individual desires. She went to the bureau drawer in the sitting-room and looked, a little scornfully, at two packages hidden there. Handkerchiefs for the schoolmaster, stockings and gloves for Solon! Shutting the drawer, she hurried out into the kitchen, snatching her scissors from the work-basket by the way. She gave herself no time to think, but went up to her flower-stand and began to cut the geranium blossoms and the rose. The fuchsias hung in flaunting grace. They were dearer to her than all. She snipped them recklessly, and because the bunch seemed meagre still, broke the top from her sweet-scented geranium and disposed the flowers hastily in the midst. Her posy was

sweet-smelling and good; it spoke to the heart.
Putting a shawl over her head, she rolled the
flowers in her apron from the frost, and stepped
out into the brilliant day. The little cross-
track between her house and the other was
snowed up; but she took the road and, hurrying between banks of carven whiteness, went
up Solon's path to the side door. She walked
in upon him where he was standing over the
kitchen stove, warming his hands at the first
blaze. Susan's cheeks were red with the challenge of the stinging air, but she had the look
of one who, living by a larger law, has banished
the foolishness of fear. She walked straight
up to him and proffered him her flowers.

"Here, Solon," she said, "it's Christmas. I
brought you these."

Solon looked at her and at them, in slow surprise. He put out both hands and took them
awkwardly.

"Well!" he said. "Well!"

Susan was smiling at him. It seemed to her
at that moment, that the world was a very rich
place, because you may take all you want and
give all you choose, while nobody is the wiser.

"Well," remarked Solon again, "I guess I'll
put 'em into water." He laid them down on
a chair. "Susan, do you remember that time
I walked over to Pine Hill to pick you some
mayflowers, when you was gittin' over the lung
fever?"

She nodded.

"Susan," said he desperately, "what if I should ask you to forgit old scores an' begin all over?"

"I ain't laid up anything," answered Susan, looking him full in the face with her brilliant smile.

"There's suthin' I've wanted to tell ye, this two year. I never s'posed you knew, but that night I kissed your sister in the entry an' asked her, I thought 't was you."

"Yes, I knew that well enough. I was in the buttery and heard it all. There, le's not talk about it."

Solon came a step nearer.

"But will you, Susan?" he persisted. "Will you? I know Jenny'd like it."

"I guess she would, too," said Susan. "There! we don't need to talk no further! You come over to breakfast, won't you? I'm goin' to fry chicken. It's Christmas mornin'." She nodded at him and went out, walking perhaps more proudly than usual down the shining path. Solon, regardless of his cooling kitchen, stood at the door and watched her. Solon never said very much, but he felt as if life were beginning all over again, just as he had wished to make it at the very start. He forgot his gray hair and furrowed face, just as he forgot the cold and snow. It was the spring of the year.

When Miss Susan entered her kitchen, the schoolmaster had come down and was putting a stick of wood into the stove.

" Merry Christmas ! " he called, " and here's something for you."

A long white package lay on the table at the end where her plate was always set.   She opened it with delicate touches, it seemed so precious.

" My sake ! " said she.   " It's a fan ! "   She lifted it out, and the fragrance of an Eastern wood filled all the room.   She swept open the feathers.   They were white and wonderful.

" It was never used except by one very beautiful woman," said the schoolmaster, without looking at her.   " She was a good deal older than I; but somehow she seemed to belong to me.   She died, and I thought I should like to have you keep this."

Susan was waving it back and forth before her face, stirring the air to fragrance.   Her eyes were full of dreams.   " My ! ain't it rich ! " she murmured.   " The Queen o' Sheba never had no better.   An' Solon's comin' over to breakfast."

A SECOND MARRIAGE

AMELIA PORTER sat by her great open fire-place, where the round, consequential black kettle hung from the crane, and breathed out a steamy cloud to be at once licked up and absorbed by the heat from a snatching flame below. It was exactly a year and a day since her husband's death, and she had packed herself away in his own corner of the settle, her hands clasped across her knees, and her red-brown eyes brooding on the nearer embers. She was not definitely speculating on her future, nor had she any heart for retracing the dull and gentle past. She had simply relaxed hold on her mind ; and so, escaping her, it had gone wandering off into shadowy prophecies of the immediate years. For, as Amelia had been telling herself for the last three months, since she had begun to outgrow the habit of a dual life, she was not old. Whenever she looked in the glass, she could not help noting how free from wrinkles her swarthy face had been kept, and that the line of her mouth was still scarlet over white, even teeth. Her crisp black hair, curling in those tight fine rolls which a bashful admirer had once commended as "full of little jerks," showed not a trace of gray. All this evidence of her senses read her a fair tale of the possibilities of the morrow; and without once saying, "I will take up a new life," she did tacitly acknowledge that life was not over.

It was a "snapping cold" night of early spring, so misplaced as to bring with it a certain dramatic excitement. The roads were frozen hard, and shone like silver in the ruts. All day sleds had gone creaking past, set to that fine groaning which belongs to the music of the year. The drivers' breath ascended in steam, the while they stamped down the probability of freezing, and yelled to Buck and Broad until that inner fervor raised them one degree in warmth. The smoking cattle held their noses low, and swayed beneath the yoke.

Amelia, shut snugly in her winter-tight house, had felt the power of the day without sharing its discomforts; and her eyes deepened and burned with a sense of the movement and warmth of living. To-night, under the spell of some vague expectancy, she had sat still for a long time, her sewing laid aside and her room scrupulously in order. She was waiting for what was not to be acknowledged even to her own intimate self. But as the clock struck nine, she roused herself, and shook off her mood in impatience and a disappointment which she would not own. She looked about the room, as she often had of late, and began to enumerate its possibilities in case she should desire to have it changed. Amelia never went so far as to say that change should be; she only felt that she had still a right to speculate upon it, as she had done for many years, as a form of harmless enjoyment. While every other house in the neighborhood had gone from the consistently good to the prosperously bad in the matter of refurnishing, John Porter had kept his precisely as his grandfather had left it to him. Amelia had never once complained; she had observed toward her husband an unfailing deference, due, she felt, to his twenty years' seniority; perhaps, also, it stood in her own mind as the only amends she could offer him for having married him without love. It was her father who made the match; and Amelia had succumbed, not through the obedience claimed by parents of an elder day, but from hot jealousy and the pique inevitably born of it. Laurie Morse had kept the singing-school that winter. He had loved Amelia; he had bound himself to her by all the most holy vows sworn from aforetime, and then, in some wanton exhibit of power — gone home with another girl. And for Amelia's responsive throb of feminine anger, she had spent fifteen years of sober country living with a man who had wrapped her about with the quiet tenderness of a strong nature, but who was not of her own generation either in mind or in habit; and

Laurie had kept a music-store in Saltash, seven miles away, and remained unmarried.

Now Amelia looked about the room, and mentally displaced the furniture, as she had done so many times while she and her husband sat there together. The settle could be taken to the attic. She had not the heart to carry out one secret resolve indulged in moments of impatient bitterness, — to split it up for fire-wood. But it could at least be exiled. She would have a good cook-stove, and the great fireplace should be walled up. The tin kitchen, sitting now beside the hearth in shining quaint-ness, should also go into the attic. The old clock — But at that instant the clash of bells shivered the frosty air, and Amelia threw her vain imaginings aside like a garment, and sprang to her feet. She clasped her hands in a spontaneous gesture of rapt attention ; and when the sound paused at her gate, with one or two sweet, lingering clingles, "I knew it!" she said aloud. Yet she did not go to the window to look into the moonlit night. Stand-ing there in the middle of the room, she awaited the knock which was not long in coming. It was imperative, insistent. Amelia, who had a spirit responsive to the dramatic exigencies of life, felt a little flush spring into her face, so hot that, on the way to the door, she involuntarily put her hand to her cheek and held it there. The door came open grumblingly.

It sagged upon the hinges, but, well-used to its vagaries, she overcame it with a regardless haste.

"Come in," she said, at once, to the man on the step. "It's cold. Oh, come in!"

He stepped inside the entry, removing his fur cap, and disclosing a youthful face charged with that radiance which made him, at thirty-five, almost the counterpart of his former self. It may have come only from the combination of curly brown hair, blue eyes, and an aspiring lift of the chin, but it always seemed to mean a great deal more. In the kitchen, he threw off his heavy coat, while Amelia, bright-eyed and breathing quickly, stood by, quite silent. Then he looked at her.

"You expected me, did n't you?" he asked.

A warmer color surged into her cheeks. "I did n't know," she said perversely.

"I guess you did. It's one day over a year. You knew I'd wait a year."

"It ain't a year over the services," said Amelia, trying to keep the note of vital expectancy out of her voice. "It won't be that till Friday."

"Well, Saturday I'll come again." He went over to the fire and stretched out his hands to the blaze. "Come here," he said imperatively, "while I talk to you."

Amelia stepped forward obediently, like a good little child. The old fascination was still as dominant as at its birth, sixteen years ago. She realized, with a strong, splendid sense of the eternity of things, that always, even while it would have been treason to recognize it, she had known how ready it was to rise and live again. All through her married years, she had sternly drugged it and kept it sleeping. Now it had a right to breathe, and she gloried in it.

"I said to myself I would n't come to-day," went on Laurie, without looking at her. A new and excited note had come into his voice, responsive to her own. He gazed down at the fire, musing the while he spoke. "Then I found I could n't help it. That's why I'm so late. I stayed in the shop till seven, and some fellows come in and wanted me to play. I took up the fiddle, and begun. But I had n't more 'n drew a note before I laid it down and put for the door. 'Dick, you keep shop,' says I. And I harnessed up, and drove like the devil."

Amelia felt warm with life and hope; she was taking up her youth just where the story ended.

"You ain't stopped swearin' yet!" she remarked, with a little excited laugh. Then, from an undercurrent of exhilaration, it occurred to her that she had never laughed so in all these years.

"Well," said Laurie abruptly, turning upon her, "how am I goin' to start out? Shall we hark back to old scores? I know what come between us. So do you. Have we got to talk it out, or can we begin now?"

"Begin now," replied Amelia faintly. Her breath choked her. He stretched out his arms to her in sudden passion. His hands touched her sleeves and, with an answering rapidity of motion, she drew back. She shrank within herself, and her face gathered a look of fright. "No! no! no!" she cried strenuously.

His arms fell at his sides, and he looked at her in amazement.

"What's the matter?" he demanded.

Amelia had retreated, until she stood now with one hand on the table. She could not look at him, and when she answered, her voice shook.

"There's nothin' the matter," she answered. "Only you must n't — yet."

A shade of relief passed over his face, and he smiled.

"There, there!" he said, "never you mind. I understand. But if I come over the last of the week, I guess it will be different. Won't it be different, Milly?"

"Yes," she owned, with a little sob in her throat, "it will be different."

Thrown out of his niche of easy friendliness with circumstance, he stood there in irritated consciousness that here was some subtile barrier which he had not foreseen. Ever since John

Porter's death, there had been strengthening in
him a joyous sense that Milly's life and his
own must have been running parallel all this
time, and that it needed only a little widening
of channels to make them join. His was no
crass certainty of finding her ready to drop into
his hand; it was rather a childlike, warm-
hearted faith in the permanence of her affection
for him, and perhaps, too, a shrewd estimate of
his own lingering youth compared with John
Porter's furrowed face and his fifty-five years.
But now, with this new whiffling of the wind,
he could only stand rebuffed and recognize his
own perplexity.

"You do care, don't you, Milly?" he asked,
with a boy's frank ardor. "You want me to
come again?"

All her own delight in youth and the warm
naturalness of life had rushed back upon her.

"Yes," she answered eagerly. "I'll tell
you the truth. I always did tell you the truth.
I do want you to come."

"But you don't want me to-night!" He
lifted his brows, pursing his lips whimsically;
and Amelia laughed.

"No," said she, with a little defiant movement of her own crisp head, "I don't know as
I do want you to-night!"

Laurie shook himself into his coat. "Well,"
he said, on his way to the door, "I'll be round
Saturday, whether or no. And Milly," he added

significantly, his hand on the latch, "you've got to like me then!"

Amelia laughed. "I guess there won't be no trouble!" she called after him daringly.

She stood there in the biting wind, while he uncovered the horse and drove away. Then she went shaking back to her fire; but it was not altogether from cold. The sense of the consistency of love and youth, the fine justice with which nature was paying an old debt, had raised her to a stature above her own. She stood there under the mantel, and held by it while she trembled. For the first time, her husband had gone utterly out of her life. It was as though he had not been.

"Saturday!" she said to herself. "Saturday! Three days till then!"

Next morning, the spring asserted itself, — there came a whiff of wind from the south and a feeling of thaw. The sled-runners began to cut through to the frozen ground, and about the tree-trunks, where thin crusts of ice were sparkling, came a faint musical sound of trickling drops. The sun was regnant, and little brown birds flew cheerily over the snow and talked of nests.

Amelia finished her housework by nine o'clock, and then sat down in her low rocker by the south window, sewing in thrifty haste. The sun fell hotly through the panes, and when she looked up, the glare met her eyes. She seemed

to be sitting in a golden shower, and she liked
it.   No sunlight ever made her blink, or screw
her face into wrinkles.   She throve in it like
a rose-tree.   At ten o'clock, one of the slow-
moving sleds, out that day in premonition of
a " spell o' weather," swung laboriously into her
yard and ground its way up to the side-door.
The sled was empty, save for a rocking-chair
where sat an enormous woman enveloped in
shawls, her broad face surrounded by a pumpkin
hood.   Her dark brown front came low over
her forehead, and she wore spectacles with wide
bows, which gave her an added expression of
benevolence.   She waved a mittened hand to
Amelia when their eyes met, and her heavy
face broke up into smiles.

" Here I be! " she called in a thick, gurgling
voice, as Amelia hastened out, her apron thrown
over her head.   " Did n't expect me, did ye ?   Nobody looks for an old rheumatic creatur'.   She's
more out o' the runnin' 'n a last year's bird's-
nest."

"Why, aunt Ann! " cried Amelia, in unmis-
takable joy.   " I 'm tickled to death to see you.
Here, Amos, I 'll help get her out."

The driver, a short, thick-set man of neutral,
ashy tints and a sprinkling of hair and beard,
trudged round the oxen and drew the rocking-
chair forward without a word.   He never once
looked in Amelia's direction, and she seemed
not to expect it ; but he had scarcely laid hold
of the chair when aunt Ann broke forth : —

"Now, Amos, ain't you goin' to take no notice of 'Melia, no more 'n if she wa'n't here? She ain't a bump on a log, nor you a born fool."

Amos at once relinquished his sway over the chair, and stood looking abstractedly at the oxen, who, with their heads low, had already fallen into that species of day-dream whereby they compensate themselves for human tyranny. They were waiting for Amos, and Amos, in obedience to some inward resolve, waited for commotion to cease.

"If ever I was ashamed, I be now!" continued aunt Ann, still with an expression of settled good-nature, and in a voice all jollity though raised conscientiously to a scolding pitch. "To think I should bring such a creatur' into the world, an' set by to see him treat his own relations like the dirt under his feet!"

Amelia laughed. She was exhilarated by the prospect of company, and this domestic whirlpool had amused her from of old.

"Law, aunt Ann," she said, "you let Amos alone. He and I are old cronies. We understand one another. Here, Amos, catch hold! We shall all get our deaths out here, if we don't do nothin' but stand still and squabble."

The immovable Amos had only been awaiting his cue. He lifted the laden chair with perfect ease to one of the piazza steps, and then to another; when it had reached the top-

most level, he dragged it over the sill into the
kitchen, and, leaving his mother sitting in colossal triumph by the fire, turned about and took
his silent way to the outer world.

"Amos," called aunt Ann, "do you mean to
say you 're goin' to walk out o' this house without speakin' a civil word to anybody? Do you
mean to say that?"

"I don't mean to say nothin'," confided
Amos to his worsted muffler, as he took up his
goad, and began backing the oxen round.

Undisturbed and not at all daunted by a reply
for which she had not even listened, aunt Ann
raised her voice in cheerful response: "Well,
you be along 'tween three an' four, an' you 'll
find me ready."

"Mercy, aunt Ann!" said Amelia, beginning
to unwind the visitor's wraps, "what makes you
keep houndin' Amos that way? If he hasn't
spoke for thirty-five years, it ain't likely he 's
goin' to begin now."

Aunt Ann was looking about her with an
expression of beaming delight in unfamiliar sur-
roundings. She laughed a rich, unctuous laugh,
and stretched her hands to the blaze.

"Law," she said contentedly, "of course it
ain't goin' to do no good. Who ever thought
't would? But I 've been at that boy all these
years to make him like other folks, an' I ain't
goin' to stop now. He never shall say his own
mother didn't know her duty towards him.

Well, 'Melia, you *air* kind o' snug here, arter all!
Here, you hand me my bag, an' I 'll knit a
stitch.   I ain't a mite cold."

Amelia was bustling about the fire, her mind
full of the possibilities of a company dinner.

" How 's your limbs?" she asked, while aunt
Ann drew out a long stocking, and began to
knit with an amazing rapidity of which her fat
fingers gave no promise.

"Well, I ain't allowed to forgit 'em very
often," she replied comfortably.   " Rheumatiz
is my cross, an' I 've got to bear it.   Sometimes
I wish 't had gone into my hands ruther 'n my
feet, an' I could ha' got round.   But there! if
't ain't one thing, it 's another.   Mis' Eben
Smith 's got eight young ones down with the
whoopin'-cough.   Amos dragged me over there
yisterday ; an' when I heerd 'em tryin' to see
which could bark the loudest, I says, 'Give me
the peace o' Jerusalem in my own house, even
if I don't stir a step for the next five year no
more 'n I have for the last.'   I dunno what 't
would be if I had n't a darter. I 've been greatly
blessed."

The talk went on in pleasant ripples, while
Amelia moved back and forth from pantry to
table.   She brought out the mixing-board, and
began to put her bread in the pans, while the
tin kitchen stood in readiness by the hearth.
The sunshine flooded all the room, and lay in-
solently on the paling fire ; the Maltese cat sat

in the broadest shaft of all, and, having lunched from her full saucer in the corner, made her second toilet for the day.

"'Melia," said aunt Ann suddenly, looking down over her glasses at the tin kitchen, "ain't it a real cross to bake in that thing?"

"I always had it in mind to buy me a range," answered Amelia reservedly, "but somehow we never got to it."

"That's the only thing I ever had ag'inst John. He was as grand a man as ever was, but he did set everything by such truck. Don't turn out the old things, I say, no more 'n the old folks; but when it comes to makin' a woman stan' quiddlin' round doin' work back side foremost, that beats me."

"He'd have got me a stove in a minute," burst forth Amelia in haste, "only he never knew I wanted it!"

"More fool you not to ha' said so!" commented aunt Ann, unwinding her ball. "Well, I s'pose he would. John wa'n't like the common run o' men. Great strong creatur' he was, but there was suthin' about him as soft as a woman. His mother used to say his eyes 'd fill full o' tears when he broke up a settin' hen. He was a good husband to you, — a good provider an' a good friend."

Amelia was putting down her bread for its last rising, and her face flushed.

"Yes," she said gently, "he *was* good."

"But there!" continued aunt Ann, dismissing all lighter considerations, "I dunno 's that 's any reason why you should bake in a tin kitchen, nor why you should need to heat up the brick oven every week, when 't was only done to please him, an' he ain't here to know. Now, 'Melia, le's see what you could do. When you got the range in, 't would alter this kitchen all over. Why don't you tear down that old-fashioned mantelpiece in the fore-room?"

"I could have a marble one," responded Amelia in a low voice. She had taken her sewing again, and she bent her head over it as if she were ashamed. A flush had risen in her cheeks, and her hand trembled.

"Wide marble! real low down!" confirmed aunt Ann, in a tone of triumph. "So fur as that goes, you could have a marble-top table." She laid down her knitting, and looked about her, a spark of excited anticipation in her eyes. All the habits of a lifetime urged her on to arrange and rearrange, in pursuit of domestic perfection. People used to say, in her first married days, that Ann Doby wasted more time in planning conveniences about her house than she ever saved by them "arter she got 'em." In her active years, she was, in local phrase, "a driver." Up and about early and late, she directed and managed until her house seemed to be a humming hive of industry and thrift. Yet there was never anything too urgent in that

sway. Her beaming good-humor acted as a
buffer between her and the doers of her will;
and though she might scold, she never rasped
and irritated. Nor had she really succumbed
in the least to the disease which had practically
disabled her. It might confine her to a chair
and render her dependent upon the service of
others, but over it, also, was she spiritual victor.
She could sit in her kitchen and issue orders;
and her daughter, with no initiative genius of
her own, had all aunt Ann's love of "springin'
to it." She cherished, besides, a worshipful admiration for her mother; so that she asked no
more than to act as the humble hand under that
directing head. It was Amos who tacitly rebelled. When a boy in school, he virtually gave
up talking, and thereafter opened his lips only
when some practical exigency was to be filled.
But once did he vouchsafe a reason for that
eccentricity. It was in his fifteenth year, as
aunt Ann remembered well, when the minister
had called; and Amos, in response to some remark about his hope of salvation, had looked
abstractedly out of the window.

"I'd be ashamed," announced aunt Ann,
after the minister had gone, — "Amos, I *would*
be ashamed, if I could n't open my head to a
minister o' the gospel!"

"If one head's open permanent in a house, I
guess that fills the bill," said Amos, getting up
to seek the woodpile. "I ain't goin' to interfere with nobody else's contract."

His mother looked after him with gaping lips, and, for the space of half an hour, spoke no word.

To-day she saw before her an alluring field of action; the prospect roused within her energies never incapable of responding to a spur.

"My soul, 'Melia!" she exclaimed, looking about the kitchen with a dominating eye, "how I should like to git hold o' this house! I al'ays did have a hankerin' that way, an' I don't mind tellin' ye. You could change it all round complete."

"It's a good house," said Amelia evasively, taking quick, even stitches, but listening hungrily to the voice of outside temptation. It seemed to confirm all the long-suppressed ambitions of her own heart.

"You're left well on 't," continued aunt Ann, her shrewd blue eyes taking on a speculative look. "I'm glad you sold the stock. A woman never undertakes man's work but she comes out the little eend o' the horn. The house is enough, if you keep it nice. Now, you've got that money laid away, an' all he left you besides. You could live in the village, if you was a mind to."

A deep flush struck suddenly into Amelia's cheek. She thought of Saltash and Laurie Morse.

"I don't want to live in the village," she

said sharply, thus reproving her own errant mind. "I like my home."

"Law, yes, of course ye do," replied aunt Ann easily, returning to her knitting. "I was only spec'latin'. The land, 'Melia, what you doin' of? Repairin' an old coat?"

Amelia bent lower over her sewing. "'T was his," she answered in a voice almost inaudible. "I put a patch on it last night by lamplight, and when daytime come, I found it was purple. So I'm takin' it off, and puttin' on a black one to match the stuff."

"Goin' to give it away?"

"No, I ain't," returned Amelia, again with that sharp, remonstrant note in her voice. "What makes you think I'd do such a thing as that?"

"Law, I didn't mean no harm. You said you was repairin' on 't, — that's all."

Amelia was ashamed of her momentary outbreak. She looked up and smiled sunnily.

"Well, I suppose it *is* foolish," she owned, — "too foolish to tell. But I've been settin' all his clothes in order to lay 'em aside at last. I kind o' like to do it."

Aunt Ann wagged her head, and ran a knitting-needle up under her cap on a voyage of discovery.

"You think so now," she said wisely, "but you'll see some time it's better by fur to give 'em away while ye can. The time never'll come when it's any easier. My soul, 'Melia,

how I should like to git up into your chambers!
It 's six year now sence I 've seen 'em."

Amelia laid down her work and considered
the possibility.

"I don't know how in the world I could h'ist
you up there," she remarked, from an evident
background of hospitable good-will.

"H'ist me up? I guess you could n't! You 'd
need a tackle an' falls. Amos has had to come
to draggin' me round by degrees, an' I don't go
off the lower floor. Be them chambers jest the
same, 'Melia?"

"Oh, yes, they 're just the same. Everything
is. You know he did n't like changes."

"Blue spread on the west room bed?"

"Yes."

"Spinnin'-wheels out in the shed chamber,
where his gran'mother Hooper kep' 'em?"

"Yes."

"Say, 'Melia, do you s'pose that little still 's
up attic he used to have such a royal good
time with, makin' essences?"

Amelia's eyes filled suddenly with hot, un-
manageable tears.

"Yes," she said; "we used it only two
summers ago. I come across it yesterday.
Seemed as if I could smell the peppermint I
brought in for him to pick over. He was too
sick to go out much then."

Aunt Ann had laid down her work again,
and was gazing into vistas of rich enjoyment.

"I'll be whipped if I should n't like to see that little still!"

"I'll go up and bring it down after dinner," said Amelia soberly, folding her work and taking off her thimble. "I'd just as soon as not."

All through the dinner hour aunt Ann kept up an inspiring stream of question and reminiscence.

"You *be* a good cook, 'Melia, an' no mistake," she remarked, breaking her brown hot biscuit. "This your same kind o' bread, made without yeast?"

"Yes," answered Amelia, pouring the tea. "I save a mite over from the last risin'."

Aunt Ann smelled the biscuit critically. "Well, it makes proper nice bread," she said, "but seems to me that's a terrible shif'less way to go about it. However'd you happen to git hold on 't? You wa'n't never brought up to 't."

"His mother used to make it so. 'T was no great trouble, and 't would have worried him if I'd changed."

When the lavender-sprigged china had been washed and the hearth swept up, the room fell into its aspect of afternoon repose. The cat, after another serious ablution, sprang up into a chair drawn close to the fireplace, and coiled herself symmetrically on the faded patchwork cushion. Amelia stroked her in passing. She liked to see puss appropriate that chair; her purr from it renewed the message of domestic content.

"Now," said Amelia, "I'll get the still."

"Bring down anything else that's ancient!" called aunt Ann. "We've pretty much got red o' such things over t' our house, but I kind o' like to see 'em."

When Amelia returned, she staggered under a miscellaneous burden : the still, some old swifts for winding yarn, and a pair of wool-cards.

"I don't believe you know so much about cardin' wool as I do," she said, in some triumph, regarding the cards with the saddened gaze of one who recalls an occupation never to be resumed. "You see, you dropped all such work when new things come in. I kept right on because he wanted me to."

Aunt Ann was abundantly interested and amused.

"Well, now, if ever!" she repeated over and over again. "If this don't carry me back! Seems if I could hear the wheel hummin' an' gramma Balch steppin' back an' forth as stiddy as a clock. It's been a good while sence I've thought o' such old days."

"If it's old days you want" — began Amelia, and she sped upstairs with a fresh light of resolution in her eyes.

It was a long time before she returned, — so long that aunt Ann exhausted the still, and

turned again to her thrifty knitting. Then
there came a bumping noise on the stairs, and
Amelia's shuffling tread.

"What under the sun be you doin' of?"
called her aunt, listening, with her head on one
side. "Don't you fall, 'Melia! Whatever 't is,
I can't help ye."

But the stairway door yielded to pressure
from within : and first a rim of wood appeared,
and then Amelia, scarlet and breathless, stag-
gering under a spinning-wheel.

"Forever!" ejaculated aunt Ann, making
one futile effort to rise, like some cumbersome
fowl whose wings are clipped. "My land alive!
you 'll break a blood-vessel, an' then where 'll
ye be?"

Amelia triumphantly drew the wheel to the
middle of the floor, and then blew upon her
dusty hands and smoothed her tumbled hair.
She took off her apron and wiped the wheel
with it rather tenderly, as if an ordinary duster
would not do.

"There!" she said. "Here's some rolls
right here in the bedroom. I carded them myself, but I never expected to spin any more."

She adjusted a roll to the spindle, and, quite
forgetting aunt Ann, began stepping back and
forth in a rhythmical march of feminine service.
The low hum of her spinning filled the air, and
she seemed to be wrapped about by an atmosphere of remoteness and memory. Even aunt

Ann was impressed by it; and once, beginning to speak, she looked at Amelia's face, and stopped. The purring silence continued, lulling all lesser energies to sleep, until Amelia, pausing to adjust her thread, found her mood broken by actual stillness, and gazed about her like one awakened from dreams.

"There!" she said, recalling herself. "Ain't that a good smooth thread? I 've sold lots of yarn. They ask for it in Sudleigh."

"'T is so!" confirmed aunt Ann cordially. "An' you 've al'ays dyed it yourself, too!"

"Yes, a good blue; sometimes tea-color. There, now, you can't say you ain't heard a spinnin'-wheel once more!"

Amelia moved the wheel to the side of the room, and went gravely back to her chair. Her energy had fled, leaving her hushed and tremulous. But not for that did aunt Ann relinquish her quest for the betterment of the domestic world. Her tongue clicked the faster as Amelia's halted. She put away her work altogether, and sat, with wagging head and eloquent hands, still holding forth on the changes which might be wrought in the house: a bay window here, a sofa there, new chairs, tables, and furnishings. Amelia's mind swam in a sea of green rep, and she found herself looking up from time to time at her mellowed four walls, to see if they sparkled in desirable yet somewhat terrifying gilt paper.

At four o'clock, when Amos swung into the
yard with the oxen, she was remorsefully conscious of heaving a sigh of relief; and she bade
him in to the cup of tea ready for him by the
fire with a sympathetic sense that too little was
made of Amos, and that perhaps only she, at
that moment, understood his habitual frame of
mind. He drank his tea in silence, the while
aunt Ann, with much relish, consumed doughnuts and cheese, having spread a wide handkerchief in her lap to catch the crumbs. Amos
never varied in his rôle of automaton; and
Amelia talked rapidly, in the hope of protecting
him from verbal avalanches. But she was not to
succeed. At the very moment of parting, aunt
Ann, enthroned in her chair, with a clogging
stick under the rockers, called a halt, just as the
oxen gave their tremulous preparatory heave.

"Amos!" cried she, "I'll be whipped if
you've spoke one word to 'Melia this livelong
day! If you ain't ashamed, I be! If you
can't speak, I can!"

Amos paused, with his habitual resignation
to circumstances, but Amelia sped forward and
clapped him cordially on the arm; with the
other hand, she dealt one of the oxen a futile
blow.

"Huddup, Bright!" she called, with a swift,
smiling look at Amos. Even in kindness she
would not do him the wrong of an unnecessary
word. "Good-by, aunt Ann! Come again!"

Amos turned half about, the goad over his
shoulder. His dull-seeming eyes had opened
to a gleam of human feeling, betraying how
bright and keen they were. Some hidden spring
had been touched, though only they would tell
its story. Amelia thought it was gratitude.
And then aunt Ann, nodding her farewells in
assured contentment with herself and all the
world, was drawn slowly out of the yard.

When Amelia went indoors and warmed her
chilled hands at the fire, the silence seemed
to her benignant. What was loneliness before
had miraculously translated itself into peace.
That worldly voice, strangely clothing her own
longings with form and substance, had been
stilled; only the clock, rich in the tranquillity
of age, ticked on, and the cat stretched herself
and curled up again. Amelia sat down in the
waning light and took a last stitch in her work ;
she looked the coat over critically with an artistic satisfaction, and then hung it behind the
door in its accustomed place, where it had
remained undisturbed now for many months.
She ate soberly and sparingly of her early supper, and then, leaving the lamp on a side-table,
where it brought out great shadows in the
room, she took a little cricket and sat down by
the fire. There she had mused many an evening which seemed to her less dull than the
general course of her former life, while her husband occupied the hearthside chair and told

her stories of the war. He had a childlike
clearness and simplicity of speech, and a self-
forgetful habit of reminiscence. The war was
the war to him, not a theatre for boastful individual action; but Amelia remembered now
that he had seemed to hold heroic proportions
in relation to that immortal past. One could
hardly bring heroism into the potato-field and
the cow-house; but after this lapse of time, it
began to dawn upon her that the man who had
fought at Gettysburg and the man who marked
out for her the narrow rut of an unchanging existence were one and the same. And as if the
moment had come for an expected event, she
heard again the jangling of bells without, and
the old vivid color rushed into her cheeks, reddened before by the fire-shine. It was as though
the other night had been a rehearsal, and as if
now she knew what was coming. Yet she only
clasped her hands more tightly about her knees
and waited, the while her heart hurried its
time. The knocker fell twice, with a resonant
clang. She did not move. It beat again, the
more insistently. Then the heavy outer door
was pushed open, and Laurie Morse came in,
looking exactly as she knew he would look —
half angry, wholly excited, and dowered with
the beauty of youth recalled. He took off his
cap and stood before her.

"Why did n't you come?" he asked imperatively. "Why did n't you let me in?"

The old wave of irresponsible joy rose in her at his presence; yet it was now not so much a part of her real self as a delight in some influence which might prove foreign to her. She answered him, as she was always impelled to do, dramatically, as if he gave her the cue, calling for words which might be her sincere expression, and might not.

"If you wanted it enough, you could get in," she said perversely, with an alluring coquetry in her mien. "The door was unfastened."

"I did want to enough," he responded. A new light came into his eyes. He held out his hands toward her. "Get up off that cricket!" he commanded. "Come here!"

Amelia rose with a swift, feminine motion, but she stepped backward, one hand upon her heart. She thought its beating could be heard.

"It ain't Saturday," she whispered.

"No, it ain't. But I could n't wait. You knew I could n't. You knew I 'd come to-night."

The added years had had their effect on him; possibly, too, there had been growing up in him the strength of a long patience. He was not an heroic type of man; but noting the sudden wrinkles in his face and the firmness of his mouth, Amelia conceived a swift respect for him which she had never felt in the days of their youth.

"Am I goin' to stay," he asked sternly, "or shall I go home?"

As if in dramatic accord with his words, the bells jangled loudly at the gate. Should he go or stay?

"I suppose," said Amelia faintly, "you're goin' to stay."

Laurie laid down his cap, and pulled off his coat. He looked about impatiently, and then, moving toward the nail by the door, he lifted the coat to place it over that other one hanging there. Amelia had watched him absently, thinking only, with a hungry anticipation, how much she had needed him; but as the garment touched her husband's, the real woman burst through the husk of her outer self, and came to life with an intensity that was pain. She sprang forward.

"No! no!" she cried, the words ringing wildly in her own ears. "No! no! don't you hang it there! Don't you! don't you!" She swept him aside, and laid her hands upon the old patched garment on the nail. It was as if they blessed it, and as if they defended it also. Her eyes burned with the horror of witnessing some irrevocable deed.

Laurie stepped back in pure surprise. "No, of course not," said he. "I'll put it on a chair. Why, what's the matter, Milly? I guess you're nervous. Come back to the fire. Here, sit down where you were, and let's talk."

The cat, roused by a commotion which was insulting to her egotism, jumped down from the

cushion, stretched into a fine curve, and made
a silhouette of herself in a corner of the hearth.
Amelia, a little ashamed, and not very well understanding what it was all about, came back,
with shaking limbs, and dropped upon the settle, striving now to remember the convention-
alities of saner living. Laurie was a kind man.
At this moment, he thought only of reassuring
her. He drew forward the chair left vacant by
the cat, and beat up the cushion.

"There," said he, "I 'll take this, and we 'll
talk."

Amelia recovered herself with a spring. She
came up straight and tall, a concluded resolution
in every muscle. She laid a hand upon his arm.

"Don't you sit there!" said she. "Don't
you!"

"Why, Amelia!" he ejaculated, in a vain
perplexity. "Why, Milly!"

She moved the chair back out of his grasp,
and turned to him again.

"I understand it now," she went on rapidly.
"I know just what I feel and think, and I thank
my God it ain't too late. Don't you see I can't
bear to have your clothes hang where his belong? Don't you see 't would kill me to have
you sit in his chair? When I find puss there,
it 's a comfort. If 't was you — I don't know
but I might do you a mischief!" Her voice
sank, in awe of herself and her own capacity for
passionate emotion.

Laurie Morse had much swift understanding of the human heart. His own nature partook of the feminine, and he shared its intuitions and its fears.

"I never should lay that up against you, Milly," he said kindly. "But we would n't have these things. You 'd come to Saltash with me, and we 'd furnish all new."

"Not have these things!" called Amelia, with a ringing note of dismay, — "not have these things he set by as he did his life! Why, what do you think I 'm made of, after fifteen years? What did *I* think I was made of, even to guess I could? You don't know what women are like, Laurie Morse, — you don't know!"

She broke down in piteous weeping. Even then it seemed to her that it would be good to find herself comforted with warm human sympathy; but not a thought of its possibility remained in her mind. She saw the boundaries beyond which she must not pass. Though the desert were arid on this side, it was her desert, and there in her tent must she abide. She began speaking again between sobbing breaths : —

"I did have a dull life. I used up all my young days doin' the same things over and over, when I wanted somethin' different. It *was* dull ; but if I could have it all over again, I 'd work my fingers to the bone. I don't know how it would have been if you and I 'd come together then, and had it all as we planned ; but now I 'm a different woman. I can't any more go back than you could turn Sudleigh River, and coax it to run uphill. I don't know whether 't was meant my life should make me a different woman; but I *am* different, and such as I am, I 'm his woman. Yes, till I die, till I 'm laid in the ground 'longside of him !" Her voice had an assured ring of triumph, as if she were taking again an indissoluble marriage oath.

Laurie had grown very pale. There were forlorn hollows under his eyes ; now he looked twice his age.

"I didn't suppose you kept a place for me," he said, with an unconscious dignity. "That would n't have been right, and him alive. And I did n't wait for dead men's shoes. But somehow I thought there was something between you and me that could n't be outlived."

Amelia looked at him with a frank sweetness which transfigured her face into spiritual beauty.

"I thought so, too," she answered, with that simplicity ever attending our approximation to the truth. "I never once said it to myself; but all this year, 'way down in my heart, I knew you 'd come back. And I wanted you to come. I guess I 'd got it all planned out how we 'd make up for what we 'd lost, and build up a new life. But so far as I go, I guess I did n't lose by what I 've lived through. I guess I gained

somethin' I 'd sooner give up my life than even
lose the memory of."

So absorbed was she in her own spiritual inheritance that she quite forgot his pain. She
gazed past him with an unseeing look ; and
striving to meet and recall it, he faced the vision
of their divided lives. To-morrow Amelia would
remember his loss and mourn over it with maternal pangs; to-night she was oblivious of all but
her own. Great human experiences are costly
things; they demand sacrifice, not only of ourselves, but of those who are near us. The room
was intolerable to Laurie. He took his hat and
coat, and hurried out. Amelia heard the drag-
ging door closed behind him. She realized,
with the numbness born of supreme emotion,
that he was putting on his coat outside in the
cold; and she did not mind. The bells stirred,
and went clanging away. Then she drew a long
breath, and bowed her head on her hands in an
acquiescence that was like prayer.

It seemed a long time to Amelia before she
awoke again to temporal things. She rose,
smiling, to her feet, and looked about her as if
her eyes caressed every corner of the homely
room. She picked up puss in a round, comfortable ball, and carried her back to the hearthside chair; there she stroked her until her
touchy ladyship had settled down again to purring content. Then Amelia, still smiling, and
with an absent look, as if her mind wandered

through lovely possibilities of a sort which can never be undone, drew forth the spinning-wheel, and fitted a roll to the spindle. She began stepping back and forth as if she moved to the measure of an unheard song, and the pleasant hum of her spinning broke delicately upon the ear. It seemed to waken all the room into new vibrations of life. The clock ticked with an assured peace, as if knowing it marked eternal hours. The flames waved softly upward without their former crackle and sheen; and the moving shadows were gentle and rhythmic ones come to keep the soul company. Amelia felt her thread lovingly.

"I guess I 'll dye it blue," she said, with a tenderness great enough to compass inanimate things. "He always set by blue, did n't he, puss ?"

THE FLAT-IRON LOT

THE fields were turning brown, and in the dusty gray of the roadside, closed gentians gloomed, and the aster burned like a purple star. It was the finest autumn for many years. People said, with every clear day, "Now this must 'be a weather-breeder;" but still the storm delayed. Then they anxiously scanned the heavens, as if, weeks beforehand, the signs of the time might be written there; for this was the fall of all others when wind and sky should be kind to Tiverton. She was going to celebrate her two hundred and fiftieth anniversary, and she was big with the importance of it.

On a still afternoon, over three weeks before that happy day, a slender old man walked erectly along the country road. He carried a cane over his shoulder, and, slung upon it, a small black leather bag, bearing the words, painted in careful letters, "Clocks repaired by N. Oldfield." As he went on, he cast a glance, now and then, to either side, from challenging blue eyes, strong yet in the indomitable quality of youth. He knew every varying step of the road, and could have numbered, from memory,

the trees and bushes that fringed its length;
and now, after a week's absence, he swept the
landscape with the air of a manorial lord, to
see what changes might have slipped in unawares. At one point, a flat triangular stone
had been tilted up on edge, and an unprac-
ticed hand had scrawled on it, in chalk, "4 M
to Sudleigh." The old man stopped, took the
bag from his shoulder, and laid it tenderly on
a stone of the wall. Then, with straining
hands, he pulled the rock down into the worn
spot where it had lain, and gave a sigh of relief when it settled into its accustomed place,
and the tall grass received it tremulously.
Now he opened his bag, took from it a cloth,
carefully folded, and rubbed the rock until
those defiling chalk marks were partially effaced.

"Little varmints!" he said, apostrophizing
the absent school children who had wrought
the deed. "Can't they let nothin' alone?"
He took up his bag, and went on.

Nicholas Oldfield, as he walked the road
that day, was a familiar figure to all the
county round. He had a smooth, carefully
shaven face, with a fine outline of nose and
chin, and his straight gray hair shone from
faithful brushing. He was almost aggressively
clean. Even his blue eyes had the appearance
of having just been washed, like a spring day
after a shower. It was a frequent remark that

he looked as if he had come out of a bandbox ;
and one critic even went so far as to assert
that on Sundays he sandpapered his eyes and
gave a little extra polish to his bones. But
these were calumnies; though to-day his suit
of home-made blue was quite speckless, and
the checked gingham neckerchief, which made
his ordinary wear, still kept its stiff, starched
creases.

"Dirt don't stick to *you*, Mr. Oldfield," once
said a seeking widow. "Your washing can't
be much. I guess anybody'd be glad to undertake it for you." Mr. Oldfield nodded gravely,
as one receiving the tribute which was justly
his, and continued to do his washing himself.

As he walked the dusty road, bearing his
little bag, so he had walked it for years, sometimes within a few miles of home, and again at
the extreme limit of the county edge. The
clocks of the region were all his clients, some
regarded with compassion ("ramshackle
things" that needed perpetual tinkering) and
others with a holy awe. "The only thing
Nicholas Oldfield bows the knee before is
a double-back-action clock a thousand years
old," said Brad Freeman, the regardless.
"That's how he reads Ancient of Days."
The justice of the remark was acknowledged,
though, as touching Mr. Oldfield, it was felt
to be striking rather too keenly at the root of
things. For Nicholas Oldfield was looked

upon with a respect not so much inspired by
his outward circumstances as by his method
of taking them.   There are, indeed, ways and
ways among us who serve the public.   When
Tom O'Neil went round peddling essences,
children saw him from afar, ran to meet him,
and, falling on his pack, besought him for
" two-three-drops-o'-c'logne " with such fervor
that the mothers had to haul them off by
main force, in order themselves to approach
his redolence ; but when the clock-mender appeared, with his little bag, propriety walked
before him, and the naughtiest scion of the
flock would come soberly in, to announce : —

"Mother, here 's Mr. Oldfield."

It is true that this little old man did exem-
plify the dignity and restraint of life to such
a degree that, had it not been for his one colossal weakness, the town might have condemned
him, in good old Athenian fashion.   Clock-
mending was a legitimate industry ; but there
were those who felt it to be, in his case, a mere
pretext for nosing round and identifying ridic-
ulous old things which nobody prized until
Nicholas Oldfield told them it was conformable
so to do.   Some believed him and some did
not ; but it was known that a MacDonough's
Victory tea-set drove him to an almost out-
spoken rapture, and that the mere mention of
the Bay Psalm Book (a copy of which he sought
with the haggard fervor of one who worships

but has ceased to hope) was enough to make him "wild as a hawk." Old papers, too, drew him by their very mildew; and when his towns-folk were in danger of respecting him too tedi-ously, they recalled these amiable puerilities, drew a breath of relief, and marked his value down.

Many facts in his life were not in the least understood, because he never saw the possi-bility of talking about them. For example, when at the marriage of his son, Young Nick, he made over the farm, and kept his own residence in the little gambrel-roofed house where he had been born, and his father and grandfather before him, the act was, for a time, regarded somewhat gloomily by the public at large. There were Young Nick and his Hattie, living in the big new house, with its spacious piazza and cool green blinds; there the two daughters were born and bred, and the elder of them was married. The new house had its hired girl and man; and meantime the other Nicholas (nobody ever dreamed of calling him Old Nick) was cooking his own meals, and even, of a Saturday, scouring his kitchen floor. It was easy to see in him the pathetic symbol of a bygone generation relegated to the past. A little wave of sympathy crept to his very feet, and then, finding itself unnoted, ebbed away again. Only one village censor dared speak, saying slyly to Young Nick's Hattie: —

"Ain't no room for grandpa in the new house, is there?"

Hattie opened her eyes wide at this discovery, though now she realized that echoes of a like benevolence had reached her ears before. She went home very early from the quilting, and that night she said to her husband, as they sat on the doorstone, waiting for the milk to cool : —

"Nicholas, little things I've got hold of, first an' last, make me conclude folks pity father. Do you s'pose they do?"

Young Nick selected a fat plantain spike, and began stripping the seeds.

"Well, I dunno what for," said he, after consideration. "Father seems to be pretty rugged."

Hattie was one of those who find no quicker remedy than that of plentiful speech; and later in the evening, she sped over to the little house, across the dewy orchard. Mr. Oldfield had come home only that afternoon, and now he had drawn up at his kitchen table, which was covered by a hand-woven cloth, beautifully ironed, and set with old-fashioned dishes. He had hot biscuits and apple-pie, and the odor of them rose soothingly to Hattie's nostrils, dissipating, for a moment, her consciousness of tragedy and wrong. A man could not be quite forlorn who cooked such "victuals," and sat before them so serenely.

"See here, father," said she, with the desperation of speaking her mind for the first time to one from whom she had hitherto kept awesomely remote; "when we moved into the new house, I dunno 's there was any talk about your comin', too. I guess it never entered into our heads you'd do anything but to stick to the old place. An' now, after it 's all past an' gone, the neighbors say " —

Nicholas Oldfield had been smiling his slight, dry smile. At this point, he took up a knife, and cut a careful triangle of pie. He did all these things as if each one were very important.

"Here, Hattie," said he, "you taste o' this dried apple. I put a mite o' lemon in."

Hattie, somehow abashed by the mental impact of the little man, ate her pie meekly, and thenceforth waived the larger issue. All the same, she knew the neighbors "pitied father," and that they would continue to pity him so long as he lived alone in the little peaceful house, doing his own washing and making his own pie.

To-night was a duplication of many another when Nicholas Oldfield had turned the corner and come in sight of his own home; but often as it had been repeated, the experience was never the same. Some would have named his springing emotion delight; but it neither quickened his pace nor made him draw his breath the faster. Perhaps he even walked a little more slowly, to enjoy the taste, for he was a saving man. There was the little house, white as paint could make it, and snug in bowering foliage. He noted, with an approving eye, that the dahlias in the front yard, set in stiff nodding rows, were holding their own bravely against the dry fall weather, and that the asters were blooming profusely, purple and pink. A rare softness came over his features when he stepped into the yard; and though he examined the roof critically in passing, it was with the eye of love. He fitted the key in the lock; the sound of its turning made music in his ears, and, setting his foot upon the sill, he was a man for whom that little was enough. Nicholas Oldfield was at home.

He laid down his bag, and went, without an instant's pause, straight through to the sitting-room, and stood before the tall eight-day clock. He put his hand on the woodwork, as if it might have been the shoulder of a friend, and looked up understandingly in its face.

"Well, here we be," said he. "You'd ha' hil' out till mornin', though."

For wherever he might travel, he always made it a point to be home in time to wind the clocks; and however early he might hurry away again, under stress of some antiquarian impulse, they were left alive and pulsing behind him. There was one in each room, besides the tall eight-day in the parlor, and they were all soft-voiced and leisurely, reminiscent of another age than ours. Though three of them had been inherited, it almost seemed as if Nicholas must have selected the entire company, so harmonious were they, so serenely fitted to the calm decorum of his own desires.

In half an hour he had accomplished many things, and his fire sent a spiral breath toward heaven. The dark old kitchen lay open, door and window, to the still opulent sun, and from the pantry and a corner cupboard came gleams of color, to delight the eye. Here were riches, indeed : old India china, an unbroken set of Sheltered Peasant, and, on the top shelf, little mugs and cups of a pink lustre, soft and sweet as flowers. Many a collector had wooed Nicholas Oldfield to part with his china (for the fame of it had spread afar,) but his only response to solicitation was to open the doors more widely on his treasures, remarking, without emphasis : —

"I guess they might as well stay where they be."

So passive was he, that many among merchants judged they had impressed him, and returned again and again to the charge ; but when they found always the same imperturbable front, the same mild neutrality of demeanor, they melted sadly away, and were seen no more, leaving their places to be taken by others equally hopeful and as sure to be betrayed.

One creature only was capable of rousing Nicholas Oldfield from that calm wherein he went ticking on through life. She it was who, by some natal likeness, understood him wholly ; and to-night, just as he was sitting down to his supper of " cream o' tartar " biscuits and smoking tea, her clear voice broke upon his solitude.

" Gran'ther," called Mary Oldfield from the door, " mother says, ' Won't you come over to supper ?' She saw your smoke."

Nicholas pushed back his chair a little ; he felt himself completed.

" You had yours ?" he asked, in his usual even tones.

" No. I waited for you."

" Then you come right in an' git it. Take your mug — here, I 'll reach it down for ye — an' there 's the Good-Girl plate."

Mary Oldfield was a tall, pleasant looking maid of sixteen, and standing quietly by, while her grandfather got out her own plate and mug, she was an amazingly faithful copy of him. They smiled a little at each other, in sitting down, but there was no closer greeting between them. They were exceedingly well content to be together again, and this was so simple and natural a state that there was nothing to say about it. Only Nicholas looked at her from time to time — her capable

brown hands and careful braids of hair, — and
nodded briefly, as he had a way of nodding at
his clocks.

"You know what I told you, Mary, about
the Flat-Iron Lot?" he asked, while Mary
buttered her biscuit.

She looked at him in assent.

"Well, I 've proved it."

"You don't say !"

Mary had certain antique methods of speech,
which the new-fangled school teacher, not liking to pronounce them vulgar, had tactfully
dubbed "obsolete." "If we used 'em all the
time they would n't get obsolete, would they?"
asked Mary; and the school teacher, being a
logical person, made no answer. So Mary went
on plying them with a conscientious calmness like one determined to keep a precious
and misprized metal in circulation. She even
called Nicholas gran'ther, because he liked it,
and because he had called his own grandfather
so.

"Ye see," said Nicholas, " the fust rec'ids
were missin'. 'Burnt up!' says that town
clerk over to Sudleigh. 'Burnt when the old
meetin'-house ketched fire, arter the Injun
raid.' 'Burnt up!' thinks I. 'The cat's
foot! I guess so, when the communion service was carried over fifteen mile an' left in
a potato sullar.' So I says to myself, 'What
become o' that fust communion set?' Why,

before the meetin'-house was repaired, they
all rode over to what 's now Saltash, to worship
in Square Billin's's kitchen. Now, when Square
Billin's died of a fever, that same winter, they
hove all his books into that old lumber-room
over Sudleigh court-house. So, when I was
fixin' up the court-house clock, t' other day, I
clim' up to that room, an' shet myself in there.
An', Mary, I found them rec'ids!" He looked
at her with that complete and awe-stricken triumph which nobody else had ever seen upon
his face. Her own reflected it.

"Where are they, gran'ther?" asked Mary.
But she was the more excited; she could only
whisper.

"They 're loose sheets o' paper," returned
Nicholas, "an' *they 're in my bag!*"

Mary made an involuntary movement toward
the bag, which lay, innocently secretive, on a
neighboring chair. Even its advertising legend
had a knowing look. Nicholas followed her
glance.

"No," said he firmly, "not now. We 'll
read 'em all over this evenin', when I 've done
the dishes. But, Mary, I 'll tell ye this much:
it 's got the whole story of the settlers comin'
into town, an' which way they come, an' all
about it, writ down by Simeon Gerry, the fust
minister, the one that killed five Injuns, stop-
pin' to load an' fire, an' then opened on the
rest with bilin' fat. An', Mary, the fust set-

tler of all was Nicholas Oldfield, haulin' his
wife on a kind of a drag made o' withes ; an'
the path they took led straight over our Flat-
Iron Lot.   An', Mary, 't was there they rested,
an' offered up prayer to God."

"O my soul, gran'ther!" breathed Mary,
clasping her little brown hands.   "O my
soul!"   Her face grew curiously mature.   It
seemed to mirror his.   She leaned forward, in
a deadly earnestness.   "Gran'ther," said she,
"did they settle here first?   Or — or was it
Sudleigh?"

Now, indeed, was Nicholas Oldfield the herald of news good both to tell and hear.

"The fust settlement," said he, as if he read
it from the book of fate, "was made in Tiverton, on the sixteenth day of the month ; the
second in Sudleigh, on the twenty-fifth."

"So, when you guessed at the date, and
told parson to have the celebration then, you
got it right?"

"I got it right," replied Nicholas quietly.
"But pa'son shall see the rec'ids, an' I 'll recom-
mend him to put 'em under lock an' key."

The two sat there and looked at each other,
with an outwelling of great content.   Then
Mary passed her mug, and while Nicholas
filled it, he gave her an oft-repeated charge:—

"Don't you open your head now, Mary.
All this is between you an' me.   I 'll just mention it to pa'son, an' make up my mind whether

he sees the meanin' on 't. But don't you say
one word to your father an' mother. To them
it don't signify."

Mary nodded wisely. She knew, with the
philosophy of a much older experience, that
she and gran'ther lived alone in a nest of
kindly aliens. As if their mention evoked a
foreign presence, her mother's voice sounded
that instant from the door : —

" Mary, why under the sun did n't you come
back ? I sent word for you to run over with
her, father, an' have some supper. Well, if
you two ain't thick ! "

" We 're havin' a dish o' discourse," returned Nicholas quietly.

Young Nick's Hattie was forty-five, but she
looked much younger. Extreme plumpness
had insured her against wrinkles, and her light
brown hair was banded smoothly back. Hattie's
originality lay in a desire for color, and therein
she overstepped the bounds of all decorum.
It was customary to see her barred across with
enormous plaids, or stripes going the broad
way ; and so long had she lived under such
insignia that no one would have known her
without them. She came in with soft, heavy
footfalls, and sat down in the little rocking-
chair at Mr. Oldfield's right hand. She smiled
at him, somewhat nervously.

" Well, father," said she, " you got home ! "

Nicholas helped himself to another half cup

of tea, after holding the teapot tentatively
across to Mary's mug.

"Yes," he answered, in his dry and gentle
fashion, "I've got home."

Hattie began rocking, in a rapid staccato, to
punctuate her speech.

"Well," she began, "I'll say my say an' done
with it. There's goin' to be a town-meetin'
to-night, an' Nicholas sent me over to mention
it. 'Father'll want to be on hand,' says he."

Mr. Oldfield pushed back his cup, and then
his chair. He bent his keen blue eyes upon
her.

"Town meetin' this time o' year?" said he.
"What for?"

"Oh, it's about the celebration. Old Mr.
Eaton" —

"What Eaton?"

"William W."

"He that went away in war time, an' made
money in wool? Old War-Wool Eaton?"

Nicholas nodded, at her assent, and his look
blackened. He knew what was coming.

"Well, he sent word he meant to give us a
clock, same as he had other towns, an' he
wanted we should have it up before the celebration."

"Yes," said Nicholas Oldfield, "he'll give
us a clock, will he? I knew he would. I've
said 't was comin'. He give one to Saltash;
he's gi'n 'em all over the county. Do you

know what them clocks be? They've got
letters round the dial, in place o' figgers; an'
the letters spell out, 'In Memory of Me.' An'
down to Saltash they've gi'n up sayin' it's
quarter arter twelve, or the like o' that. They
say it's O minutes past I."

He glared at her. Young Nick's Hattie
thought she had never heard father speak with
such bitterness; and indeed it was true. Never
before had he been assailed on his own ground;
it seemed as if the whole township now con-
spired to bait him.

"Well" she remarked weakly, "I dunno 's it
does any hurt, so long as they can tell what
they mean by it."

Nicholas threw her a pitying glance. He
scorned to waste eternal truth on one so dull.

"Well," she went on, in desperation, "that
ain't all, neither. I might as well say the
whole, an' done with it. He wants 'em to set
up the clock on the meetin'-house; an' seeing
the tower might n't be firm enough, he 'll build
it up higher, an' give 'em a new bell."

Now, indeed, Nicholas Oldfield was in the
case of Shylock, when he learned his daughter's
limit of larceny. "The curse never fell upon
our nation till now," so he might have quoted.
"I never felt it till now."

He rose from his chair.

"In the name of God Almighty," he asked
solemnly, "what do they want of a new bell?"

Young Nick's Hattie gave an involuntary cry.

"O father!" she entreated, "don't say such words. I never see you take on so. What under the sun has got into you?"

Nicholas made no reply. Slowly and methodically he was putting the dishes into the wooden sink. When he touched Mary's pink mug, his fingers trembled a little; but he did not look at her. He knew she understood. Young Nick's Hattie rolled her hands nervously in her apron, and then unrolled them, and smoothed the apron down. She gathered herself desperately.

"Well, father," she said, "I've got another arrant. I said I'd do it, an' I will; but I dunno how you'll take it."

"O mother!" cried Mary, "don't!"

"What is it?" asked Nicholas, folding the tablecloth in careful creases. "Say your say an' git it over."

Hattie rocked faster and faster. Even in the stress of the moment Nicholas remembered that the old chair was well made, and true to its equilibrium.

"Well," said she, "Luella an' Freeman Henry come over here this very day, an' Freeman Henry's possessed you should sell him the Flat-Iron Lot."

"Wants the Flat-Iron Lot, does he?" inquired Nicholas grimly. "What's he made up his mind to do with it?"

"He wants to build," answered Hattie, momentarily encouraged. "He says he'll be glad to ride over to work, every mornin' of his life, if he can only feel 't he's settled in Tiverton for good. An' there's that lot on high ground, right near the meetin'-house, as sightly a place as ever was, an' no good to you, — there ain't half a load o' hay cut there in a season, — an' he'd pay the full vally" —

"Stop!" called Nicholas; and though his tone was conversational, Hattie paused, open-mouthed, in full swing. He turned and faced her. "Hattie," said he, "did you know that the fust settlers of this town had anything to do with that lot o' land?"

"No, I didn't know it," answered Hattie blankly.

"I guess you didn't," concurred Nicholas. He had gone back to his old gentleness of voice. "An' 't wouldn't ha' meant nothin' to ye, if ye had known it. Now, you harken to me! It's my last word. That Flat-Iron Lot stays under this name so long as I'm above ground. When I'm gone, you can do as ye like. Now, I don't want to hurry ye, but I'm goin' down to vote."

Hattie rose, abashed and nearly terrified. "Well!" said she vacantly. "Well!" Nicholas had taken the broom, under pretext of brushing up the crumbs, and he seemed literally to be sweeping her away. It was a wind of destiny; and scudding softly and heavily before it, she disappeared in the gathering dusk.

"Mary!" she called from the gate, "Mary! Guess you better come along with me."

Mary did not hear. She was standing by Nicholas, holding the edge of his sleeve. The unaccustomed action was significant; it bespoke a passionate loyalty. Her blue eyes were on fire, and two hot tears stood in them, unstanched. "O gran'ther!" she cried, "don't you let 'em have it. I wish I was father. I'd see!"

Nicholas Oldfield stood quite still, obedient to that touch upon his arm.

"It's the name, Mary," said he. "Why, Freeman Henry's a Titcomb! He can't help that. But he need n't think he can buy Oldfield land, an' set up a house there, as if 't was all in the day's work. Why, Mary, I meant to leave that land to you! An' p'raps you won't marry. Nobody knows. Then, 't would stand in the name a mite longer."

Mary blushed a little, but her eyes never wavered.

"No, gran'ther," said she firmly, "I sha'n't ever marry anybody."

"Well, ye can't tell," responded Nicholas, with a sigh. "Ye can't tell. He might take your name if he wanted ye enough; but I should call it a poor tool that would do that."

He sighed again, as he reached for his hat,
and Mary and he went out of the house together, hand in hand.　At the gate they
parted, and Nicholas took his way to the
schoolhouse, where the town fathers were already assembled.

Since he passed over it that afternoon, the
road had changed, responsive to twilight and
the coming dark.　Nicholas knew it in all its
phases, from the dawn of spring, vocal with
the peeping of frogs, to the revery of winter,
the silence of snow, and a hopeful glow in the
west.　Just here, by the barberry bush at the
corner, he had stood still under the spell of
Northern Lights.　That was the night when
his wife lay first in Tiverton churchyard; and
he remembered, as a part of the strangeness
and wonder of the time, how the north had
streamed, and the neighboring houses had been
rosy red.　But at this hour of the brooding,
sultry fall, there was a bitter fragrance in the
air, and the world seemed tuned to the som-
nolent sound of crickets, singing the fields to
sleep.　That one little note brooded over the
earth, and all the living things upon it: hovering, and crooning, and lulling them to the rest
decreed from of old.　The homely beauty of it
smote upon him, though it could not cheer.
A hideous progress seemed to threaten, not
alone the few details it touched, but all the
sweet, familiar things of life.　Old War-Wool

Eaton, in assailing the town's historic peace, menaced also the crickets and the breath of asters in the air. He was the rampant spirit of an awful change. So, in the bitterness of revolt, Nicholas Oldfield marched on, and stepped silently into the little schoolhouse, to meet his fellows. They were standing about in groups, each laying down the law according to his kind. The doors were wide open, and Nicholas felt as if he had brought in with him the sounds of coming night. They kept him sane, so that he could hold his own, as he might not have done in a room full of winter brightness.

"Hullo!" cried Caleb Rivers, in his neutral voice. "Here's Mr. Oldfield. Well, Mr. Oldfield, there's a good deal on hand."

"Called any votes?" asked Nicholas.

"Well, no," said Caleb, scraping his chin. "I guess we're sort o' takin' the sense o' the meetin'."

"Good deal like a quiltin' so fur," remarked Brad Freeman indulgently. "All gab an' no git there!"

"They tell me," said Uncle Eli Pike, approaching Nicholas as if he had something to confide, "that out west, where they have them new-fangled clocks, they're all lighted up with 'lectricity."

"Do they so?" asked Caleb, but Nicholas returned, with an unwonted fierceness: —

"Does that go to the right spot with you? Do you want to see a clock-face starin' over Tiverton, like a full moon, chargin' ye to keep Old War-Wool Eaton in memory?"

"Well, no," replied Eli gently, "I dunno's I do, an' I dunno *but* I do."

"Might set a lantern back o' the dial, an' take turns lightin' on 't," suggested Brad Freeman.

"Might carve out a jack-o'-lantern like Old Eaton's face," supplemented Tom O'Neil irreverently.

"Well," concluded Rivers, "I guess, when all's said and done, we might as well take the clock, an' bell, too. When a man makes a fair offer, it's no more 'n civil to close with it. Ye can't rightly heave it back ag'in."

"My argyment is," put in Ebenezer Tolman, who knew how to lay dollar by dollar, "if he's willin' to do one thing for the town, he's willin' to do another. S'pose he offered us a new brick meetin'-house — or a fancy gate to the cemet'ry! Or s'pose he had it in mind to fill in that low land, so 't we could bury there! Why, he could bring the town right up! Or, take it t' other way round; he could put every dollar he's got into Sudleigh."

Nicholas Oldfield groaned, but in the stress of voices no one heard him. He slipped about from one group to another, and always the sentiment was the same. A few smiled at Old

War-Wool Eaton, who desired so urgently to be remembered, when no one was likely to forget him; but all agreed that it was, at the worst, a harmless and natural folly.

"Let him be remembered," said one, with a large impartiality. "'T won't do us no hurt, an' we shall have the clock an' bell."

Just as the meeting was called to order, Nicholas Oldfield stole away, and no one missed him. The proceedings began with some animated discussion, all tending one way. Cupidity had entered into the public soul, and everybody professed himself willing to take the clock, lest, by refusing, some golden future should be marred. Let Old Eaton have his way, if thereby they might beguile him into paving theirs. Let the town grow. Talk was very full and free; but when the moment came for taking a vote, an unexpected sound broke roundly on the air. It was the bell of the old church. One! it tolled. Each man looked at his neighbor. Had death entered the village, and they unaware? Two! three! it went solemnly on, the mellow cadence scarcely dying before another stroke renewed it. The sexton was Simeon Pease, a little red-headed man, a hunchback, abnormally strong. Suddenly he rose in amazement. His face looked ashen.

"Suthin's tollin' the bell!" he gasped. "The bell's a-tollin' an' *I ain't there!*"

A new element of mystery and terror sprang to life.

"The sax'on's here!" whispered one and another. But nobody stirred, for nobody would lose count. Twenty-three! the dead was young. Twenty-four! and so it marched and marched, to thirty and thirty-five. They looked about them, taking a swift inventory of familiar faces, and more than one man felt a tightening about his heart, at thought of the women-folk at home. The record climbed to middle-age, and tolled majestically beyond it, like a life ripening to victorious close. Sixty! seventy! eighty-one!

"It ain't Pa'son True!" whispered an awe-struck voice.

Then on it beat, to the completed century.

The women of Tiverton, in afterwards weighing the immobility of their public representatives under this mysterious clangor, dwelt upon the fact with scorn.

"Well, I should think you was smart!" cried sundry of them in turn. "Set there like a bump on a log, an' wonder what's the matter! Never heard of anything so numb in all my born days. If I was a man, I guess I'd see!"

It was Brad Freeman who broke the spell, with a sudden thought and cry, —

"By thunder! maybe's suthin's afire!"

He leaped to his feet, and with long, loping

strides made his way up the hill to Tiverton church. The men, in one excited, surging rabble, followed him. The women were before them. They, too, had heard the tolling for the unknown dead, and had climbed a quicker way, leaving fire and cradle behind. At the very moment when they were pressing, men and women, to the open church door, the last lingering clang had ceased, the bell lay humming itself to rest, and Nicholas Oldfield strode out and faced them. By this time, factions had broken up, and each woman instinctively sought her husband's side, assuring herself of protection against the unresting things of the spirit. Young Nick's Hattie found her lawful ally, with the rest.

"My soul!" said she in a whisper, "it's father!"

Nicholas touched her arm in warning, and stood silent. He felt that the waters were troubled, as he had known them to be once or twice in his boyhood.

"He's got his mad up," remarked Young Nick to himself. "Stan' from under!"

Nicholas strode through the crowd, and it separated to let him pass. There was about him at that moment an amazing physical energy, apparent even in the dark. He seemed a different man, and one woman whispered to another, "Why, that can't be Mr. Oldfield! It's a head taller."

He walked across the green, and the crowd
turned also, to follow him. There, just opposite the church, lay his own Flat-Iron Lot, and
he stepped into it, over the low stone bound-
ary, and turned about.

"Don't ye come no nearer," called he.
"This is my land. Don't ye set foot on it."

The Flat-Iron Lot was a triangular piece of
ground, rich in drooping elms, and otherwise
varied only by a great boulder looming up
within the wall nearest the church. Nicholas
paused for a moment where he was; then
with a thought of being the better heard, he
turned, ran up the rough side of the boulder,
and faced his fellows. As he stood there,
illumined by the rising moon, he seemed
colossal.

"He'll break his infernal old neck!" said
Brad Freeman admiringly. But no one answered, for Nicholas Oldfield had begun to
speak.

"Don't ye set foot on my land!" he repeated. "Ye ain't wuth it. Do you know
what this land is? It belonged to a man that
settled in a place that knows enough to celebrate its foundin', but don't know enough to
prize what's fell to it. Do you know what I
was doin' of, when I tolled that bell? I'll tell
ye. I tolled a hunderd an' ten strokes. That's
the age of the bell you're goin' to throw aside
to flatter up a man that made money out o' the

war. A hunderd an' twelve years ago that
bell was cast in England ; a hunderd an' ten
years ago 't was sent over here."

"Now, how 's father know that ? " whispered
Hattie disparagingly.

"I 've cast my vote. Them hunderd an'
ten strokes is all the voice I 'll have in the
matter, or any matter, so long as I live in this
God-forsaken town. I 'd ruther die than talk
over a thing like that in open meetin'. It 's
an insult to them that went before ye, an' fit
hunger and cold an' Injuns. I 've got only
one thing more to say," he continued, and
some fancied there came a little break in his
voice. "When ye take the old bell down,
send her out to sea, an' sink her ; or bury her
deep enough in the woods, so 't nobody 'll git
at her till the Judgment Day."

With one descending step, he seemed to
melt away into the darkness; and though
every one stood quite still, expectant, there
was no sound, save that of the crickets and
the night. He had gone, and left them trembling. Well as they knew him, he had all the
effect of some strange herald, freighted with
wisdom from another sphere.

"Well, I swear ! " said Brad Freeman, at
length, and as if a word could shiver the spell,
men and woman turned silently about and went
down the hill. When they reached a lower
plane, they stopped to talk a little, and once

indoors, discussion had its way. Young Nick
and Hattie had walked side by side, feeling
that the eyes of the town were on them, reading
their emblazoned names. But Mary marched
behind them, solemnly and alone. She held
her head very high, knowing what her kins-
folk thought: that gran'ther had disgraced
them. A passionate protest rose within her.

That night, everybody watched the old
house in the shade of the poplars, to see if
Nicholas had "lighted up." But the windows
lay dark, and little Mary, slipping over across
the orchard, when her mother thought her
safe in bed, tried the door in vain. She
pushed at it wildly, and then ran round to the
front, charging against the sentinel hollyhocks,
and letting the knocker fall with a desperate
and repeated clang. The noise she had herself evoked frightened her more than the stillness, and she fled home again, crying softly,
and pursued by all the unresponsive presences
of night.

For weeks Tiverton lay in a state of hushed
expectancy ; one miracle seemed to promise
another. But Nicholas Oldfield's house was
really closed; the windows shone blankly at
men and women who passed, interrogating it.
Young Nick and his Hattie had nothing to
say, after Hattie's one unguarded admission
that she did n't know what possessed father.
The village felt that it had been arraigned be-

fore some high tribunal, only to be found lack-
ing. It had an irritated conviction that, meaning no harm, it should not have been dealt
with so harshly ; and was even moved to declare that, if Nicholas Oldfield knew so much
about what was past and gone, he need n't
have waited till the trump o' doom to say so.
But, somehow, the affair of clock and bell
could not be at once revived, and a vague letter was dispatched to the prospective donor
stating that, in regard to his generous offer,
no decision could at the moment be reached ;
the town was too busy in preparing for its
celebration, which would take place in something over two weeks ; after that the question would be considered. The truth was
that, at the bottom of each heart, still lurked
the natural cupidity of the loyal citizen who
will not see his town denied ; but side by side
with that desire for the march of progress,
walked the spectre of Nicholas Oldfield's wrath.
The trembling consciousness prevailed that he
might at any moment descend again, wrapped
in that inexplicable atmosphere of loftier
meanings.

Still, Tiverton was glad to put the question
by, for she had enough to do. The celebration knocked at the door, and no one was
ready. Only Brad Freeman, always behind-
hand, save at some momentary exigency of rod
or gun, was fulfilling the prophecy that the

last shall be first. For he had, out of the
spontaneity of genius, elected to do one deed
for that great day, and his work was all but
accomplished. In public conclave assembled
to discuss the parade, he had offered to make
an elephant, to lead the van. Tiverton roared,
and then, finding him gravely silent, remained,
with gaping mouth, to hear his story. It
seemed, then, that Brad had always cherished
one dear ambition. He would fain fashion
an elephant ; and having never heard of
Frankenstein, he lacked anticipation of the
dramatic finale likely to attend a meddling
with the creative powers. He did not confess,
save once to his own wife, how many nights
he had lain awake, in their little dark bedroom, planning the anatomy of the eastern
lord ; he simply said that he "wanted to make
the critter," and he thought he could do it.
Immediately the town gave him to understand
that he had full power to draw upon the public
treasury, to the extent of one elephant ; and
the youth, who always flocked adoringly about
him, intimated that they were with him, heart
and soul. Thereupon, in Eli Pike's barn,
selected as of goodly size, creation reveled,
the while a couple of men, chosen for their
true eye and practiced hand, went into the
woods, and chopped down two beautiful slender trees for tusks. For many a day now, the
atmosphere of sacred art had hung about that

barn. Brad was a maker, and everybody felt
it. Fired by no tradition of the horse that
went to the undoing of Troy, and with no plan
before him, he set his framework together,
nailing with unerring hand. Did he need a
design, he who had brooded over his bliss these
many months when Tiverton thought he was
"jest lazin' round?" Nay, it was to be "all
wrought out of the carver's brain," and the
brain was ready.

Often have I wished some worthy chronicler
had been at hand when Tiverton sat by at
the making of the elephant ; and then again
I have realized that, though the atmosphere
was highly charged, it may have been void of
homely talk. For this was a serious moment,
and even when Brad gave sandpaper and glass
into the hands of Lothrop Wilson, the cooper,
bidding him smooth and polish the tusks, there
was no jealousy : only a solemn sense that Mr.
Wilson had been greatly favored. Brad's wife
sewed together a dark slate-colored cambric,
for the elephant's hide, and wet and wrinkled
it, as her husband bade her, for the shambling
shoulders and flanks. It was she who made the
ears, from a pattern cunningly conceived ; and
she stuffed the legs with fine shavings brought
from the planing-mill at Sudleigh. Then there
came an intoxicating day when the trunk took
shape, the glass-bottle eyes were inserted, and
Brad sprung upon a breathless world his one

surprise.   Between the creature's fore-legs, he
disclosed an opening, saying meantime to the
smallest Crane boy, —

"You crawl up there!"

The Crane boy was not valiant, but he reasoned that it was better to seek an unguessed
fate within the elephant than to refuse immortal glory.   Trembling, he crept into the hole,
and was eclipsed.

"Now put your hand up an' grip that rope
that's hangin' there," commanded Brad.
Perhaps he, too, trembled a little.   The heart
beats fast when we approach a great fruition.

"Pull it!   Easy, now! easy!"

The boy pulled, and the elephant moved his
trunk.   He stretched it out, he drew it in.
Never was such a miracle before.   And Tiverton, drunk with glory, clapped and shouted
until the women-folk clutched their sunbon-
nets and ran to see.   No situation since the
war had ever excited such ferment.   Brad was
the hero of his town.   But now arose a natural
rivalry, the reaction from great, impersonal
joy in noble work.   What lad, on that final
day, should ride within the elephant, and move
his trunk?   The Crane boy contended passionately that he held the right of possession.
Had he not been selected first?   Others wept
at home and argued the case abroad, until it
became a common thing to see two young
scions of Tiverton grappling in dusty roadways,

or stoning each other from afar. The public
accommodated itself to such spectacles, and
grown-up relatives, when they came upon little
sons rolling over and over, or sitting triumphantly, the one upon another's chest, would
only remark, as they gripped two shirt collars,
and dragged the combatants apart : —

"Now, what do you want to act so for?
Brad 'll pick out the one he thinks best.
He's got the say."

In vain did mothers argue, at twilight time,
when the little dusty legs in overalls were still,
and stubbed toes did their last wriggling for
the day, that the boy who moved the trunk
could not possibly see the rest of the procession. The candidates, to a boy, rejected that
specious plea.

"What do I want to see anything for, if I
can jest set inside that elephant?" sobbed the
Crane boy angrily. And under every roof the
wail was repeated in many keys.

Meantime, the log cabin had been going
steadily up, and a week before the great day,
it was completed. This was a typical scene-
setting, — the cabin of a first settler, — and
through one wild leap of fancy it became suddenly and dramatically dignified.

"For the land's sake!" said aunt Lucindy,
when she went by and saw it standing, in
modest worth, "ain't they goin' to *do* anythin'
with it? Jest let it set there? Why under

the sun don't they have a party of Injuns
tackle it ?"

The woman who heard repeated the remark
as a sample of aunt Lucindy's desire to have
everything " all of a whew ; " but when it came
to the ears of a certain young man who had
sat brooding, in silent emulation, over the birth
of the elephant, he rose, with fire in his eye,
and went to seek his mates. Indians there
should be, and he, by right of first desire,
should become their leader. Thereupon, turkey feathers came into great demand, and
wattled fowl, once glorious, went drooping de-
jectedly about, while maidens sat in doorways
sewing wampum and leggings for their favored
swains. The first rehearsal of this aboriginal
drama was not an entire success, because the
leader, being unimaginative though faithful,
decreed that faces should be blackened with
burnt cork ; and the result was a tribe of the
African race, greatly astonished at their own
appearance in the family mirror. Then the
doctor suggested walnut juice, and all went
conformably again. But each man wanted to
be an Indian, and no one professed himself
willing to suffer the attack.

" I 'll stay in the cabin, if I can shoot, an'
drop a redskin every time," said Dana Marden
stubbornly ; but no redskin would consent to
be dropped, and naturally no settler could
yield. It would ill befit that glorious day to

see the log cabin taken; but, on the other
hand, what loyal citizen could allow himself to
be defeated, even as a skulking redman, at the
very hour of Tiverton's triumph? For a time
a peaceful solution was promised by the doctor,
who proposed that a party of settlers on horse-
back should come to the rescue, just when a
settler's wife, within the cabin, was in danger
of immolation. That seemed logical and right,
and for days thereafter young men on astonished farm horses went sweeping down Tiverton Street, alternately pursuing and pursued,
while Isabel North, as Priscilla, the Puritan
maiden, trembled realistically at the cabin door.
Just why she was to be Priscilla, a daughter
of Massachusetts, Isabel never knew; the
name had struck the popular fancy, and she
made her costume accordingly. But one day,
when young Tiverton was galloping about the
town, to the sound of ecstatic yells, a farmer
drew up his horse to inquire : —

"Now see here! there's one thing that's
got to be settled. When the day comes, who's
goin' to beat?"

An Indian, his face scarlet with much sound,
and his later state not yet apparent, in that
his wampum, blanket, and horsehair wig lay
at home, on the best-room bed, made answer
hoarsely, "We be!"

"Not by a long chalk!" returned the other,
and the settlers growled in unison. They had

all a patriot's pride in upholding white blood against red.

"Well, by gum! then you can look out for your own Injuns!" returned their chief. "*My* last gun 's fired."

Settlers and Indians turned sulkily about; they rode home in two separate factions, and the streets were stilled. Isabel North went faithfully on, making her Priscilla dress, but it seemed, in those days, as if she might remain in her log cabin, unattacked and undefended. Tiverton was to be deprived of its one dramatic spectacle. Young men met one another in the streets, remarked gloomily, "How are ye?" and passed by. There were no more curdling yells at which even the oxen lifted their dull ears; and one youth went so far as to pack his Indian suit sadly away in the garret, as a jilted girl might lay aside her wedding gown. It was a sullen and all but universal feud.

Now in all this time two prominent citizens had let public opinion riot as it would, — the minister and the doctor. The minister, a grave-faced, brown-bearded young man, had seen fit to get run down, and have an attack of slow fever, from which he was just recovering; and the doctor had been spending most of his time in Saltash, with an epidemic of mumps. But the mumps subsided, and the minister gained strength; so, being public-spirited men, these two at once concerned themselves in village affairs. The first thing the minister did was to call on Nicholas Old-field, and Young Nick's Hattie saw him there, knocking at the front door.

"Mary! Mary!" cried she, "if there ain't the young pa'son over to your grandpa's. I dunno when anybody's called there, he's away so much. Like as not he's heard how father carried on that night, an' now he's got out, he's come right over, first thing, to tell him what folks think."

Mary looked up from the serpentine braid she was crocheting.

"Well, I guess he'd better not," she threatened. And her mother, absorbed by curiosity, contented herself with the reproof implied in a shaken head and pursed-up lips.

A sad and curious change had befallen Mary. She looked older. One week had dimmed her brightness, and little puckers between her eyes were telling a story of anxious care. For gran'-ther had been home without her seeing him. Mary felt as if he had repudiated the town. She knew well that he had not abandoned her with it, but she could guess what the loss of larger issues meant to him. Young Nick, if he had been in the habit of expressing himself, would have said that father's mad was still up. Mary knew he was grieved, and she grieved also. She had not expected him until the end

of the week. Then watching wistfully, she saw
the darkness come, and knew next day would
bring him; but the next day it was the same.
One placid afternoon, a quick thought assailed
her, and stained her cheek with crimson. She
laid down the sheet which was her "stent"
of over-edge, and ran with flying feet to the
little house. Hanging by her hands upon the
sill of the window nearest the clock, she laid
her ear to the glass. The clock was ticking
serenely, as of old. Gran'ther had been home
to wind it. So he had come in the night, and
slipped away again in silence !

"There ! he 's gi'n it up !" cried Hattie, still
watching the minister. "He 's turnin' down
the path. My land ! he 's headed this way.
He 's comin' here. You beat up that cushion,
an' throw open the best-room door. My soul !
if your grandpa's goin' to set the whole town
by the ears, I wisht he 'd come home an' fight
his own battles ! "

Hattie did not look at her young daughter ;
but if she had looked, she might have been
amazed. Mary stood firm as iron ; she was
more than ever a chip o' the old block.

When the young minister had somewhat
weakly climbed the two front steps, he elected
not to sit in the best room, for he was a little
chilly, and would like the sun. Presently he
was installed in the new cane-backed rocker,

and Mrs. Oldfield had offered him some currant wine.

"Though I dunno's you would," said she, anxiously flaunting a principle righteous as his own. "I s'pose you're teetotal."

The minister would not have wine, and he could not stay.

"I've really come on business," said he. "Do you know anything about Mr. Oldfield?"

So strong was the family conviction that Nicholas had involved them in disgrace, that Mary glanced up fiercely, and her mother gave an apologetic cough.

"Well," said Young Nick's Hattie, "I dunno's I know anything particular about father."

"Where is he, I mean," asked the minister. "I want to see him. I've got to."

"Gran'ther's gone away," announced Mary, looking up at him with hot and loyal eyes. "We don't know where." Her fingers trembled, and she lost her stitch. She was furious with herself for not being calmer. It seemed as if gran'ther had a right to demand it of her. The minister bent his brows impatiently.

"Why, I depended on seeing Mr. Oldfield," said he, with the fractiousness of a man recently ill. "This sickness of mine has put me back tremendously. I've got to make the address, and I don't know what to say. I

meant to read town records and hunt up old
stories; and then when I was sick I thought,
' Never mind! Mr. Oldfield will have it all at
his tongue's end.' And now he is n't here,
and I 'm all at sea without him."

This was perhaps the first time that Young
Nick's Hattie had ever looked upon her father's
pursuits with anything but a pitying eye. A
frown of perplexity grew between her brows.
Her brain ached in expanding. Mary leaned
forward, her face irradiated with pure delight.

"Why, yes," said she, at once accepting the
minister for a friend, "gran'ther could tell you,
if he was here. He knows everything."

"You see," continued the minister, now ad-
dressing her, "there are facts enough that are
common talk about the town, but we only half
know them. The first settlers came from
Devon. Well, where did they enter the town ?
From which point ? Sudleigh side, or along by
the river ? I incline to the river. The doctor
says it would be a fine symbolic thing to take
the procession up to the church by the very
way the first settlers came in. But where was
it ? I don't know, and nobody does, unless
it 's Nicholas Oldfield."

Mary folded her hands, in proud composure.

" Yes, sir," said she, "gran'ther knows. He
could tell you, if he was here."

" I should like to inquire what makes you so
certain, Mary Oldfield," asked her mother,

with the natural irritation of the unprepared. "I should like to know how father's got hold of things pa'son and doctor ain't neither of 'em heard of?"

"Why," said the minister, rising, "he's simply crammed with town legends. He can repeat them by the yard. He's a local historian. But then, I need n't tell you that; you know what an untiring student he has been." And he went away thoughtful and discouraged, omitting, as Hattie realized with awe, to offer prayer.

Mary stepped joyously about, getting supper and singing "Hearken, Ye Sprightly!" in an exultant voice; but her mother brooded. It was not until dusk, when the three sat before the clock-room fire, "blazed" rather for company than warmth, that Young Nick's Hattie opened her mouth and spoke.

"Mary," said she, "how'd you find out your grandpa was such great shakes?"

Mary was in some things much older than her mother. She answered demurely, "I don't know as I can say."

"Nick," continued Hattie, turning to her spouse, "did you ever hear your father was smarter 'n the minister an' doctor put together, so 't they had to run round beseechin' him to tell 'em how to act?"

Nicholas knocked his pipe against the andiron, and rose, to lay it carefully on the shelf.

"I can't say 's I did," he returned. Then he set forth for Eli Pike's barn, where it was customary now to stand about the elephant and prophesy what Tiverton might become. As for Hattie, realizing how little light she was likely to borrow from those who were nearest and dearest her, she remarked that she should like to shake them both.

The next day began a new and exciting era. It was bruited abroad that the presence of Nicholas Oldfield was necessary for the success of the celebration; and now young men but lately engaged in unprofitable warfare rode madly over the county in search of him. They inquired for him at taverns; they sought him in farmhouses where he had been wont to lodge. He gained almost the terrible notoriety of an absconding cashier; and the current issue of the Sudleigh "Star" wore a flaming headline, "No Trace of Mr. Oldfield Yet!"

Mary at first waxed merry over the pursuit. She knew very well why gran'ther was staying away; and her pride grew insolent at seeing him sought in vain. But when his loss flared out at her in sacred print, she stared for a moment, and then, after that wide-eyed, piteous glance at the possibilities of things, walked with a firm tread to her little room. There she knelt down, and buried her face in the bed, being careful, meanwhile, not to rumple the valance. At last she knew the truth; he was dead, and village gossip seemed a small thing in comparison.

It would have been difficult, as time went on, to convince the rest of the township that Mr. Oldfield was not in a better world.

"They 'd ha' found him, if he 's above ground," said the fathers, full of faith in the detective instinct of their coursing sons. It seemed incredible that sons should ride so fast and far, and come to nothing. "Never was known to go out o' the county, an' they 've rid over it from one eend to t'other. Must ha' made way with himself. He wa'n't quite right, that time he tolled the bell."

They found ominous parallels of peddlers who had been murdered in byways, or stuck in swamps, and even cited a Tivertonian, of low degree, who was once caught beneath the chin by a clothes-line, and remained there, under the impression that he was being hanged, until the family came out in the morning, and tilted him the other way.

"But then," they added, "he was a drinkin' man, an' Mr. Oldfield never was known to touch a drop, even when he had a tight cold."

Dark as the occasion waxed, what with feuds and presentiments of ill, there was some casual comfort in rolling this new tragedy as a sweet morsel under the tongue, and a mournful plea-sure in referring to the night when poor Mr. Oldfield was last seen alive. So time went on to the very eve of the celebration, and it was as well that the celebration had never been. For kindly as Tiverton proved herself, in the main, and closely welded in union against rival towns, now it seemed as if the hand of every man were raised against his brother. Settlers and Indians were still implacable ; neither would ride, save each might slay the other. The Crane boy tossed in bed, swollen to the eyes with an evil tooth ; and his exulting mates so besieged Brad Freeman for preferment, that even that philosopher's patience gave way, and he said he'd be hanged if he'd take the elephant out at all, if there was going to be such a to-do about it. Even the minister sulked, though he wore a pretense of dignity ; for he had concocted a short address with very little history in it, and that all hearsay, and the doctor had said lightly, looking it over, "Well, old man, not much of it, is there ? But there's enough of it, such as it is."

It was in vain for the doctor to declare that this was a colloquialism which might mean much or little, as you chose to take it. The minister, justly hurt, remarked that, when a man was in a tight place, he needed the support of his friends, if he had any ; and the doctor went whistling drearily away, conscious that he could have said much worse about the address, without doing it justice.

The only earthly circumstance which seemed

to be fulfilling its duty toward Tiverton was the weather. That shone seraphically bright. The air was never so soft, the skies were never so clear and far, and they were looking down indulgently on all this earthly turmoil when, something before midnight, on the fateful eve, Nicholas Oldfield went up the path to his side-door, and stumbled over despairing Mary on the step.

"What under the heavens" — he began; but Mary precipitated herself upon him, and held him with both hands. The moral tension, which had held her hopeless and rigid, gave way. She was sobbing wildly.

"O gran'ther!" she moaned, over and over again. "O gran'ther!"

Nicholas managed somehow to get the door open and walk in, hampered as he was by the clinging arms of his tall girl. Then he sat down in the big chair, taking Mary there too, and stroked her cheek. Perhaps he could hardly have done it in the light, but at that moment it seemed very natural. For a long time neither of them spoke. Mary had no words, and it may be that Nicholas could not seek for them. At last she began, catching her breath tremulously : —

"They've hunted everywhere, gran'ther. They've rode all over the county; and after the celebration, they're going to — dr— drag the pond!"

"Well, I guess I can go out o' the county if I want to," responded Nicholas calmly. "I come across a sheet in them rec'ids that told about a pewter communion set over to Rocky Ridge, an' I 've found part on 't in a tavern there. Who put 'em up to all this work? Your father?"

"No," sobbed Mary. "The minister."

"The minister? What 's he want?"

"He 's got to write an address, and he wants you to tell him what to say."

Then, in the darkness of the room, a slow smile stole over Nicholas Oldfield's face, but his voice remained quite grave.

"Does, does he?" he remarked. "Well, he ain't the fust pa'son that 's needed a lift; but he 's the fust one ever I knew to ask for it. I 've got nothin' for 'em, Mary. I come home to wind up the clocks; but I ain't goin' to stand by a town that 'll swaller a Memory-o'-Me timekeeper an' murder the old bell. You can say I was here, an' they need n't go to muddyin' up the ponds; but as to their doin's, they can carry 'em out as they may. I 've no part nor lot in 'em."

Mary, in the weakness of her kind, was wiser than she knew. She drew her arms about his neck, and clung to him the closer. All this talk of plots and counter-plots seemed very trivial now that she had him back; and being only a child, wearied with care and

watching, she went fast asleep on his shoulder.
Nicholas felt tired too ; but he thought he had
only dozed a little when he opened his eyes on
a gleam of morning, and saw the doctor come
striding into the yard.

"Your door's open!" called the doctor.
"You must be at home to callers. Morning,
Mary! Either of you sick?"

Mary, abashed, drew herself away, and
slipped into the sitting-room, a hand upon her
tumbled hair ; the doctor, wise in his honesty,
slashed at the situation without delay.

"See here, Mr. Oldfield," said he, "whether
you've slept or not, you've got to come right
over to parson's with me, and straighten him
out. He's all balled up. You are as bad as
the rest of us. You think we don't know
enough to refuse a clock like a comic valen-
tine, and you think we don't prize that old bell.
How are we going to prize things if nobody
tells us anything about them? And here's
the town going to pieces over a celebration
it hasn't sense enough to plan, just because
you're so obstinate. Oh, come along! Hear
that! The boys are begining to toot, and fire
off their crackers, and Tiverton's going to the
dogs, and Sudleigh'll be glad of it! Come,
Mr. Oldfield, come along!"

Nicholas stood quite calmly looking through
the window into the morning dew and mist.
He wore his habitual air of gentle indifference,

and the doctor saw in him those everlasting
hills which persuasion may not climb. Suddenly there was a rustling from the other
room, and Mary appeared in the doorway,
standing there expectant. Her face was pink
and a little vague from sleep, but she looked
very dear and good. Though Nicholas had
"lost himself" that night, he had kept time
for thought; and perhaps he realized how
precious a thing it is to lay up treasure of inheritance for one who loves us, and is truly
of our kind. He turned quite meekly to the
doctor.

"Should you think," he inquired, "should
you think pa'son would be up an' dressed?"

Ten minutes thereafter, the two were knocking at the parson's door.

Confused and turbulent as Tiverton had become, Nicholas Oldfield settled her at once.
Knowledge dripped from his finger-ends; he
had it ready, like oil to give a clock. Doctor
and minister stood breathless while he laid out
the track for the procession by local marks
they both knew well.

"They must ha' come into the town from
som'er's nigh the old cross-road," said he.
"No, 't wa'n't where they made the river road.
Then they turned straight to one side — 't was
thick woods then, you understand — an' went
up a little ways towards Horn o' the Moon.
But they concluded that would n't suit 'em,

't was so barren-like ; an' they wheeled round, took what's now the old turnpike, an' clim' right up Tiverton Hill, through Tiverton Street that now is. An' there " — Nicholas Oldfield's eyes burned like blue flame, and again he told the story of the Flat-Iron Lot.

" Indeed ! " cried the parson. " What a truly remarkable circumstance ! We might halt on that very spot, and offer prayer, before entering the church."

" 'Pears as if that would be about the rights on 't," said Nicholas quietly. " That is, if anybody wanted to plan it out jest as 't was." He could free his words from the pride of life, but not his voice ; it quivered and betrayed him.

" Your idea would be to have the services before going down for the Indian raid ? " inquired the doctor. " They 're all at loggerheads there."

But Nicholas, hearing how neither faction would forego its glory, had the remedy ready in a cranny of his brain.

" Well," said he, " you know there was a raid in '53, when both sides gi'n up an' run. A crazed creatur on a white horse galloped up an' dispersed 'em. He was all wropped up in a sheet, and carried a jack-o'-lantern on a pole over his head, so 't he seemed more 'n nine feet high. The settlers thought 't was a spirit ; an' as for the Injuns, Lord knows what 't was to them. 'T any rate, the raid was over."

"Heaven be praised!" cried the doctor fervently. "Allah is great, and you, Mr. Oldfield, are his prophet. Stay here and coach the parson while I start up the town."

The doctor dashed home and mounted his horse. It was said that he did some tall riding that day. From door to door he galloped, a lesser Paul Revere, but sowing seeds of harmony. It was true that the soil was ready. Indians in full costume were lurking down cellar or behind kitchen doors, swearing they would never ride, but tremblingly eager to be urged. Settlers, gloomily acquiescent in an unjust fate, brightened at his heralding. The ghost was the thing. It took the popular fancy; and everybody wondered, as after all illuminings of genius, why nobody had thought of it before. Brad Freeman was unanimously elected to act the part, as the only living man likely to manage a supplementary head without rehearsal; and Pillsbury's white colt was hastily groomed for the onslaught. Brad had at once seen the possibilities of the situation and decided, with an unerring certainty, that as a jack-o'-lantern is naught by day, the pumpkin face must be cunningly veiled. He was a busy man that morning; for he not only had to arrange his own ghostly progress, but settle the elephant on its platform, to be dragged by vine-wreathed oxen, and also, at the doctor's instigation, to make the sledge on which the first Nicholas

Oldfield should draw his wife into town.   The
doctor sought out Young Nick, and asked him
to undertake the part, as tribute to his illus-
trious name; but he was of a prudent nature
and declined.   What if the town should laugh!
"I guess I won't," said he.

But Mary, regardless of maternal cacklings,
sped after the doctor as he turned his horse.

"O doctor!" she besought, "let me be the
first settler's wife!   Please, *please* let me be
Mary Oldfield!"

The doctor was glad enough.   All the tides
of destiny were surging his way.   Even when
he paused, in his progress, to pull the Crane
boy's tooth, it seemed to work out public harmony.   For the victim, cannily anxious to
prove his valor, insisted on having the opera-
tion conducted before the front window; and
after it was accomplished, the squads of boys
waiting at the gate for his apotheosis or down-
fall, gave an unwilling yet delighted yell.   He
had not winced; and when, with the fire of a
dear ambition still shining in his eyes, he held
up the tooth to them, through the glass, they
realized that he, and he only, could with justice
take the crown of that most glorious day.   He
must ride inside the elephant.

So it came to pass that when the procession
wound slowly up from the cross-road, preceded
by the elephant, lifting his trunk at rhythmic intervals, Nicholas Oldfield saw his little

Mary, her eyes shining and her cheeks aglow, sitting proudly upon a sledge, drawn by the handsomest young man in town. A pang may have struck the old man's heart, realizing that Phil Marden was so splendid in his strength, and that he wore so sweet a look of invitation; but he remembered Mary's vow and was content. A great pride and peace enwrapped him when the procession halted at the Flat-Iron Lot, and the minister, lifting up his voice, explained to the townspeople why they were called upon to pause. The name of Oldfield sounded clearly on the air.

"Now," said the minister, "let us pray." The petition went forth, and Mr. Oldfield stood brooding there, his thoughts running back through a long chain of ancestry to the Almighty, Who is the fount of all.

When heads were covered again, and this little world began to surge into the church, young Nick's Hattie moved closer to her husband and shot out a sibilant whisper : —

"Did you know that ? — about the Flat-Iron Lot ? "

Young Nick shook his head. He was entirely dazed.

"Well," continued Hattie, full of awe, " I guess I never was nearer my end than when I let myself be go-between for Freeman Henry. I wonder father let me get out alive."

The minister's address was very short and unpretending. He dwelt on the sacredness of the past, and all its memories, and closed by saying that, while we need not shrink from signs of progress, we should guard against tampering with those ancient landmarks which serve as beacon lights, to point the brighter way. Hearing that, every man steeled his heart against Memory-of-Me clocks, and resolved to vote against them. Then the minister explained that, since he had been unable to prepare a suitable address, Mr. Oldfield had kindly consented to read some precious records recently discovered by him. A little rustling breath went over the audience. So this amiable lunacy had its bearing on the economy of life! They were amazed, as may befall us at any judgment day, when grays are strangely alchemized to white.

Mr. Oldfield, unmoved as ever, save in a certain dominating quality of presence, rose and stood before them, the records in his hands. He read them firmly, explaining here and there, his simple speech untouched by finer usage; and when the minister interposed a question, he dropped into such quaintness of rich legendry that his hearers sat astounded. So they were a part of the world! and not the world to-day, but the universe in its making.

It was long before Nicholas concluded; but the time seemed brief. He sat down, and the minister took the floor. He thanked Mr. Old-

field and then went on to say that, although it
might be informal, he would suggest that the
town, with Mr. Oldfield's permission, place an
inscription on the boulder in the Flat-Iron
Lot, stating why it was to be held historically
sacred. The town roared and stamped, but
meanwhile Nicholas Oldfield was quietly rising.

"In that case, pa'son," said he, "I should
like to state that it would be my purpose to
make over that lot to the town to be held as
public land forever."

Again the village folk outdid themselves in
applause, while Young Nick muttered, "Well,
I vum!" beneath his breath, and Hattie replied, antiphonally, "My soul!" These were
not the notes of mere surprise. They were
prayers for guidance in this exigency of finding
a despised intelligence exalted.

The celebration went on to a victorious close.
Who shall sing the sweetness of Isabel North,
as she sat by the log-cabin door, placidly spinning flax, or the horror of the moment when,
redskins swooping down on her and settlers on
them, the ghost swept in and put them all to
flight? Who will ever forget the exercises in
the hall, when the "Suwanee River" was sung
by minstrels, to a set of tableaux representing
the "old folks" at their cabin door, "playin'
wid my brudder" as a game of stick-knife, and
the "Swanny" River itself by a frieze of white
pasteboard swans in the background? There

were patriotic songs, accompanied by remarks laudatory of England; since it was justly felt that our mother-land might be wounded if, on an occasion of this sort, we fomented international differences by "America" or the reminiscent triumph of "The Sword of Bunker Hill." A very noble sentiment pervaded Tiverton when, at twilight, little groups of tired and very happy people lingered here and there before "harnessing up" and betaking themselves to their homes. The homes themselves meant more to them now, not as shelters, but as sacred shrines; and many a glance sought out Nicholas Oldfield standing quietly by — the reverential glance accorded those who find out unsuspected wealth. Young Nick approached his father with an awkwardness sitting more heavily upon him than usual.

"Well," said he, "I'm mighty glad you gi'n 'em that lot."

Old Nicholas nodded gravely, and at that moment Hattie came up, all in a flutter.

"Father," said she quite appealingly, "I wisht you'd come over to supper. Luella an' Freeman Henry'll be there. It's a great day, an'" —

"Yes, I know 't is," answered Nicholas kindly. "I'm much obleeged, but Mary's goin' to eat with me. Mebbe we might look in, along in the evenin'. Come, Mary!"

Mary, very sweet in her plain dress and

white kerchief, was talking with young Marden, her husband for the day; but she turned about contentedly.

"Yes, gran'ther," said she, without a look behind, "I'm coming!"

THE END OF ALL LIVING

THE First Church of Tiverton stands on a
hill, whence it overlooks the little village, with
one or two pine-shaded neighborhoods beyond,
and, when the air is clear, a thin blue line of
upland delusively like the sea. Set thus aus-
terely aloft, it seems now a survival of the day
when men used to go to meeting gun in hand,
and when one stayed, a lookout by the door,
to watch and listen. But this the present
dwellers do not remember. Conceding not a
sigh to the holy and strenuous past, they
lament — and the more as they grow older —
the stiff climb up the hill, albeit to rest in so
sweet a sanctuary at the top. For it is sweet
indeed. A soft little wind seems always to be
stirring there, on summer Sundays a messenger of good. It runs whispering about, and
wafts in all sorts of odors : honey of the milk-
weed and wild rose, and a Christmas tang of
the evergreens just below. It carries away
something, too — scents calculated to bewilder
the thrift-hunting bee : sometimes a whiff of
peppermint from an old lady's pew, but oftener
the breath of musk and southernwood, gathered in ancient gardens, and borne up here to

embroider the preacher's drowsy homilies, and
remind us, when we faint, of the keen savor of
righteousness.

Here in the church do we congregate from
week to week; but behind it, on a sloping
hillside, is the last home of us all, the old bury-
ing-ground, overrun with a briery tangle, and
relieved by Nature's sweet and cunning hand
from the severe decorum set ordinarily about
the dead.   Our very faithlessness has made it
fair.   There was a time when we were a little
ashamed of it.   We regarded it with affection,
indeed, but affection of the sort accorded some
rusty relative who has lain too supine in the rut
of years.   Thus, with growing ambition came,
in due course, the project of a new burying-
ground.   This we dignified, even in common
speech; it was always grandly "the Cemetery."   While it lay unrealized in the distance,
the home of our forbears fell into neglect, and
Nature marched in, according to her lavish-
ness, and adorned what we ignored.   The
white alder crept farther and farther from its
bounds; tansy and wild rose rioted in pro-
fusion, and soft patches of violets smiled to
meet the spring.   Here were, indeed, great
riches, "a little of everything" that pasture
life affords: a hardy bed of checkerberry,
crimson strawberries nodding on long stalks,
and in one sequestered corner the beloved
Linnæa.   It seemed a consecrated pasture

shut off from daily use, and so given up to pleasantness that you could scarcely walk there without setting foot on some precious outgrowth of the spring, or pushing aside a summer loveliness better made for wear.

Ambition had its fulfillment. We bought our Cemetery, a large, green tract, quite square, and lying open to the sun. But our pendulum had swung too wide. Like many folk who suffer from one discomfort, we had gone to the utmost extreme and courted another. We were tired of climbing hills, and so we pressed too far into the lowland; and the first grave dug in our Cemetery showed three inches of water at the bottom. It was in "Prince's new lot," and there his young daughter was to lie. But her lover had stood by while the men were making the grave ; and, looking into the ooze below, he woke to the thought of her fair young body there.

"God!" they heard him say, "she sha'n't lay so. Leave it as it is, an' come up into the old buryin'-ground. There's room enough by me."

The men, all mates of his, stopped work without a glance and followed him ; and up there in the dearer shrine her place was made. The father said but a word at her changed estate. Neighbors had hurried in to bring him the news ; he went first to the unfinished grave in the Cemetery, and then strode up the hill, where the men had not yet done. After watching them for a while in silence, he turned aside; but he came back to drop a trembling hand upon the lover's arm.

"I guess," he said miserably, "she'd full as lieves lay here by you."

And she will be quite beside him, though, in the beaten ways of earth, others have come between. For years he lived silently and apart; but when his mother died, and he and his father were left staring at the dulled embers of life, he married a good woman, who perhaps does not deify early dreams; yet she is tender of them, and at the death of her own child it was she who went toiling up to the graveyard, to see that its little place did not encroach too far. She gave no reason, but we all knew it was because she meant to let her husband lie there by the long-loved guest.

Naturally enough, after this incident of the forsaken grave, we conceived a strange horror of the new Cemetery, and it has remained deserted to this day. It is nothing but a meadow now, with that one little grassy hollow in it to tell a piteous tale. It is mown by any farmer who chooses to take it for a price; but we regard it differently from any other plot of ground. It is "the Cemetery," and always will be. We wonder who has bought the grass. "Eli's got the Cemetery this year," we say. And sometimes awe-stricken little squads of school children lead one another there, hand in hand, to look at the grave where Annie Prince was going to be buried when her beau took her away. They never seem to connect that heart-broken wraith of a lover with the bent farmer who goes to and fro driving the cows. He wears patched overalls, and has sciatica in winter; but I have seen the gleam of youth awakened, though remotely, in his eyes. I do not believe he ever quite forgets ; there are moments, now and then, at dusk or midnight, all his for poring over those dulled pages of the past.

After we had elected to abide by our old home, we voted an enlargement of its bounds ; and thereby hangs a tale of outlawed revenge. Long years ago "old Abe Eaton" quarreled with his twin brother, and vowed, as the last fiat of an eternal divorce, " I won't be buried in the same yard with ye ! "

The brother died first ; and because he lay within a little knoll beside the fence, Abe willfully set a public seal on that iron oath by purchasing a strip of land outside, wherein he should himself be buried. Thus they would rest in a hollow correspondence, the fence between. It all fell out as he ordained, for we in Tiverton are cheerfully willing to give the dead their way. Lax enough is the helpless hand in the fictitious stiffness of its grasp ; and we are not the people to deny it holding, by cour-

tesy at least.   Soon enough does the sceptre
of mortality crumble and fall.   So Abe was
buried according to his wish.   But when necessity commanded us to add unto ourselves another acre, we took in his grave with it, and
the fence, falling into decay, was never renewed.   There he lies, in affectionate decorum,
beside the brother he hated ; and thus does the
greater good wipe out the individual wrong.

So now, as in ancient times, we toil steeply
up here, with the dead upon his bier ; for not
often in Tiverton do we depend on that un-
couth monstrosity, the hearse.   It is not that
we do not own one, — a rigid box of that name
has belonged to us now for many a year ; and
when Sudleigh came out with a new one,
plumes, trappings, and all, we broached the
idea of emulating her.   But the project fell
through after Brad Freeman's contented remark that he guessed the old one would last
us out.   He "never heard no complaint from
anybody 't ever rode in it."   That placed our
last journey on a homely, humorous basis, and
we smiled, and reflected that we preferred going
up the hill borne by friendly hands, with the
light of heaven falling on our coffin-lids.

The antiquary would set much store by our
headstones, did he ever find them out.   Certain of them are very ancient, according to our
ideas ; for they came over from England, and
are now fallen into the grayness of age.   They

are woven all over with lichens, and the black-
berry binds them fast.   Well, too, for them!
They need the grace of some such veiling; for
most of them are alive, even to this day, with
warning skulls, and awful cherubs compounded
of bleak, bald faces and sparsely feathered
wings.   One discovery, made there on a summer day, has not, I fancy, been duplicated in
another New England town.   On six of the
larger tombstones are carved, below the grass
level, a row of tiny imps, grinning faces and
humanized animals.   Whose was the hand that
wrought?   The Tivertonians know nothing
about it.   They say there was a certain old
Veasey who, some eighty odd years ago, used
to steal into the graveyard with his tools, and
there, for love, scrape the mosses from the
stones and chip the letters clear.   He liked to
draw, "creatur's" especially, and would trace
them for children on their slates.   He lived
alone in a little house long since fallen, and he
would eat no meat.   That is all they know of
him.   I can guess but one thing more: that
when no looker-on was by, he pushed away
the grass, and wrote his little jokes, safe in the
kindly tolerance of the dead.   This was the
identical soul who should, in good old days,
have been carving gargoyles and misereres;
here his only field was the obscurity of Tiverton churchyard, his only monument these
grotesqueries so cunningly concealed.

We have epitaphs, too, — all our own as yet,
for the world has not discovered them. One
couple lies in well-to-do respectability under a
tiny monument not much taller than the conventional gravestone, but shaped on a pre-
tentious model.

"We 'd ruther have it nice," said the build-
ers, "even if there ain't much of it."

These were Eliza Marden and Peleg her husband, who worked from sun to sun, with scant
reward save that of pride in their own fore-
handedness. I can imagine them as they drove
to church in the open wagon, a couple portentously large and prosperous: their one child,
Hannah, sitting between them, and glancing
about her, in a flickering, intermittent way, at
the pleasant holiday world. Hannah was no
worker; she liked a long afternoon in the sun,
her thin little hands busied about nothing
weightier than crochet; and her mother regarded her with a horrified patience, as one
who might some time be trusted to sow all her
wild oats of idleness. The well-mated pair
died within the same year, and it was Hannah
who composed their epitaph, with an artistic
accuracy, but a defective sense of rhyme: —

> " Here lies Eliza
> She was a striver
> Here lies Peleg
> He was a select
> Man "

We townsfolk found something haunting and bewildering in the lines ; they drew, and yet they baffled us, with their suggested echoes luring only to betray. Hannah never wrote anything else, but we always cherished the belief that she could do "'most anything" with words and their possibilities. Still, we accepted her one crowning achievement, and never urged her to further proof. In Tiverton we never look genius in the mouth. Nor did Hannah herself propose developing her gift. Relieved from the spur of those two unquiet spirits who had begotten her, she settled down to sit all day in the sun, learning new patterns of crochet ; and having cheerfully let her farm run down, she died at last in a placid poverty.

Then there was Desire Baker, who belonged to the era of colonial hardship, and who, through a redundant punctuation, is relegated to a day still more remote. For some stone-cutter, scornful of working by the card, or born with an inordinate taste for periods, set forth, below her *obiit*, the astounding statement : —

"The first woman. She made the journey to Boston. By stage."

Here, too, are the ironies whereof departed life is prodigal. This is the tidy lot of Peter Merrick, who had a desire to stand well with the world, in leaving it, and whose purple and fine linen were embodied in the pomp of death. He was a cobbler, and he put his small savings

together to erect a modest monument to his
own memory. Every Sunday he visited it,
"after meetin'," and perhaps his day-dreams,
as he sat leather-aproned on his bench, were
still of that white marble idealism. The inscription upon it was full of significant blanks;
they seemed an interrogation of the destiny
which governs man.

"Here lies Peter Merrick —— " ran the unfinished scroll, "and his wife who died —— "

But ambitious Peter never lay there at all;
for in his later prime, with one flash of sharp
desire to see the world, he went on a voyage
to the Banks, and was drowned. And his wife?
The story grows somewhat threadbare. She
summoned his step-brother to settle the estate,
and he, a marble-cutter by trade, filled in the
date of Peter's death with letters English and
illegible. In the process of their carving, the
widow stood by, hands folded under her apron
from the midsummer sun. The two got excellent well acquainted, and the stone-cutter prolonged his stay. He came again in a little over
a year, at Thanksgiving time, and they were
married. Which shows that nothing is certain
in life, — no, not the proprieties of our leaving
it, — and that even there we must walk softly,
writing no boastful legend for time to annul.

At one period a certain quatrain had a great
run in Tiverton; it was the epitaph of the day.
Noting how it overspread that stony soil, you

picture to yourself the modest pride of its com-
poser ; unless, indeed, it had been copied from
an older inscription in an English yard, and
transplanted through the heart and brain of
some settler whose thoughts were ever flitting
back.   Thus it runs in decorous metre : —

> " Dear husband, now my life is passed,
> You have dearly loved me to the last.
> Grieve not for me, but pity take
> On my dear children for my sake."

But one sorrowing widower amended it, according to his wife's direction, so that it bore a new
and significant meaning.   He was charged to

> "pity take
> On my dear parent for my sake."

The lesson was patent.   His mother-in-law
had always lived with him, and she was " difficult."   Who knows how keenly the sick woman's mind ran on the possibilities of reef and
quicksand for the alien two left alone without
her guiding hand ?   So she set the warning of
her love and fear to be no more forgotten while
she herself should be remembered.

The husband was a silent man.   He said
very little about his intentions ; performance
was enough for him.   Therefore it happened
that his " parent," adopted perforce, knew nothing about this public charge until she came
upon it, on her first Sunday visit, surveying
the new glory of the stone.   The story goes
that she stood before it, a square, portentous

figure in black alpaca and warlike mitts, and
that she uttered these irrevocable words : —

"Pity on *me !* Well, I guess he won't ! I 'll
go to the poor-farm fust !"

And Monday morning, spite of his loyal dis-
suasions, she packed her "blue chist," and
drove off to a far-away cousin, who got her
"nussin'" to do. Another lesson from the
warning finger of Death : let what was life not
dream that it can sway the life that is, after
the two part company.

Not always were mothers-in-law such break-
ers of the peace. There is a story in Tiverton
of one man who went remorsefully mad after
his wife's death, and whose mind dwelt unceas-
ingly on the things he had denied her. These
were not many, yet the sum seemed to him
colossal. It piled the Ossa of his grief. Especially did he writhe under the remembrance of
certain blue dishes she had desired the week
before her sudden death ; and one night, driven
by an insane impulse to expiate his blindness,
he walked to town, bought them, and placed
them in a foolish order about her grave. It
was a puerile, crazy deed, but no one smiled,
not even the little children who heard of it
next day, on the way home from school, and
went trudging up there to see. To their stirring minds it seemed a strange departure from
the comfortable order of things, chiefly because
their elders stood about with furtive glances at

one another and murmurs of " Poor creatur' ! "
But one man, wiser than the rest, " harnessed
up," and went to tell the dead woman's mother, a mile away.   Jonas was " shackled ; " he
might " do himself a mischief."   In the late
afternoon, the guest so summoned walked
quietly into the silent house, where Jonas sat
by the window, beating one hand incessantly
upon the sill, and staring at the air.   His sister, also, had come ; she was frightened, however, and had betaken herself to the bedroom,
to sob.   But in walked this little plump, soft-
footed woman, with her banded hair, her benevolent spectacles, and her atmosphere of calm.

"I guess I 'll blaze a fire, Jonas," said she.
" You step out an' git me a mite o' kindlin'."

The air of homely living enwrapped him once
again, and mechanically, with the inertia of old
habit, he obeyed.   They had a " cup o' tea "
together ; and then, when the dishes were
washed, and the peaceful twilight began to
settle down upon them like a sifting mist, she
drew a little rocking chair to the window where
he sat opposite, and spoke.

" Jonas," said she, in that still voice which
had been harmonized by the experiences of
life, " arter dark, you jest go up an' bring home
them blue dishes.   Mary 's got an awful lot o'
fun in her, an' if she ain't laughin' over that,
I 'm beat.   Now, Jonas, you do it !   Do you
s'pose she wants them nice blue pieces out

there through wind an' weather? She'd ruther
by half see 'em on the parlor cluzzet shelves;
an' if you'll·fetch 'em home, I'll scallop some
white paper, jest as she liked, an' we'll set 'em
up there."

Jonas wakened a little from his mental
swoon. Life seemed warmer, more tangible,
again.

"Law, do go," said the mother soothingly.
"She don't want the whole township tramplin'
up there to eye over her chiny. Make her as
nervous as a witch. Here's the ha'-bushel
basket, an' some paper to put between 'em.
You go, Jonas, an' I'll clear off the shelves."

So Jonas, whether he was tired of guiding
the impulses of his own unquiet mind, or
whether he had become a child again, glad to
yield to the maternal, as we all do in our grief,
took the basket and went. He stood by, still
like a child, while this comfortable woman put
the china on the shelves, speaking warmly,
as she worked, of the pretty curving of the
cups, and her belief that the pitcher was "one
you could pour out of." She stayed on at the
house, and Jonas, through his sickness of the
mind, lay back upon her soothing will as a
baby lies in its mother's arms. But the china
was never used, even when he had come to his
normal estate, and bought and sold as before.
The mother's prescience was too keen for
that.

Here in this ground are the ambiguities of life carried over into that other state, its pathos and its small misunderstandings. This was a much-married man whose last spouse had been a triple widow. Even to him the situation proved mathematically complex, and the sumptuous stone to her memory bears the dizzying legend that "Enoch Nudd who erects this stone is her fourth husband and his fifth wife." Perhaps it was the exigencies of space which brought about this amazing elision; but surely, in its very apparent intention, there is only a modest pride. For indubitably the much-married may plume themselves upon being also the widely sought. If it is the crown of sex to be desired, here you have it, under seal of the civil bond. No baseless, windy boasting that "I might an if I would!" Nay, here be the marriage ties to testify.

In this pleasant, weedy corner is a little white stone, not so long erected. "I shall arise in thine image," runs the inscription; and reading it, you shall remember that the dust within belonged to a little hunchback, who played the fiddle divinely, and had beseeching eyes. With that cry he escaped from the marred conditions of the clay. Here, too (for this is a sort of bachelor nook), is the grave of a man 'whom we unconsciously thrust into a permanent masquerade. Years and years ago he broke into a house, — an unknown felony in

our quiet limits, — and was incontinently shot.
The burglar lost his arm, and went about at
first under a cloud of disgrace and horror, which
became, with healing of the public conscience,
a veil of sympathy. After his brief imprison-
ment indoors, during the healing of the mutilated stump, he came forth among us again, a
man sadder and wiser in that he had learned
how slow and sure may be the road to wealth.
He had sown his wild oats in one night's foolish work, and now he settled down to doing
such odd jobs as he might with one hand. We
got accustomed to his loss. Those of us who
were children when it happened never really
discovered that it was disgrace at all; we
called it misfortune, and no one said us nay.
Then one day it occurred to us that he must
have been shot "in the war," and so, all un-
wittingly to himself, the silent man became a
hero. We accepted him. He was part of our
poetic time, and when he died, we held him
still in remembrance among those who fell
worthily. When Decoration Day was first observed in Tiverton, one of us thought of him,
and dropped some apple blossoms on his grave;
and so it had its posy like the rest, although it
bore no flag. It was the doctor who set us
right there. "I would n't do that," he said,
withholding the hand of one unthinking child;
and she took back her flag. But she left the
blossoms, and, being fond of precedent, we still

do the same; unless we stop to think, we know not why. You may say there is here some perfidy to the republic and the honored dead, or at least some laxity of morals. We are lax, indeed, but possibly that is why we are so kind. We are not willing to "hurt folks' feelings" even when they have migrated to another star; and a flower more or less from the overplus given to men who made the greater choice will do no harm, tossed to one whose soul may be sitting, like Lazarus, at their riches' gate.

But of all these fleeting legends made to hold the soul a moment on its way, and keep it here in fickle permanence, one is more dramatic than all, more charged with power and pathos. Years ago there came into Tiverton an unknown man, very handsome, showing the marks of high breeding, and yet in his bearing strangely solitary and remote. He wore a cloak, and had a foreign look. He came walking into the town one night, with dust upon his shoes, and we judged that he had been traveling a long time. He had the appearance of one who was not nearly at his journey's end, and would pass through the village, continuing on a longer way. He glanced at no one, but we all stared at him. He seemed, though we had not the words to put it so, an exiled prince. He went straight through Tiverton Street until he came to the parsonage; and something about it (perhaps its garden, hot with flowers, larkspur, coreopsis, and the rest) detained his eye, and he walked in. Next day the old doctor was there also with his little black case, but we were none the wiser for that ; for the old doctor was of the sort who intrench themselves in a professional reserve. You might draw up beside the road to question him, but you could as well deter the course of nature. He would give the roan a flick, and his sulky would flash by.

"What's the matter with so-and-so?" would ask a mousing neighbor.

"He's sick," ran the laconic reply.

"Goin' to die?" one daring querist ventured further.

"Some time," said the doctor.

But though he assumed a right to combat thus the outer world, no one was gentler with a sick man or with those about him in their grief. To the latter he would speak ; but he used to say he drew his line at second cousins.

Into his hands and the true old parson's fell the stranger's confidence, if confidence it were. He may have died solitary and unexplained ; but no matter what he said, his story was safe. In a week he was carried out for burial ; and so solemn was the parson's manner as he spoke a brief service over him, so thrilling his enunciation of the words "our brother," that we dared not even ask what else he should be called. And we never knew. The headstone,

set up by the parson, bore the words "Pec-
cator Maximus." For a long time we thought
they made the stranger's name, and judged
that he must have been a foreigner; but a new
schoolmistress taught us otherwise. It was
Latin, she said, and it meant "the chiefest
among sinners." When that report flew round,
the parson got wind of it, and then, in the pulpit one morning, he announced that he felt it
necessary to say that the words had been used
"at our brother's request," and that it was his
own decision to write below them, "For this
cause came I into the world."

We have accepted the stranger as we accept
many things in Tiverton. Parson and doctor
kept his secret well. He is quite safe from our
questioning; but for years I expected a lady,
always young and full of grief, to seek out his
grave and shrive him with her tears. She will
not appear now, unless she come as an old, old
woman, to lie beside him. It is too late.

One more record of our vanished time, —
this full of poesy only, and the pathos of farewell. It was not the aged and heartsick alone
who lay down here to rest. We have been no
more fortunate than others. Youth and beauty
came also, and returned no more. This, where
the white rose-bush grows untended, was the
young daughter of a squire in far-off days: too
young to have known the pangs of love or the
sweet desire of Death, save that, in primrose

time, he always paints himself so fair. I have thought the inscription must have been borrowed from another grave, in some yard shaded by yews and silent under the cawing of the rooks; perhaps, from its stiffness, translated from a stately Latin verse. This it is, snatched not too soon from oblivion; for a few more years will wear it quite away : —

"Here lies the purple flower of a maid
Having to envious Death due tribute paid.
Her sudden Loss her Parents did lament,
And all her Friends with grief their hearts did Rent.
Life's short. Your wicked Lives amend with care,
For Mortals know we Dust and Shadows are."

"The purple flower of a maid!" All the blossomy sweetness, the fragrant lamenting of Lycidas, lies in that one line. Alas, poor love-lies-bleeding! And yet not poor according to the barren pity we accord the dead, but dowered with another youth set like a crown upon the unstained front of this. Not going with sparse blossoms ripened or decayed, but heaped with buds and dripping over in perfume. She seems so sweet in her still loveliness, the empty promise of her balmy spring, that for a moment fain are you to snatch her back into the pageant of your day. Reading that phrase, you feel the earth is poorer for her loss. And yet not so, since the world holds other greater worlds as well. Elsewhere she may have grown to age and stature; but here she lives yet in beauteous permanence, — as true a part of youth and joy and rapture as the immortal figures on the Grecian Urn. While she was but a flying phantom on the frieze of time, Death fixed her there forever, — a haunting spirit in perennial bliss.

Americans in Fiction

*A series of reprints of 19th century American novels important
to the study of American folklore, culture and literary history*